Praise for Penny Richards's book,

AN UNTIMELY FROST

Lilly Long Mystery #1

"Penny Richards has created a fascinating heroine, a great mystery, and an exceptional play on history. For any lover of history and or mystery, this is must-read author!"
— New York Times bestselling author Heather Graham, on *An Untimely Frost*

"A strong heroine and the intriguing Pinkertons make this historical mystery a cozy way to spend a weekend. Lilly Long's independence and stubborn spirit will immediately endear her to many readers. The case is well constructed, and the tone of the prose casts an almost gothic mood over the story. This is a solid start to a new series, and the introduction of a potential work and romantic partner for Lilly adds an extra element of appeal for a variety of readers."
— *RT Book Reviews,* 4 Stars

"[A] riveting series launch . . . Strange undercurrents of sorrow and menace swirl around our intrepid heroine, drawing her into a vortex of cruelty and long-buried evil. Richards provides just the right amount of melodrama in this lively tale."
— *Publishers Weekly*

"Penny Richards has written a fun, feisty protagonist in Lilly Long. The prose is crisp and the tempo paces nicely to a finish that sees Lilly needing every bit of her cunning."
— Historical Novel Society

Lilly Long Mysteries

AN UNTIMELY FROST

THOUGH THIS BE MADNESS

Published by Kensington Publishing Corporation

THOUGH THIS
BE MADNESS

PENNY RICHARDS

KENSINGTON BOOKS
www.kensingtonbooks.com

KENSINGTON BOOKS are published by

Kensington Publishing Corp.
119 West 40th Street
New York, NY 10018

All Kensington titles, imprints, and distributed lines are available at special quantity discounts for bulk purchases for sales promotion, premiums, fundraising, educational, or institutional use.

Special book excerpts or customized printings can also be created to fit specific needs. For details, write or phone the office of the Kensington Sales Manager: Kensington Publishing Corp., 119 West 40th Street, New York, NY 10018. Attn. Sales Department. Phone: 1-800-221-2647.

Kensington and the K logo Reg. U.S. Pat. & TM Off.

eISBN-13: 978-1-4967-0605-8
eISBN-10: 1-4967-0605-6
First Kensington Electronic Edition: May 2017

ISBN-13: 978-1-4967-0604-1
ISBN-10: 1-4967-0604-8
First Kensington Trade Paperback Printing: May 2017

10 9 8 7 6 5 4 3 2 1

Printed in the United States of America

[Aside] *Though this be madness, yet there is method in't.*
—Lord Polonius, *Hamlet,* act 2, scene 2

CHAPTER 1

1881
89 Dearborn, Chicago
Pinkerton Offices

"I bloody well won't do it!" The declaration came from the man pacing the floor of William Pinkerton's office. "I'm a Pinkerton agent, not a blasted nanny."

William Pinkerton pinned the young operative with an unrelenting look from beneath heavy brows. "You haven't any choice, McShane."

Andrew Cadence McShane faced his boss with a defiant expression. "What? I haven't yet groveled enough for you and your father?"

William stifled his own irritation at the bold statement. McShane was a loose cannon, and if it were up to William, he'd fire the man on the spot. Indeed, Allan *had* fired him a year ago, for drinking and brawling and behaving in a way that was unacceptable to Pinkerton's code of conduct. But, claiming that he had his life together at last, McShane had come asking for his job back about the same time the young actress, Lilly Long, had applied for a position. Allan, who had always thought the Irishman was one of his best agents, had rehired him on a provisional basis.

"You know exactly what I mean," William said in a measured tone. "No one was holding a gun to your head when you agreed to the terms of our rehiring you, which, as you no doubt recall, was probation for an undetermined length of time."

Feeling a certain amount of uneasiness over his father's decision to hire McShane and Miss Long, William had suggested that McShane be assigned to keep an eye out for the inexperienced new operative on her first mission, which would—Lord willing—keep him too preoccupied to get into any more scrapes. Allan had agreed.

So while new agent Lilly Long tried to locate the Reverend Harold Purcell, a preacher who had stolen from his congregation and disappeared from his home near Vandalia, Illinois, McShane had kept tabs on her by pretending to be part of a traveling boxing troupe. He'd been no happier about the job than Miss Long had been about her missing person assignment, but they'd both known they were in no position to object, just as neither had any say about this new arrangement.

"Until we feel confident that you will not resort to your previous unacceptable behavior, you will partner with Miss Long."

McShane's eyes went wide with something akin to shock. "It was a barroom brawl, sir. I did not reveal any secrets or compromise my assignment in any way."

"We've been through all this before, McShane, and I refuse to revisit it." William's gaze shied away from the younger man's, which had lost its belligerence and grown as bleak as the stormy spring morning.

William cleared his throat. "Believe me, I understand that on a personal level you were going through an extremely rough patch at the time, and for that you have my sympathy, but you must understand that the agency cannot have our operatives behaving in ways that make us look bad. We have a sterling reputation, and we will do what we must to make sure it stays that way. If you continue to do well, you'll soon be on your own again."

All the fiery irritation seemed to drain from the younger man. "Yes, sir."

"Actually, this assignment is one that will be best served by a man and woman working together."

Seemingly resigned, McShane took a seat in the chair across from William's desk. "Tell me about it."

"I prefer to explain things to you and Miss Long together," William said. "She should be here any minute. But I will tell you this much. The two of you will be going to New Orleans."

The rain had stopped . . . at least for the moment, but thick black clouds still roiled uneasily in the sky when Lilly's cab pulled up in front of the five-story building that housed the Pinkerton offices. She paid the driver and, careful to step around the puddles, entered the structure with a feeling of elation.

Since returning from her first assignment just a week ago, she'd been riding the wave of her success in bringing her first case to a satisfactory conclusion and basking in the knowledge that she would continue to be employed by the prestigious detective firm. She'd been more than a little surprised when she received a message that morning stating that William wanted to see her at once.

Though she knew she had a long way to go before becoming a seasoned agent, the praise she'd received from both William and Allan was, to paraphrase the bard, "the stuff that dreams were made of." When her missing person assignment had evolved into solving a twenty-year-old murder, it had been satisfying to know that she'd helped bring about justice. And Allan, who loved correcting what he perceived as social wrongdoing, had been quite satisfied that things had been made as right as humanly possible. She was eager to embark on her next mission.

Pausing outside the doorway, she tucked a loose strand of red hair beneath the brim of the straw hat she'd purchased as a treat for herself the day before. The soft green of the grosgrain ribbons was the exact hue of her new walking dress with its high stand-up collar topped with the wide, heavy white lace that marched down the front. The off-the-ground hem of her narrow skirt showed the pointed toes of her matching shoes and was trimmed with a wide band of the lace.

She stepped through the door to the outer office, where William's clerk, Harris, pounded on the keys of the Remington typewriter, using the hunt-and-peck system. The morning sunshine behind him illuminated the long, thin wisps of graying hair that had been combed over to help disguise his balding pate.

Hearing her at the door, he looked up. "Good morning, Miss Long," he said with a polite smile. "You're looking chipper today."

"Hello, Harris," she replied. "I am chipper this morning. I'm anxious to get back to work."

Harris stood. "I'll just let them know you're here," he said.

Them. Lilly smiled. Oh, good. Allan was going to be involved in her next project. She had the feeling that the intrepid lawman supported her hiring, even though William was ambivalent at best about his father's determination to hire female agents.

"Miss Long is here," Harris said, moving aside for Lilly to enter.

When she stepped through the aperture, William was already coming around the desk, his hand extended in greeting. But it wasn't William who caught Lilly's attention. It was the man who had risen from a chair as she entered the room. It wasn't Allan Pinkerton who stood when she stepped through the doorway. It was Cadence McShane.

With her attention focused on the other man, she barely heard William's words of welcome. The last time she'd seen McShane was after the completion of the Heaven's Gate assignment. He'd made a cryptic comment and disappeared into the crowd. She thought she'd seen the last of him, so what was he doing here, she wondered as he took her hand in greeting. His palm was rough and warm, and his words and smile were pleasant, but the coldness in his sapphire-blue eyes was undeniable.

What the devil was going on? she wondered again, her lively imagination steering her toward a conclusion that was not the least bit acceptable. Seeking an answer to the questions churning around in her head, Lilly turned her puzzled gaze to William. Allan Pinkerton's son was noted for his speed in assessing situations, and he did not miss the query on Lilly's face or the disdain on McShane's.

"Have a seat, Miss Long," he said, gesturing toward the chair Cade had vacated at her arrival.

Clutching her purse in her lap, Lilly did his bidding.

"My father and I have decided on your next assignment," William told her, wasting no time getting to the point. "You and McShane will be going to New Orleans."

"What!" Lilly's gaze flew to McShane's. If the grim twist of his lips and the blatant annoyance in his eyes were any indication, he was no happier than she.

"Do you really feel this is necessary, sir?" she protested. "While I appreciate the fact that you were concerned about my inexperience, I understood the agency was happy with my work in Vandalia."

"We were extremely pleased," William assured her, "but one successful assignment does not afford you any vast field knowledge. While you were the one who rooted out the truth about the Purcells, if it had not been for McShane, you might very well be dead."

She could not deny that there was a kernel of truth in William's statement. She'd been trapped in the attic of the Purcell home, and though she'd been in the process of trying to free herself by jumping from a small window onto a steep roof, her plan might have gone very wrong. McShane had rescued her from a sticky situation.

"Keeping your youth and inexperience in mind, my father and I feel that, at least for the next few assignments, you and McShane should work together. It will give you a chance to hone your skills."

Lilly looked askance at the man now lounging with apparent indolence on the settee, though the set of his jaw and the jewel hardness in his sapphire-hued eyes left no doubt of his true feelings.

She made one last attempt to change the course of her task, indeed, the course of her life . . . at least for the foreseeable future. "And is Agent McShane agreeable to this arrangement?" she asked.

William's calm gaze flickered over the younger man. "McShane is a professional, Miss Long," he said in a no-nonsense tone. "He accepts his obligations and gives this agency his best." Though he was speaking to her, she could not shake the notion that his words were directed to her new partner as well.

Lilly sighed. Disappointment, anger, and frustration vied for supremacy. Clearly, neither she nor McShane had a choice in the matter, and to argue it further would only make her appear contrary and disagreeable. As she had with her first assignment, she would accept the situation, do her best, and hope that soon she would be trusted to go it alone.

With a lift of her chin, she said, "So we go to New Orleans." The statement told her employer that she had resigned herself to her fate and was ready to hear the details of the operation.

"Yes, actually, Miss Long, I believe you will embrace the case once you hear about it," William told her, stepping from behind the desk and handing each of them a copy of the journal they were given at the beginning of each case. The book held the name of the client, the situation, and the agency's ideas for following through. As per Pinkerton protocol, the persons seeking help would not be introduced to the agents or have any idea how the help they sought might come about.

"If indeed there is a crime involved, it is against a woman, so I know you'll derive a great deal of satisfaction from investigating it," William said to Lilly.

"A brief overview of what you'll find in the journal is this: Just days ago, we received a special-delivery letter from one Mrs. Etienne Fontenot, whose name is LaRee . . . LaRee Fontenot. She and the legitimacy of her concern have been confirmed by her long-time attorney, Mr. Armand DeMille."

William looked from Lilly to McShane. "Mrs. Fontenot believes that her grandson's widow, Patricia Ducharme, has been wrongly committed to an insane asylum by her new husband, Henri."

Lilly's irritation at being paired with Cade faded as she gave her attention to William's tale. "Are you saying she believes there is nothing wrong with her granddaughter-in-law?" Lilly asked.

"That is exactly what she believes."

"Why?" The question came from Cade, who, like Lilly, seemed to have lost his animosity as his interest in the case grew.

"Mrs. Fontenot is convinced that Patricia's new husband's, Dr. Henri Ducharme's, true purpose is to gain control of the family fortune, which, according to Mr. DeMille, is extensive and which all the Fontenot males have gone to great lengths to keep safe for future generations."

"I don't understand," Lilly said. "Wouldn't it pass down to the remaining heirs?"

"Indeed. Louisiana operates under the Napoleonic Code, which means that the closest male relative handles the business and monetary affairs of their womenfolk, who are considered little more than chattel to their fathers and husbands."

Lilly felt herself bristling. Once again, a male-dominated world sought to keep the fairer sex under its thumb. No doubt they felt that feeble female brains were incapable of comprehending, much less dealing with, anything beyond regular feminine pursuits.

"I see you take umbrage at that notion, Miss Long, as I suspected you would," William said with a nod and a slight smile. "As you know, social injustice is one thing that infuriates my father, so he was immediately drawn to this case. It's also common knowledge that he has strong beliefs in a woman's capabilities, or he would not hire female operatives.

"But I digress. When LaRee Fontenot's husband, Etienne, suffered a stroke at a relatively young age, he began to consider ways to insure the money he'd amassed stayed within the family. With Mr. DeMille's legal advice, Etienne transferred all his business holdings, as well as a house on Rampart Street and a plantation called River Run, to his son, Grayson, in whose capabilities he had complete trust. All this before his death.

"By all accounts, LaRee Fontenot was quite a lovely woman in her youth, and Etienne feared that after his death she would fall for some unscrupulous ne'er-do-well, who would take control of the family fortune."

"Let me see if I understand," Cade said. "Etienne hoped that by giving everything to his son before his own death, he could avoid the possibility of his family losing everything he'd worked so hard to gain, should his wife marry unwisely after he died."

"Exactly," William said, nodding. "He knew Grayson would be generous and fair in providing for his womenfolk, yet they would have no money of their own."

"It doesn't sound as if Etienne had much faith in his wife's ability to choose a suitable husband," Lilly said.

William smiled and shrugged. "In any case, LaRee Fontenot never remarried. According to DeMille, the arrangement worked well, and the same agreement was set up between Grayson and his son, Garrett, who lost no time expanding the family holdings—timber in this case—into Arkansas, where he made his home most of the year.

"Garrett was unmarried when his father passed away, and on a visit to his grandmother in New Orleans, he met and fell in love with Patricia Galloway. After they married, they went back to Arkansas to make their home."

"Is this the same Patricia who is now in the insane asylum?" Lilly queried.

"The same," William corroborated. "Garrett and Patricia had two daughters, Cassandra and Suzannah. He died four years ago with no son to inherit. Like his father, he felt that some women are as intelligent and business savvy as men, since his grandmother had regularly and successfully interjected her thoughts and ideas into the running of the various family endeavors."

"You said his grandmother *had* interjected her thoughts and ideas," Cade said. "Why isn't she still?"

"We're getting there," William said. "Bear with me."

"As a resident of Arkansas, Garrett was not bound by Louisiana law. In accordance with the Married Women's Property Act, which admittedly is haphazardly enforced, depending on who sits in the seat of power, Patricia became heir to everything the male Fontenots had amassed from Etienne's time until the present."

"Ah," Cade said with a nod. "And it was Patricia, not LaRee, who fell for the unscrupulous man, this Henri Ducharme."

"It appears so, yes," William told them.

"If Patricia and her daughters lived in Arkansas, how did she meet Ducharme and lose control?" Lilly asked.

"She was lonely in Arkansas without her husband, and she and her girls had moved in with Mrs. Fontenot. She and Henri met soon afterward. To the dismay of the entire family, they were married as soon as her year of mourning ended."

"You say that Ducharme is a doctor, and yet Mrs. Fontenot doubts his diagnosis in Patricia's case," Cade said. "Why?"

"Yes, Cassandra, the older daughter, confided to Mrs. Fontenot that her mother was mere months into her new marriage when she began to suspect she'd made a dreadful mistake and had put the family fortune in her new husband's grasping hands—Mrs. Fontenot's words, not mine," William clarified.

"I can certainly relate to that," Lilly said in a voice laced with bitterness. She ignored the questioning look her partner shot her way.

"According to Cassandra, it appears that her stepfather's sole intent in life is to spend them into poverty."

Lilly gave another huff of disgust.

"To further upset the family," William continued, "within ten months of the marriage, Patricia found herself with child— what is commonly referred to as a 'change of life baby.' The confinement was troublesome, and Patricia got little comfort from her husband, who constantly warned that something could go wrong because of her age."

"Job's comforter," Cade muttered.

William nodded. "As it happened, something did go wrong. The baby, a boy, was stillborn some eighteen months ago, which sent Patricia into a deep melancholy, from which, Mrs. Fontenot claims, she seemed to be emerging little by little, until she received another blow."

As Lilly listened, she thought of her own mother's murder that resulted in the death of the baby she'd been carrying. She wondered if she would always be reminded of their deaths at odd times like this, with nothing but a snippet of conversation bringing back the painful memory.

Cade leaned forward in interest. "What was that?"

"Four months ago, in an effort to cheer her mother, Cassandra urged Patricia to attend a suffragist gathering with her and her sister, Suzannah, who somehow became separated from them in the crush. They looked for her to no avail, and she was located two days later by some hobo in an alley. She had been molested and killed."

There was an apologetic expression on William's face as he looked at Lilly, but though her heart gave a lurch of empathetic pain for Patricia Ducharme's loss and Suzannah's suffering, she was no shrinking violet to go into a swoon from hearing such brutal truths.

"The murder has not been solved, and the New Orleans police have little hope of ever knowing who committed the crime. Needless to say, this tragedy on top of the loss of her infant son strained Patricia's emotions to the limit."

"It would strain anyone's emotions," Lilly said.

William nodded. "Henri claimed she was so overcome with grief and anger that she became abusive, striking him on several occasions.

"Mrs. Fontenot admits that Patricia's emotions seesawed between bouts of depression and something near normalcy, but she never witnessed the"—William referred to the letter in his hand—" 'howling, screeching creature hell-bent on physical injury.' That last was Henri's description as Mrs. Fontenot recalls it.

"Ducharme claims he had no recourse but to administer small doses of laudanum. Fearful of making her a fiend, he discontinued the drug after the funeral, at which time Patricia began to alternate between forgetfulness and belligerence. She began to imagine things that were not so and accused him of everything from hiding things to lying to her."

"The poor thing," Lilly said, thinking that it certainly sounded as if the woman's sanity had fled.

"And so he had her committed," Cade said.

William nodded. "A month after burying Suzannah, Henri committed Patricia to the City Insane Asylum there in New Orleans."

"I've heard of it," Cade said. "I thought it was for indigents, not the crème de la crème of New Orleans society. I can't imagine Mrs. Fontenot choosing such a place for a loved one."

"You're right, McShane," William said with a dry smile. "But there is a certain method in her madness, if you'll pardon the dreadful pun. Henri wanted to put Patricia in a state institution, but Mrs. Fontenot put down her foot and insisted that Patricia be placed in a private home or left in the city until her true mental state could be evaluated by professionals. That way she would be close enough for the family to visit, and"—his smile deepened—"with the Fontenot bank account, Mrs. Fontenot could arrange for special privileges and care for her granddaughter-in-law."

"I understand the special privileges, but not the other," Lilly confessed.

"By law—anyone, including policemen, family members, clergy, literally anyone—can leave someone for evaluation at the New Orleans facility for a certain length of time. If they get better, they're released, but if they don't, they're sent to the East Louisiana State Hospital in Jackson."

"From what you've told us, it seems Dr. Ducharme's fears

are well-founded," Lilly mused. "Why does Mrs. Fontenot doubt his judgment?"

"She admits she has no proof that Henri is up to anything nefarious," William told them. "But with Cassandra's statement about her mother's concerns over her new husband and Mrs. Fontenot's own feeling that too many disasters have befallen Patricia since her marriage, she feels she has justification for her suspicions."

Lilly understood LaRee Fontenot's intuitive feelings perfectly. She recalled feeling that people were withholding the truth during her previous investigation. She also remembered the feeling of certainty that Cadence McShane was not the person who intended her harm after she'd almost been run down by a buggy, even though her intellect reminded her that he'd been in the area when other dodgy things had taken place.

"Cassandra also believes that her stepfather is somehow responsible for Patricia's mental state," William was saying. "She and her great-grandmother fear that Henri will bypass them and send Patricia to an even worse place and that leaving her in an asylum truly will drive her over the edge."

"So our job," Cade said, glancing at Lilly, "is to try to disprove the notion of Patricia Ducharme's insanity?"

"Yes, and to do everything in your power to find out whether or not Dr. Henri Ducharme is the villain Mrs. Fontenot and Cassandra believe he is. And do it as quickly as possible."

Lilly was feeling a bit overwhelmed by the task set before her and her disgruntled partner, especially since they needed to move without delay. She shot Cade a sharp glance. His dark eyebrows were drawn together in a frown as he looked over the notes he'd been taking.

"Does Mrs. Fontenot know anything at all about Henri's past?" she asked. "We could use someplace to start looking."

"The doctor is, by Mrs. Fontenot's grudging admission, an attractive and charming man, forty-seven years old, and has been married before. She has no idea to whom he was married," William supplied. "She believes the first wife died."

"Am I correct in assuming that we will be employed by Mrs. Fontenot at the house on Rampart Street?"

William nodded. "You will be hired as a married couple."

Cade and Lilly shared a stunned look.

"We've arranged things so that it is almost a given that you will be hired."

Mouth set in a hard line, Cade nodded in compliance. "Who else lives in the house besides Mrs. Fontenot?"

"The doctor, of course, and an array of servants."

"Cassandra?"

"No," William said. "She met and married an attorney"— he shuffled the pages of the letter again—"one Preston Easterling, fifteen months after her mother married Ducharme. They live on the family plantation, River Run, a half-day's trip from New Orleans; however, they are frequent visitors to the house on Rampart Street."

"Does Mrs. Fontenot's attorney . . ." Cade paused, searching through his notes for a name.

"Armand DeMille."

"Yes. Does Mr. DeMille have any input about the family's finances, or has he discovered any financial shenanigans that can be attributed to Ducharme?" Cade asked.

"DeMille has been in the dark since soon after Cassandra married Preston, and Henri suggested that it made more sense to have all the family affairs handled by someone in the family. He turned over everything to Preston."

At the seemingly innocuous comment, Cade's head came up like a hound on the scent of its prey.

"I see you find that interesting, too, McShane," William said with a nod of approval.

"Very."

"I want you and Miss Long to become an integral part of that household," William instructed, looking from one to the other. "You will, of course, interact on some level with all the people we've discussed today, though as you know, not even Mrs. Fontenot is to have any idea who you are."

Agency policy dictated that the clients never meet the operatives working their case. It was a practice that made a lot of sense to Lilly. William's steady gaze met hers, then moved to Cade. At that moment, Lilly saw Allan Pinkerton's determination and drive reflected in his son's eyes.

"Within reason and the law, you are to use every means possible to find out everything you can about Dr. Ducharme. If he is as corrupt as the Fontenot ladies and Mr. DeMille seem to think he is, I want you to nail the scoundrel's hide to the wall."

CHAPTER 2

After clearing up a few more details about the case, Lilly and Cade exited the Pinkerton building into the dismal spring morning. McShane plunged his hands into the pockets of his trousers and let his gaze roam over the passersby, almost as if he were looking for something or someone. Always alert.

"So," she said with a bright smile, "shall we divide the tasks more or less equally?"

"Divide the tasks?" He looked at her as if she'd gone round the bend. "Didn't you hear what William said? We will be working this case *together*. That means we work as a team."

"We will go to New Orleans together, certainly," Lilly said, eager to rid herself of her partner. "But I see no reason we can't each follow our own leads once we arrive."

"Look, Miss Long," McShane said in a voice reeking with disdain, "I understand your need to prove yourself to the agency, but when I'm given orders, I follow them."

Gone was the flirty prizefighter who a mere week ago had winked and smiled at her and made her heart pound willy-nilly. In his place stood a brooding stranger who looked as if he seldom smiled and laughed even less. The deviltry she'd seen in his blue eyes was gone, and in its place was something that looked closely akin to torment. Was he *that* upset about working with her?

"But you're no happier about being paired with me than I am with you."

His gaze was fixed on something across the busy Chicago street. "No."

Womanlike, she was torn between anger that William thought she needed coddling and a purely feminine annoyance that Cade had no desire to work with her. Knowing she was pulling the tiger's whiskers, she said, "If you're the agent he claims you are, why did William give you the job of following me around?"

McShane's icy gaze pierced hers with the sharpness of a needle. "You ask too many questions that are none of your business, Miss Long. I only acknowledge my sins in the confessional or when I'm drunk."

"Sins? Ah," she said with a slow nod of understanding. "You did something bad enough to make the Pinkertons angry, and cosseting me is your penance."

"One thing you must learn, Miss Long, is that we are forced to deal with many unpleasant things in life. As William said, I am a professional despite—or perhaps because of—my sins."

"So you consider working with me an unpleasantness?"

He gave a negligent lift of his wide shoulders. "I believe we are in agreement that neither of us is keen on the situation."

"Fine," she said, stung, though she couldn't define why. "If we are to be stuck with each other, I would prefer to have back the boxer as my partner. At least he didn't look at me as if he'd like to have my head on a platter."

Cade stared at her for a moment and, without warning,

winked and smiled his cocky smile. "Oh, he'll be around, colleen, when he's needed."

Lilly's mouth fell open and she blinked in disbelief. The transformation was immediate and startling. One minute he was distant and inflexible, the next he looked and acted as if he hadn't a care in the world.

"You do that extremely well," she said with grudging respect. "And don't call me colleen."

"I told you in Springfield that I'd been around the theater since I was a child. Did you doubt me?"

She gave a slight shrug.

"And why wouldn't you?" he said, the derisive grin still in place. "After all, we Irish have the reputation of being bad-tempered drunks, not to mention that we're greedy illiterates, and like all good Catholics, we breed like rabbits. However," he said, raising a finger for attention, "we've some fine newspapers in Chicago, and we're quite involved with the stage . . . since, as you are no doubt aware, that enterprise demands no literacy."

Lilly heard the scorn in his voice and knew he was only voicing the opinion shared by most of the country. She had seen the cartoons of R. F. Outcault and Thomas Nast, as well as stage productions that portrayed Irish immigrants as unpredictable, aggressive inebriates who were resented because they were willing to work for any wage. And even though they'd gained a certain amount of respect for their fighting skill during the Civil War, they had yet to gain full acceptance.

As angry as he made her, the feminine, nurturing part of her wanted to make things better for him. That was a weakness of hers, a vulnerability that her soon-to-be ex-husband, Timothy, had learned to exploit to his own benefit early in their marriage. She must learn to ignore it.

"I'm an actress, sir, as are my family and friends. Do you imply that we are ignorant?"

The antagonism seemed to drain from him before her very eyes. "Dear heaven, no," he said, the bleakness back. "Thank God for the stage, I say. That and the Church have saved many an Irish lad from becoming a bugger or a cracksman."

Seeing her frown of confusion, he said, "That would be a pickpocket or burglar to you."

Finally, as if they both realized that butting heads was foolish under the circumstances, they looked at each other long and hard. Cade spoke first. "We would no doubt be more effective if we at least tried to get along the next few weeks, don't you agree?"

"Yes," Lilly said with a reluctant nod. "We need to present a united front." She sighed. "But I have a request."

Cade lifted a dark eyebrow in query.

"Since you know boxing, I would like you to teach me to defend myself. My experience with Mrs. Purcell might have turned out differently had I been better prepared."

Lilly had been locked in an attic room and left to die. She had no desire to find herself in that sort of pickle again.

Instead of pooh-poohing her idea, McShane regarded her for several seconds. "All right," he said at last. "When and if we find the time, I'll show you a few tricks."

"Thank you," she said, pleased that he'd given her no argument. "Now, since you are the experienced operative, what do you suggest we do first?"

"First we'll go to a nice restaurant somewhere, order lunch, and try to assemble a past for ourselves."

A past? It had never occurred to her the importance of such a seemingly trivial thing to their undertaking. If they were to be effective in their new roles, it was imperative that they invent believable "pasts," both as individuals and as a married couple. It was another reminder that she was not quite ready to venture out on her own.

"I hadn't thought of that," she admitted.

"Nor of names either, I don't imagine," he said.

"No."

He waved and gave a sharp whistle at a cab drawn by two tired-looking mares headed their way. The driver pulled the calash to a stop, and Cade offered Lilly his arm. She wrapped her gloved hand around his biceps, feeling the hardness of tempered muscle beneath her fingertips.

"I was thinking Brona and Bran Sullivan," he said, pausing to give her a hand into the carriage. "I imagine you would be better at affecting an Irish accent than I would ridding myself of mine."

Lilly nodded and looked up at him. "Why Brona?"

He flashed her an unrepentant smile as he swung up into the cab next to her. "I considered Colleen, but for some reason, I ken you've a certain revulsion to the name."

Lilly glared at him, and he continued to smile. Then she looked away and stared at the storefronts as the carriage passed. Let him wonder, she thought, lifting her nose into the air. They might be forced to work together, but that did not mean she had to share her life story. She would keep to their business arrangement, but she would not give him the satisfaction of explaining why the name was so repugnant to her.

They found a nice but inexpensive restaurant, where they ordered steak, potatoes, and Boston baked beans with thick slabs of fresh-baked bread, topped off with apple pandowdy and hot, strong coffee. They were also served the thick, sweet Borden's condensed milk that Lilly loved in her coffee.

"One thing you must learn about telling lies is that the closer it is to the truth, the easier it is to remember. I think we both grew up here in Chicago," Cade said as they ate. "And we went to the same church, so we've known each other all of our lives."

"Hmm." Lilly eyed him beneath the sweep of her eyelashes. She braced her chin on her left palm and lifted her coffee cup to her lips. "And how many years have we been married? I am quite long in the tooth to be a newlywed, aren't I?"

Cade crossed his arms and regarded her face, taking in every detail. "What are you—all of twenty?"

When she didn't answer immediately, he gave her a wicked smile that caused her heart to race. Why was she cursed with her mother's weakness for good-looking men?

"Come, come now. You may as well acknowledge the corn. It isn't as if your age makes a bit o' difference."

"I'm twenty-two, if you must know," she said, hardening her heart against the charm he turned on and off so easily.

"Aye, I must," he said. "As any husband should."

"And you?" she countered.

"Twenty and eight for a couple of months yet," he said. "So, perhaps we should have been married three years. What do you think?"

"Sounds fine with me."

"We've been in Chicago, where we both worked in factories, but I have a brother who's been living in the South for several years. He wrote telling us of the mild Louisiana winters, and since you had a bad bout of croup last December, we decided to make the move. This job is a godsend."

"Why didn't you have the croup?" Lilly asked, just to be obstinate. "Men get sick."

"Aye, but I had to make a living."

"Ah." She took another sip of her coffee. "And what of children? If we've been married three years, why don't we have one, or at least one on the way?"

His face turned a sickly white. He swallowed hard and closed his eyes. He looked as if he were contemplating stepping off a very high ledge.

"You . . . you don't actually have a wife and children, do you?" she asked, hearing the quiver in her voice and wondering why the possibility should be so devastating.

He opened his eyes, and she saw that the desolation was back. "No," he told her. "I am not married, and I have no children." He drew a deep, almost steadying breath. When he spoke his voice sounded almost tentative. "We will say that we want children and that it is one of our greatest disappointments that God has not blessed us with a child."

Later, as Lilly lay in bed in her rented room, she thought about everything that had happened that long eventful day. She'd been furious when William announced that she and Cade were to pretend to be man and wife as they worked the case in Louisiana, even though she knew that it was the best for her to have some coaching for now.

She also knew that Andrew Cadence McShane was not only a dangerous man, he was a man who needed no one. He was knowledgeable and self-sufficient, and she figured she was right when she'd said he'd done something to get himself into trouble with the agency. Sticking him with her was his punishment.

What had he done? When he'd approached her at the theater in Springfield, she sensed there was more to him than the brash boxer he claimed to be. For all his arrogance, he was too aware of people and his surroundings. She suspected that little got by him and sensed in him both controlled anger and a bottomless pain. Perhaps even guilt.

She wondered what had caused it.

Like Lilly, Cade lay in his solitary bed, his arms folded beneath his head, thinking of the day and the strange course his life had taken. He wished he'd never allowed his grief to overtake his common sense. If he'd only kept his wits about him, he wouldn't be in this fine mess. But he hadn't, and he *was* in a mess, and there was no sense crying over spilt milk, as the saying went. There was nothing to do but what he always tried to accomplish: make the best of things.

He had to give his new partner kudos for solving her first case alone, though. He doubted that he'd have had the intuition it took to understand all the purely feminine aspects of the case she'd just solved.

William had confided in him that Lilly was divorcing the husband who'd stolen her savings and physically attacked her, but something deep in Cade's gut told him that something more than that one incident had driven her to change the entire course of her life.

She was smart and quick and very pretty with those large brown eyes and that vibrant red hair. From following her during the last assignment, he'd seen firsthand that she had spunk and potential, but on the other side of the coin, she was impetuous, filled with defiance, and carried a big chip on her shoulder, at least when it came to him. Again, he suspected there was something more behind her animosity than her desire to work alone. Perhaps she was still enraged over her husband's actions.

Well, whatever her story, it wasn't his problem, thank God. He had enough troubles of his own. As much as *he* would rather be working alone, if Lilly upheld her end of their partnership, he'd be happy.

CHAPTER 3

Three days later, Lilly got her first look at the Mississippi River and the paddle-wheeler that would carry them to New Orleans. She and Cade had taken the train from Chicago to St. Louis and would spend the next few days aboard the *Belle of Memphis,* which was making its maiden trip to New Orleans.

Her first glimpse of the *Belle* took her breath away. She'd never imagined a steamboat was so large. The side-wheeler was somewhat shorter than the average of 275 feet, but impressive nonetheless—from her three decks to the large anchor that was prominently displayed between the two towering smokestacks.

According to Cade, this was the second *Belle of Memphis* to ply the river. Unlike many of the paddle-wheelers that roamed the waterways, the first *Belle* had not succumbed to a sandbar, "sawyer," or explosion, the fate of so many of the fancy boats, but had simply been dismantled and her engines reused in her second incarnation.

The boat would make several scheduled stops along the way to New Orleans, and Lilly couldn't help the tingle of excitement that shivered through her as she boarded. It promised to be a thrilling trip, with the opportunity to enjoy, for a few days, a lifestyle she'd never before experienced.

"I paid our passage as Mr. and Mrs. Bran Sullivan so that you could have a private stateroom," Cade said, as they stood at the railing and watched the other passengers board. She glanced up from beneath the wide brim of her straw bonnet. He seemed tense to Lilly—watchful and on edge—and she had no idea why, other than that he was still miffed at being paired with her.

"We can't afford that on our daily stipend," she said, sounding very much like the wife she pretended to be.

"If we pool them both, we can."

"But where will you sleep?"

His gaze searched the crowd of people saying their good-byes while others clamored to board the boat. "I'll find a place on deck, just like a goodly number of other passengers."

Considering how he felt about this assignment, the unexpected consideration was touching. "I can't let you do that."

He finally looked at her, a wry smile slanted in her direction. "Are you offering to let me share the room with you?"

Her heart took a misstep. "Of course not!"

"I thought as much," he said, returning his gaze to the passengers. "It's too late for any objections. Believe me, it's as much for me as you. Since I'll only have deck space, it would be nice to have a private place to take a bath and change clothes. If that's acceptable to you," he added.

Thinking of the implied intimacy, Lilly felt a blush creep into her cheeks. She didn't mind him using the room for his basic needs, but she intended to make sure she was nowhere near when he did so. "I don't mind at all, under the circumstances."

Finally, he gave her the full impact of that piercing blue gaze. "Thank you."

His unfailing politeness and professionalism since the day they'd been thrown together on the Fontenot assignment was welcome, yet she wished he'd show more emotion. Irritation or anger would be preferable to his cool, unfailing civility. She chalked up her feelings to the growing realization that despite her wishes to the contrary, she was attracted to the dratted man. Lilly hated her mother's blood that flowed so hotly in her own veins.

Kate Long had been cursed with beauty, and men were undeniably attracted to her. There had been a lot of them through the years, including Pierce, the man who'd been like a father to Lilly since she was eleven and one of her mother's lovers had killed her. Recently, Pierce confessed that he'd always thought he might be her father, but there was no way he could know for certain.

Ever since she'd grown old enough to understand the attraction between men and women, she'd gone out of her way to disprove her fear that she was anything like her mother; yet no matter how hard she'd tried, there was no denying that she had fallen for the unscrupulous, thieving Timothy Warner, to whom she was still legally tied. She sighed. Now there was this unwanted fascination for Cadence McShane.

"If you've seen enough, I'll show you the main cabin."

The sound of his voice brought her back from her troubled thoughts. "Then perhaps we can find someone to show you to your room."

He pulled a pocket watch from his vest. "I believe dinner is served at seven, so you should have plenty of time to relax before we eat."

Having reached the main salon, she preceded him through the doorway. The long room had undersized, high-set windows every few feet, with small lights hung over each one. Comfortable chairs and settees were arranged for conversational seating over floral carpeting. Chandeliers were spaced throughout the room. It was as elegant as the fancy restaurant where she'd treated herself to dinner before attending Chatterton's Opera House in Springfield a few weeks earlier. She said as much to Cade.

"It is spectacular, isn't it? But I understand there are some even finer."

They watched as several men moved the conversational seating aside. Others carried in tables. A huge copper urn with spigots all around for the dispensing of water or maybe lemonade was placed in the center of a round table.

"What are they doing?"

"The main cabin doubles as the dining room," he told her. "They move things out between meals."

Left speechless by the grandeur and caught up in an excitement she'd seldom experienced, Lilly took his arm and they strolled from the room. "Would it be all right if we take a walk around the deck before we go to my room?"

Cade paused just outside the door and looked at her questioningly. She gave a little shrug, wishing she'd held her tongue. "It seems as if they're casting off now, and I've never seen a boat launching. I've only traveled by train or stagecoach until now."

He gave an abrupt nod, and they began to move around the deck. She observed the other occupants who were sitting in deck chairs or standing in groups of two or three, chatting and drinking lemonade. It made her feel very special to be part of this exciting experience.

Cade's hand tightened on her arm. She turned and saw an expression of urgency in his eyes.

"Stay here," he commanded. Without waiting for her to answer, he moved toward the stern of the boat, purpose in his long stride, determination in the set of his wide shoulders. She sighed, wondering whom he'd seen that had caused his hasty departure. Shrugging, she turned to gaze at the people around her.

He was back in a matter of minutes.

"What was it?"

"I thought I saw someone I knew."

"And?"

"I lost sight of him."

"Oh."

After a while, they found someone to show them the cabin he'd booked, and she looked around with interest. Except for the size, which couldn't be much over eight by ten feet, it had all the amenities of a fancy hotel room, including an iron bed and an oak wardrobe. One corner held a washbasin with crisp linen towels hanging above; another held a small slipper chair. Lilly experienced a twinge of guilt. Though there was barely enough room to turn around, she would be far more comfortable than Cade as he slept in a chair on the decks.

"It's very nice," she said over her shoulder. "I appreciate what you've done."

"You're welcome."

He glanced again at his pocket watch. "Why don't you try to rest awhile?"

"That sounds wonderful." She looked down at her hands that still had not healed fully from the cuts and scrapes she'd received trying to escape the attic at Heaven's Gate. "I'm not quite my old self yet."

"You had quite a time in Vandalia. Just a reminder, lass. Remember to play Brona every moment. This assignment is one requiring the utmost discretion. We can't take chances on anyone knowing who we really are or what we're about. You'd be amazed at how one small, seemingly insignificant thing can wreck everything."

His accent had grown thicker and the torment was back in his eyes. Without another word, he wheeled around and started for the door. Framed in the aperture, he turned. "I'll be back a little before seven to take you to dinner."

Before she could formulate any response other than to

thank him, he was gone. Lilly stared at the door and wondered again what it was that caused the expression of suffering she so often saw in his eyes.

Determined not to give the wretched man another moment of her thoughts, she wandered around the small room, touching the accoutrements with care. Though he'd said there were floating palaces finer than this one, she could not imagine it being true.

Smiling to herself, she untied her bonnet and hung it on a brass hook next to the mirror, which reflected the color in her cheeks and the gleam of pleasure in her brown eyes. Stripping down to her chemise and pantaloons, she stretched out on the bed and closed her eyes.

CHAPTER 4

Leaving Lilly to rest, Cade went onto the deck and lit a sweet-smelling cheroot. Wondering how he'd gotten his life in such a mess, he went to stare over the boat's railing, watching the eddies left in the wake of the wheels beating at the murky water.

After a while, he turned and rested his elbows on the railing so that he could while away some time by watching the crowd. He'd had the feeling that he and Lilly were being followed ever since they'd left Chicago, but he hadn't spotted anyone.

His gaze settled on a young couple sitting across the way, clearly in love. They must be newlyweds. A white liveried porter set a tray with two ice-filled glasses of lemonade on the small table between them. The young man, who looked no older than twenty and two, could barely drag his gaze from his beloved long enough to reach into his inside breast pocket for his wallet. He extracted a bill that he then passed to the hovering attendant.

Ah, young love. The cynical thought was pushed aside by a rush of memory . . . himself and Glenna when they were newly wed and had been equally fresh and innocent and every bit as in love as this young couple.

The pain of her loss, as hurtful now as it had been the day it happened, sliced through him with the sharpness of a stiletto. Ah, blast it! If only there were some way to excise the unbearable memories from his mind, but it was hard when he knew that part of the blame was his. He pushed the agonizing thought from his head and turned to flip the cheroot into the water.

A stealthy movement from the corner of his eye brought his attention back to the young couple. A too-thin, ragtag child had slipped around the corner and was approaching them, his hands shoved into his pockets. The expression on the boy's face looked innocent enough, but Cade recognized the urchin's actions and his face as the one he thought he'd seen earlier.

He lunged from the railing, and in half a dozen long strides was upon the boy, who chose that moment to stumble toward the young bridegroom. At precisely that moment, Cade slipped an arm around the child's narrow torso, scooping him close instead of allowing him to fall against the young man.

"So there you are, you little scamp!" Cade said, tossing an apologetic smile toward the young couple. "I've been looking all over for you."

He set the boy to his feet and clamped a hand around a thin wrist, half dragging him across the deck. The boy looked at him with a combination of surprise and fury in his eyes. "Holy mother of pearl, McShane!" he spat. "What in blazes do you think you're doing?"

"Keeping you from getting thrown off the boat and into the hoosegow, most likely," Cade said from between teeth clenched together in a fake smile aimed toward an elderly couple. He pulled the boy around the corner of the bow and pushed him against the wall. "What in blazes are *you* doing here, when to the best of my recollection I left you safe and well cared for at Seamus and Meagan's?"

"Gently, there," the boy said, straightening the collar of his scruffy jacket as if he were wearing a finely tailored suit instead of a coat at least two sizes too small.

"Well?"

The bravado slipped from the boy's face, and he gazed up at Cade with bleak brown eyes. "Aye, ya did."

"What are you doing here, Jenks?" Cade asked in a gentler tone.

The boy swallowed hard, and his gaze slid from Cade's. "I only got to see ya for a couple of hours when you come back from yer last job, and I . . . I didn't much like being left behind again." He found Cade's gaze once more. "I thought we were mates."

If Cade didn't know that the child was as tough as shoe leather, he would swear the boy's bottom lip and voice quavered the slightest bit.

"I missed spending time with you, too," he said, going straight to the heart of the matter. "And we are mates, but I'm working again, so there's no way I can spend as much time with you as I did before."

"Done with me, are ya?"

Cade knew the boy was remembering the family who'd left him sitting in a graveyard while they went "to find a bite to eat" and never came back.

"Of course I'm not done with you. I'm eternally grateful to you for all you've done for me, but I cannot take you with me when I'm working."

"I'm not going back."

Well acquainted with the child's stubbornness, Cade said, "We'll talk about it later."

The boy glared up at him, as if to say he'd said all he intended to about the matter. Cade sighed and changed the subject. "I take it you're hungry, since you were going to filch that man's wallet."

"I could use a bite," he said, his tone carefully nonchalant.

"Come along. We'll see if we can't find something to tide you over until dinner."

Cade and Jenks whiled away some time walking the decks and looking at the passing scenery. Around six, he went to wake Lilly, figuring she would need the better part of an hour to ready herself for dinner.

When he pushed open the door and stepped inside, he found her still asleep. Stripped to ruffled pantaloons and a lacy chemise, she lay on top of the pale green-and-white quilt, one hand tucked beneath her cheek, her wavy red hair loose and spread over the pristine whiteness of the pillow. Looking at the pretty picture she made, his irritation at being stuck with her dwindled. But not his curiosity.

It hadn't taken the agency long after hiring her to check into her past, and William had wasted no time passing that information on to Cade, the senior agent. They'd established that her mother had been killed by a lover when Lilly was a child, that Pierce Wainwright and his wife, Rose, had taken her in, and that she'd recently been married and even more recently filed for a divorce after the cad had stolen her savings and nearly killed Wainwright's wife. Cade couldn't say he blamed her. Nevertheless, it took a lot of spunk to fly in the face of convention in such an obvious way. The lady was definitely different from the norm, in many ways. He just wished he had more information. The last thing they needed were unexpected skeletons from her past popping up when least expected and undermining their whole operation.

Since there'd been little time for her to wind down from her first assignment, he backed out the door. He'd let her sleep. Then, knowing full well that he was inviting complications to an already complex task, but at a loss at how to handle the situation with Jenks, Cade paid the boy's way to New Orleans.

After delivering a dinner plate to Lilly's stateroom for when she awakened, he sauntered into the main cabin and joined a friendly game of cards.

Contrary to public conjecture, riverboats were not floating casinos inhabited by professional gamblers. The thought that polite society and reputable captains would condone such questionable behavior was ridiculous. While games of chance were common, for the most part they were an enjoyable way for the gentlemen onboard to pass the time, and it was common to see women included. Like any game, the stakes could get high on occasion, and there *was* the chance of a few gamblers making a trip now and again.

After playing a hand or two, Cade left the game and went on deck to check on Jenks. He was surprised to see that the boy had obeyed him for once and was sound asleep in an empty deck chair.

Cade took off his jacket and laid it over the child, then settled into the chair next to the boy. He crossed his arms over his chest to ward off the chilly nighttime air and closed his eyes. His last coherent thought was to wonder if Lilly was still sleeping and what her reaction would be to young Robert Jenkins.

CHAPTER 5

Lilly awakened with that heavy lethargy that came from sleeping too long, too hard. She covered a wide yawn and slanted a look at the light coming in through the high window, then swung her legs to the edge of the bed and stood. The engines throbbed, and though the floor was very steady, she was not unaware of the sensation of movement beneath her feet. A glance at the small watch pinned to the front of the traveling jacket she'd slung over the back of the chair confirmed that she'd slept away the entire afternoon. Why, it was almost eight! Why hadn't Cade tried to wake her?

It was then that she noticed the tray sitting on the small side table. He must have had someone bring her dinner while she was sleeping. A crystal stemmed glass with the Anchor insignia etched into its side stood next to a china plate with the same logo at the edge.

She lifted the silver cover and saw her dinner—chicken, potatoes, and fresh green beans. Her stomach growled, reminding her that it had been hours since she'd eaten. She picked up the fork and was about to lift a bite of potatoes to her mouth when the sound of a knock and the simultaneous grating of the key in the lock stopped her.

Cade stood in the doorway, his black hair slightly mussed and a day's growth of beard shadowing his lean cheeks. A raggedy, wide-eyed boy stood behind him, craning his neck to see into the room. Becoming aware of her state of undress, she snatched up the wrapper lying on the foot of the bed and slipped it on.

"I wouldn't eat that if I were you," Cade warned. "It might have gone bad since last night."

"Last night?"

"It's morning."

"Morning!" she cried, glancing up at the window again. The brighter sunshine said that it was indeed eight in the morning, instead of eight at night, when it would be much darker.

"I came to wake you for dinner, but you were sleeping so soundly I didn't have the heart to rouse you. I brought you the plate, but it can't be fit to eat by now."

She pushed the tangled hair away from her face. The boy watched her every movement as carefully as she watched his. "I must have been more tired than I thought."

"Evidently."

"Who's your friend?" she asked, since it appeared Cade had forgotten the child.

He stepped more fully into the room, taking the boy by the shoulder and propelling him inside. He offered Lilly a wry smile. "Since he is too old to be the son we have always longed for, I suppose he will have to be my younger brother."

"What?" Clearly her head was still sleep muddled, since the comment made no sense.

An ironic smile hiked one corner of her partner's mustache. "Jenks, this is my colleague, Miss Long. Lilly, meet Robert Jenkins. Better known on the streets as Jenks."

She eyed the child's scruffy attire and the dirt on his narrow face. "You know him?" she asked, somewhat aghast at the notion.

"Unfortunately."

The boy sketched a cocky bow, as if she were royalty and he didn't really give a rat's behind. "Ma'am."

Lilly inclined her head in dubious acknowledgment. "Robert."

"It ain't Robert; it's Jenks," the boy corrected. "I ain't been Robert since . . . well, since my mum . . . went away."

The child was definitely of Irish lineage. Even more apparent was the fact that he needed some parental guidance.

"Don't be so brassy when you speak to the lady," Cade told him. He scowled at the boy but spoke to Lilly. "Ever since we left Chicago, I've had the feeling we were being watched. And then yesterday afternoon I spotted him, but he got away. After I got you settled in, he became a bit careless and I nabbed him smack dab in the middle of a whisk."

"A whisk?" she asked, slanting a glance at the young ruffian.

"He was about to relieve a poor, unsuspecting gentleman of his money."

Jenks pushed out his chest in pride. "I'd figgered out the swell's wallet was in his left kick, don't cha know."

"That would be his left pocket," Cade explained.

"And how is it that you know what a left kick is?" she asked, her eyes wide with astonishment.

"Let's just say that Jenks's childhood is running parallel to mine."

Her eyes widened. "You were a pickpocket as a child?" she screeched.

"I'd have cut the president's throat if it would've meant food for my sisters and brothers," Cade said without a hint of apology.

Shocked and frowning, she looked from one male to the

other. "How is it then that you rose above your . . . upbringing and became a man who enforces the law?"

"As I said once before, you ask too many questions." His lips twisted into another of those acerbic smiles, but he added, "The good sisters did a first-rate job of convincing me I was headed straight for hell, so I went from stealing to battering other people senseless in a boxing ring to make a bit o' change."

It was the most he'd ever talked about his past, and Lilly suspected he wouldn't tell her much more. She decided to change the subject. "So he"—she glanced at the boy standing next to Cade—"has been following us all this time?"

"So it seems."

"How?"

With the assurance and worldliness of a much older person, Jenks moved past Cade and began to meander around the small cabin, touching the richness of the appointments.

"Don't even think of it," Cade warned.

The boy replied with an impudent grin. "Weren't hard. I had a bit o' money McShane left for me, but not enough to buy a ticket an' food, so I hopped one of the freight cars when you two left Chicago and I slipped onboard this tub right behind ya, I did."

Somewhat unnerved by the offhanded manner in which a mere child related how he'd followed them for hundreds of miles, Lilly shifted her gaze from the boy to Cade. "What do you propose we do with him?"

"He'll have to come with us. I can't just put him ashore at the next stop. Besides, I've already paid his fare."

"We can't take a child with us on an assignment. It would complicate things, and we will not have time to care for him. I suggest that when we stop next, we buy him a ticket back to Chicago."

"I won't go." Jenks glared up at her. "And I'm all paid up

to New Orleans. Besides, I don't need nobody to take care of me."

Cade was familiar with the boy's tone. "Steady there, lad," he said in a soothing voice, turning the boy to face him. "If you listen well and promise to do as I say, I'm sure we can work this out to everyone's satisfaction."

Lilly's arms were folded across her chest and she was regarding him with raised eyebrows.

"I told you Miss Long is my colleague. The truth of the matter is that we are traveling to New Orleans as a married couple to work a case."

She gestured toward the boy. "He knows what you do?" she asked, shocked.

"He does."

Jenks glared at Lilly and said, "I know more about him than you do, I'll wager." To Cade, he said, "What kind of case? Whatever it is, I can help."

"No doubt you'll get a chance to help. Lilly and I will be posing as Bran and Brona Sullivan." He gave him a sketchy overview of what they'd be doing. "You will be my little brother, Robbie." Cade was hoping the child would agree to go back to being called by the name he'd once confessed his mother had called him. "I think we should start getting used to calling each other by our new names."

"Robbie Sullivan, eh?" Jenks squared his shoulders, raised his pointed chin into the air, and looked at Lilly down his narrow nose. Then he swaggered toward Cade with a self-satisfied grin. "Bloody good, McShane. If that don't make me a huckleberry above a persimmon, nothing will!"

Lilly gasped at hearing the curse word coming from the child's lips.

"Oh," the boy crooned with an impish grin. "Brona don't like little Robbie, Bran."

"I don't *know* you," she snapped, resisting the urge to grind her teeth. "Suffice it to say that I am a bit taken aback by your unexpected arrival. But I do know that you should not be cursing like a grown man, and if you are to be in my—our—care, you can be sure that as your *big sister* I will wash out your mouth with soap if you do it in front of me."

To her surprise, Cade smiled. "She's right, Robbie," he said, taking the boy by the shoulders. "Listen, lad. We're a team. You, me, and Brona. We've a job to do, and we can't give it our best if we don't work together. It is very important that you don't take it upon yourself to meddle in our affairs, and it is imperative that you do as I tell you and that you mind Lilly, just as you do Meagan when you're with Seamus. If you don't, I will personally take you back to Chicago and leave you with the nuns. Do I make myself clear?"

"Aye," the boy said, hearing the explicit warning in Cade's voice.

"Then let's shake on it." They shook hands all around. "You might be interested to know that Brona has asked that I teach her how to defend herself on the street."

The child's eyes bugged in disbelief. "You're joshing me."

"Would that I were. I'm sure that there are things you can teach her that might come in handy, too. There will be plenty for you to do."

He gave Lilly a considering look. "I might be willin' to pass on a trick or two if you think she can take it."

"She can take it," Cade assured the boy. "She's pretty tough for a colleen."

Despite his use of the hated name, Lilly could not find it in herself to chastise him. It promised to be a long few weeks, and when it came to her association with Cadence McShane, she doubted Robbie Jenkins would be the only thing she'd have to deal with.

CHAPTER 6

Dressed in a plain white blouse and the olive-hued skirt she'd worn for one of her interviews with the Pinkertons, Lilly, now fully invested as the character of Brona, along with her two male escorts, left behind the wonderful time aboard the *Belle of Memphis.*

After days of hearing nothing but the thrashing of the paddle wheels, feeling the lift and fall of the boat, and seeing the lush landscape along the Mississippi slip by, the raucous activity at the Canal Street wharf was somewhat grating. The smell was unpleasant as well, she thought, hoping the shallow breaths she took would lessen the sickening odor of decaying fish and vegetation and God knew what else that hung in the humid atmosphere. The heavy air seemed too moisture-laden to even breathe, though they were still weeks from the oppressive heat of summer. But despite the uncommon trials associated with her arrival, she could not in truth say the ordeal lacked interest.

Since this was the *Belle's* maiden voyage, the curiosity seekers were out in full force. Inquisitive about the engines and eager to reconnect with friends and hear the latest gossip, well-dressed men made their way onboard while their feminine counterparts wandered along the dock, discreetly studying the ladies who disembarked. Fancy buggies waited to take fares to the local hotels.

Robbie stood at the railing, an expression of longing on his face as he watched children running and playing among the stacks of new wagon wheels and grain-filled tow sacks, and between the dark, sweating roustabouts unloading barrels and crates of merchandise. When the wagons were loaded, they would take the goods into town to distribute among various merchants. Seeing the wistful look on his face, Lilly wondered if the boy had ever had the opportunity to partake of the simple pleasures of childhood. If he'd ever had a real friend until Cade.

Cade whistled for a cab and Robbie's attention darted back to his mentor. The yearning gaze she'd seen in his dark eyes had been replaced with one of studied nonchalance as Cade assisted them into the buggy, helped load their trunks, and climbed in himself, instructing the driver to take them to the nearest telegraph office.

The diversity of the city was fascinating, Lilly thought as they made their way to the Louisiana Telegraph Company. The architecture, wrought-iron fencing, and aboveground sepulchers were things she could look at indefinitely. She glanced at Robbie, who she'd learned was ten, though he often seemed as jaded as someone three times that age. Caught up in the sights and sounds, he was unable to squelch his excitement. Cade's face showed no marked emotion, but as usual, she had the impression that he was taking in every sight, noise, and nuance around him, something she had yet to learn.

The telegraph office was situated near the railroad depot, a practice that had been in place since someone noted that the two activities complemented each other. Most telegraph companies strung their lines along railroad rights-of-way, and when, for whatever reason, it became necessary to deviate, the lines followed established stagecoach routes.

She watched as Cade disappeared through the door of the telegraph office. As befitting his new station in life, he was dressed in heavy work boots, brown twill trousers with braces, and a white collarless shirt. A cloth cap with a bill sat atop his dark hair. She had to admit he looked every inch the young Irish worker.

While he sent news to William of their arrival and the new addition to their "family," Lilly wondered again about the relationship between her partner and the boy. He'd assuaged part of her curiosity, explaining that the two had met at pivotal times in each other's lives, and that the child had become a bit possessive, which was natural since he had no family of his own. So far, she hadn't developed enough spine to question either of them about that time in any detail. When she'd asked Cade if William Pinkerton knew Robbie, he informed her curtly that the two had met.

She sneaked surreptitious glances at the boy standing next to the waiting buggy. Much to his chagrin, she'd seen to it that he received a bath the previous day, and she'd paid one of the service women to mend and wash his dirty clothing. He now wore the spare chambray shirt he'd brought in the knapsack holding his meager belongings. Although the sleeves were so short his bony wrists stuck out like sharp little knobs, the shirt was at least clean, pressed, and free of tears.

Though he flatly refused the use of brilliantine to tame his hair's unruliness, Lilly herself had cut his shaggy mane prior to his bath, and it now fell short of his collar and barely brushed his dark eyebrows. At least, she thought with a sigh, she'd seen no signs of head lice, and the thick, unruly mop was out of his eyes.

"What are ya lookin' at?" he asked, catching her staring at him.

It was no secret that even though he understood Cade's rules about the two of them getting along, he had little love for his new "sister." By no stretch of the imagination could his attitude toward her be described as anything beyond tolerance.

Very aware of the tension between them and determined to do her best to bring him around, she smiled. "I was just thinking we look like a nice family, and that I hope the housekeeper thinks well enough of us to hire us."

Robbie made a sound that could have been derision or agreement.

She stifled a little sigh. She'd apologized and done her best to explain to the child that her reactions when she'd first seen him in her doorway had been surprise and a simple loss as to how to deal with the situation. She did not tell him that once her shock had worn off, she had come to the realization that had it not been for Pierce and Rose taking her in, she herself might have wound up like Robbie.

Her heart had gone out to him, though she hadn't spoken a word of those tender feelings or shown him any overt kindnesses. Some innate instinct told her that, like Cade, Robbie would not appreciate any foolish, sentimental overtures. He was a tough little character, used to being on his own, living by his quick wits and quicker hands. He claimed he could take care of himself and that he needed no one "fawnin'" over him.

But he needed Cade, Lilly thought as she watched the boy's avid brown gaze fasten on his mentor as he stepped through the doorway of the telegraph office. He needed a father to guide him. In fact, the two were like father and son in many ways. No, Cade wasn't nearly as strict as she felt a father should be. He treated Robbie more like the indulged younger brother they pretended he was.

She was still skeptical about how his addition to their little family would work out, but Cade insisted it would be fine, that Robbie was quick as a steel trap and he'd seen the boy whip his weight in wildcats on more than one occasion—to which Lilly had intoned that Cade should not encourage such behavior. Instead, he should see to it that the child was taught Biblical principles and some semblance of manners.

To her surprise, her partner had offered her one of his rare, true smiles and said, "Ah, but that would be your job, dear wife."

She knew they all needed to get to know each other better if they were to fool the residents on Rampart Street, and since she was determined to successfully complete the job William Pinkerton had sent her to do, she tried once more to break through the child's armadillo hide.

"Were you scared riding in the boxcar from Chicago to St. Louis?" she asked, doing her best to draw the strange, adult-like child into a conversation. "I'd have been terrified."

Robbie gave her a look of disdain. "Weren't no picnic," he admitted. "It got a bit cold at night, and me with no coat and nothing but my knapsack for a pillow. Me and another kid snuggled together to keep warm, we did."

"There was another boy with you?"

"Aye, Tommy McDougal. He was goin' to St. Louis."

Genuinely troubled by Robbie's circumstances, she said, "I'm sorry you've had to live in such a way."

He shot her a sharp glance. "No fault of yours," he said. "I didn't have to come. I should have stayed with Seamus and Meagan like I was told ta do. Seamus is Cade's brother and a policeman, if you're a mind to know," he added. "But Meagan favors nagging more than a wee bit, and I couldn't let McShane leave me behind again. He needs me to look after him."

"Look after him?" Lilly echoed in amazement. "What do you mean? It seems to me that he should be looking after you."

"Isn't that what he's doing, then?" Robbie asked, cocking an eyebrow at her. "Isn't that why I'm here instead of on the next boat going upriver?"

"I suppose it is," she agreed. "What do you mean? How do you look after him?"

"You'll have to ask him that, won't ya?" Robbie said. "I figure if he wants ya to know, he'll tell ya."

He was loyal; she'd give him that. The notion of asking Cade about his past association with the tough little guy sitting next to her was not one that seemed appealing. She could still hear him telling her that she asked too many questions and that he confided his sins to no one unless he was drunk or in the confessional. She heaved a deep sigh. She would not be asking Cadence McShane anything more about his past in the near future.

They were soon rolling through the heart of the French Quarter, exclaiming over every new and wonderful sight they passed. The thriving city was filled with history. It seemed there was a vibration to it, a vital pulse of the many nationalities that had settled there, blending their cultures into one unique heart that beat with every rumble of wagon, every vendor's call, every smile she encountered. She was glad she'd come and hoped she would have a chance to explore the city in more detail while she was here.

A quick lunch was something spicy called gumbo, filled with sausage, chicken, shrimp, peppers, onions, and a vegetable itself called gumbo, or okra, in a tasty brown sauce served over a bed of rice. Vastly different from anything she'd ever eaten, Lilly loved the blend of flavors. The hearty dish was followed with a deep-fried, fruit-filled dough called a *fritter*. Soon afterward, Cade instructed the driver to take them to the Fontenot home, which was situated on the edge of the French Quarter.

The driver turned onto St. Anne, took a left on Royal for one block, and then made another right at St. Peter, where he stayed for a distance before turning onto Rampart Street. The Fontenot home was somewhat narrow and deep, a perfect example of how well the front gable style conformed to the restrictive size of the city lots.

Having longed for a home of her own the past few years, Lilly had taken more than a passing interest in architectural styles and thought she recognized an Italianate influence. Its wooden façade boasted two stories, the upper supported by decorative brackets instead of posts or pillars.

The full-length windows were topped by flattened arches. The front porch steps spanned three quarters of its length, and the posts and upper railing were painted a pristine white that contrasted nicely with the sedate steel gray of the house. The lower porch had no railings.

Though narrow, the yard was shaded by several huge oak trees. A plethora of shrubs and flowers bordered the house and created a lacy edging down the front path. The driver pulled alongside the house and around back. When Lilly looked askance at Cade, he offered a wry smile.

"We're here to interview as the hired help, Brona, and don't you forget it," he told her.

The back door opened as soon as he alighted. A tall woman, somewhere on the shady side of forty, exited the house. Clad in unrelenting black save for the pristine white apron covering the front of her simply styled gown, she stood in the aperture, her back ramrod straight, her blue gaze probing, and her thin lips downturned with what could only be described as disapproval.

Her graying blond hair was scraped into a tight bun atop

her head. Lilly had the feeling that not a single hair of the woman's head would have had the audacity to straggle. She also thought that with a different hairstyle and a smile she could be passably attractive.

Cade helped Lilly down; Robbie jumped down by himself. Donning the boxer's persona, Cade approached the woman with a friendly smile, his hand extended. "Mrs. Abelard? I'm Bran Sullivan." He gestured toward Lilly and Robbie. "This is my wife, Brona, and my little brother, Robbie. We're here to see about the positions my brother said might be available."

The woman ignored his outstretched hand. "I am Hedda Abelard," she said with a thick German accent. Her stony gaze moved to Robbie. "Your brother made no mention of a child."

"I am aware of that," Cade said in his most apologetic tone, "but since I last spoke with him, our mother has died and there was no one in Chicago to look after the boy."

He turned to Robbie, and Lilly saw the warning in Cade's eyes.

"He's a good lad and a hard worker."

Lilly kept her eyes downcast. She fully expected a lightning bolt to come from the cloudless sky at the blatant lie and knock them all into eternity.

"If we are hired, I'll see to it that he pulls his weight." Cade gave Mrs. Abelard another of those bone-melting smiles.

The woman visibly softened, revealing a hint of that restrained prettiness. Lilly resisted the urge to groan. Even the seemingly inflexible Hedda Abelard was no challenge for a handsome, smooth-talking man.

"Normally," Mrs. Abelard intoned, finding her professional persona once more, "I would not be so accommodating; however, the last couple who was here found higher-paying employment and left us more than a month ago without giving notice. We have been muddling through with part-time help, but we need reliable, full-time staff, especially since this is Holy Week and Easter Sunday is upon us."

"It is unfortunate, but those things happen," Cade said in a sympathetic tone. "But I can assure you that we are dependable employees. We have our latest reference." He turned and held out a hand toward Lilly, who reached into her reticule and withdrew a sealed envelope. He passed it to Mrs. Abelard, who opened the letter and began to read.

Lilly knew exactly what the letter said, since it had been composed by William Pinkerton and typed up by Harris on his trusty Remington typewriter. Posing as the Sullivans' last employer, Mr. Terrence Turner, William had recounted Bran and Brona's hard work, their loyalty and honesty, ending with the tongue-in-cheek promise that Bran could "whip things into shape," and Brona would "get to the bottom of things" and would do their jobs well. Finished, Mrs. Abelard sighed and divided a severe look between Cade and Lilly.

"Fine, then. Your wife will be helping Lamartine in the kitchen as well as with other household duties that I deem necessary. You, Mr. Sullivan, will be working with Amos, Lamartine's husband, doing whatever needs to be done outside, as well as tending the horses and carriages."

She looked at Robbie, whose sharp-eyed expression had been miraculously transformed into the countenance of an angel. Lilly wondered if he, too, had acting experience.

The housekeeper gave the boy a hard look. "Since I have nowhere else to put you, you will stay with Bernard, Amos and Lamartine's son. You, Mr. and Mrs. Sullivan, will occupy a room at the top of the servant's stairs, across from Amos and Lamartine."

Lilly shot a wide-eyed look at Cade, who only smiled that

infuriating smile, and told the housekeeper that it all sounded perfect.

Mrs. Abelard told them what they would be making per week, that they would be paid on Fridays, and that they would have Mondays off. "Come along to the stables," she said, the matter settled to everyone's satisfaction, "and I will introduce you to Amos."

Amos Lagasse was a huge man, and as handsome as sin. Tall and broad and sleekly muscled, his dark skin had a definite copper hue, and his features were noble and finely wrought. His cheekbones were as high as those Lilly had seen in renderings of the proud Indian chiefs, his nose straight and chiseled.

He and Cade shook hands, and Amos introduced his son, Bernard, a lad of thirteen who was the spitting image of his father. Eager to see everyone settled, the housekeeper told Amos that as soon as Bran and Brona met Lamartine and Madam Fontenot and were settled in, Bran could come out and have his duties explained more fully.

"No doubt Madam is up from her afternoon rest," the German woman told them as they made their way through a well-tended herb garden toward the kitchen. "She has been having some stomach issues from time to time, and she is getting on in years and tires more easily than she would like. Dinner is at seven. Brona, you will please do the serving for Madam and the doctor."

"B–but I've never served dinner before," Lilly blurted, remembering at the last moment to adopt an Irish accent.

Mrs. Abelard shot her a sharp look.

"I have only just cleaned and been a ladies' maid," Lilly told her. "I am quite good with doing hair and choosing outfits."

Mrs. Abelard gave a sigh of exasperation. "Then you must learn. I will show you tonight, but from then on you will be doing all of those things—making the beds, cleaning, serving, and helping with whatever else Lamartine or I need you to do."

"Yes, ma'am. I'm a quick study," Lilly said truthfully, as, with her hand tucked into the crook of Cade's arm, they followed the older woman into the kitchen. "I'll soon get the hang of what you require."

The sweet aromas of butter and brown sugar blended in the afternoon air, wafting from the open doorway. Lamartine, the cook, was just taking a cake of some sort from the oven of a brand-new wood-burning stove. Turning toward her, his back to the housekeeper, Cade rolled his eyes in an imitation of swooning ecstasy that made Lilly's lips twitch with the longing to smile. The boxer had made the briefest of appearances.

Schooling her features to solemnity and digging her fingernails into his arm, she pressed her lips together and let her gaze roam the room, spying two freshly plucked chickens in a bowl of water, waiting to be plunked into one of the copper pots that hung from a rack on the ceiling, or cut up, dredged in flour, and fried in the huge cast-iron skillet sitting on the stove.

The cook was as tall as Mrs. Abelard, but where the German housekeeper was all angles and planes, with mostly unremarkable features, Lamartine Lagasse was all rounded flesh and curves and as exotically beautiful as her husband was handsome.

Her skin was the color of the café au lait Lilly had drunk with her fritter earlier. What hair that was not hidden by the brightly hued tignon wrapped around her head was honey brown. Her nose was narrow, with the slightest bit of a flare at the nostrils, and her eyes, a startling light gray-blue, were framed with thick, sooty lashes. Her lips were full and enticing. Without a doubt she was one of the most beautiful women Lilly had ever seen. No wonder Bernard was so handsome.

Despite her regal bearing and a strange expression in her eyes that Lilly could not quite place, there was a smile of welcome on Lamartine's face when Mrs. Abelard made the introductions.

"We're pleased to have you," she said in the soft New Orleans patois they'd heard so much of in the few hours since they had docked.

While Mrs. Abelard explained that Brona needed some tutoring in serving, Lilly's gaze roamed the spotless kitchen with its wood floors and round oak table with a bowl of brown eggs in the middle. A hand pump with a copper basin sat beneath the window that was draped with calico curtains, eliminating the need to go outside for water. It was truly the home of the wealthy.

Robbie, who had had a peek at his room, rejoined them. Lilly was pleased to see that he was still on good behavior. Satisfied that the Sullivans' room was ready and that things were on schedule for dinner, Mrs. Abelard inclined her head toward a doorway and said, "Follow me, please. I will introduce you to Madam Fontenot. The doctor will not be home until just before dinner."

They followed the housekeeper through a dining room with windows looking out over a sun-dappled side yard, where plump cherubs and stately angels played peekaboo from behind carefully trimmed shrubbery. An ornately carved table sat in front of the window. A huge black cat sprawled across the delicate needlepoint runner next to a jade-green vase filled with sweet-smelling roses.

As they entered the room, the feline raised its head and considered them with narrowed eyes. Its left ear was missing a chunk, and a jagged scar ran from the ear across an eye to the bridge of the feline's nose. The injury had left the eye milky white. Deciding they were not worth expending any further energy on, the beast lay its massive head back down on its paws and began to purr.

Taking it as a sign of acceptance, Robbie reached out to give the fellow a pat. The feline instantly lifted his head, hissed a warning, and made a flashing slash with his right paw. Robbie jerked back his hand just in time to avoid a nasty scratch and turned to look at Cade and Lilly with wide eyes. The cat was quick.

"Have a care for that one, young man," Mrs. Abelard said, pointing at the cat. "That is Lucifer, and he does not take kindly to anyone but Madam."

"Yes, ma'am." For once, Robbie looked as if he would take the warning to heart.

Sliding aside pocket doors that were at least ten feet in height, the housekeeper ushered them through the drawing room and down a hall to a library where a tiny woman with snow-white hair sat at a desk, the skirts of her eggplant-hued gown spread over the Oriental carpet as she pored over a book of some sort, a quill in her right hand that glittered with rings.

"Madam."

The woman jumped. "Damnation, Mrs. Abelard, must you sneak up on a body?" the old woman asked, blotting at a large spot of ink.

"I beg your pardon, Madam. I didn't mean to startle you. The Sullivans have arrived, and as you suggested, I've taken the liberty to hire them, since their referral appears impeccable and we are so near Easter."

LaRee Fontenot rose in one smooth motion, the grace of her movements belying her age. As she approached them, Lilly took the opportunity to study the woman who had requested the help of the Pinkertons.

She was short—not quite five feet if Lilly had to guess—

and there was not an ounce of extra flesh on her small frame. Her face was a network of wrinkles, powdered and rouged, but with exquisite care. Her hair was curly and as white as a fresh-washed bedsheet, with unruly tendrils escaping to frame her delicate features. Her eyes were as black as Lucifer and filled with a quiet intelligence. Unlike the cat, Lilly suspected that everything that went on in the house was of interest to the petite woman.

"Mr. and Mrs. Sullivan, Madam Fontenot. Madam, Mr. Bran Sullivan, his wife, Brona, and his brother, Robbie."

The mistress of the house gave them each a quick once-over with those sharp dark eyes and then, smiling a smile of welcome, she said, "Welcome to New Orleans and my home. We are so very glad you're here."

CHAPTER 7

After a brief visit with Mrs. Fontenot, who seemed quite taken with young Robbie, the boy went off with Bernard to the room they would share, and Cade carried his and Lilly's bags to their new room. Situated on the north side of the house, it overlooked the shaded backyard with the stables beyond.

An iron bedstead up against one wall and covered with a colorful quilt was the room's focal point, and a narrow and simply crafted pine armoire was placed across from it. A plain pine chest of drawers and a shaving stand with a mirror atop sat on either side. A comfortable-looking chair sat near the window. Matching rag rugs lay on either side of the bed, which Lilly eyed with a sense of trepidation.

Seeing the expression on her face, Cade gave what could only be described as a disgusted snort. "Have no fear for your virtue, madam. I will be perfectly happy to sleep on the floor." He gave her a rueful smile. "Well, perhaps happy is a bit over-stating it."

"If you think humor and a smile will soften my heart and

I will agree to letting you share this bed, you are sorely mistaken," she snapped, though the image that filled her mind left her feeling a trifle shaky.

He sobered in an instant. "I can assure you, Brona, I have seen little in our short acquaintance that leads me to believe that your heart can be softened. Whoever the man was who hurt you left nothing behind to work with."

Lilly sucked in a sharp breath, both at the callousness and insight of his words. Was her disillusionment so obvious? Biting her lower lip, she pivoted toward the window. "The condition of my heart, sir, is none of your concern."

"You're right. It isn't."

She turned at the sound of him flopping onto the bed. He lay on his back, his fingers laced behind his head. "So what do you think so far?"

Lilly's forehead puckered as she sorted out her impressions. She was hesitant to tell him anything since she preferred to make as much headway as possible on this case by her own wit and skill. As far as she was concerned, her "partner" was just a nuisance she had to deal with along the way.

When he just lay there regarding her with an enigmatic expression, she said, "I think Mrs. Abelard will be a hard taskmaster and that Mrs. Fontenot may be old, but she has a very sharp mind. I'm glad Bernard is here for Robbie, even though he is a bit older."

"I agree all around," Cade concurred. "You'll be working a lot with Lamartine. She and Amos should be a good source of information about the family."

She nodded. "Pierce has always maintained that the servants know as much about what goes on in a household as the homeowners, and it's been my experience that, in general, women like to talk."

"Tread lightly with your questions," Cade warned. "We don't want to rouse any suspicion."

"Certainly," Lilly said with a hint of asperity. Did the wretched man think she was a total nincompoop?

"I'll do the same with Amos. He'll know a lot about the doctor's habits. And don't forget Robbie."

"Robbie?" She'd never thought of him as any real help to the investigation. She'd been more worried about him pilfering some valuable trinket and all of them getting the boot or going to jail before they could accomplish their goals.

"Yes, Robbie," Cade said, sitting up abruptly and resting his forearms on his raised knees. "He's very good at making himself inconspicuous. He's also an excellent judge of character, and he has an uncanny way of finding out the most obscure things."

"How?"

Cade's wry smile was tinged with grimness. "I don't know, and I'm fairly certain I'd rather not be told." Without missing a beat, he asked, "Tell me about Pierce."

"Pierce?" she echoed. "Why?"

"Because for all intents and purposes, we're man and wife, and the more we know about each other's pasts, the more believable we'll be."

"Pierce is Sir Pierce Wainwright. He's the manager of the troupe I've been with for several years."

"But he isn't your father?"

"He's the only father I've ever known, and his wife, Rose, has been my mother since I was eleven."

"What happened to your real mother?"

"Did anyone ever tell you that you ask too many questions, McShane?" she said, hitting him with the same reply he had given her on more than one occasion.

"Touché." In a sudden move, as if he were suddenly tired of the conversation, he stood, the motion smooth and fluid for a man his size.

"She was murdered."

Lilly had no idea what had prompted her to give him the information, when it was a topic of conversation she'd avoided for half her life. But ever since her memory of that day had returned at Heaven's Gate, it seemed there was no reason to avoid the subject. The pain was there, would always be there, but time had dulled all but the sharpest and most vivid recollections.

Cade, who was tucking his shirt into his trousers more tightly, paused. "Murdered?"

"Yes."

He was about to respond when there was a rapid knocking on the door and, without waiting for a summons, Robbie poked his head in. "Don't nobody like the doctor," he said with a triumphant smile.

Cade glanced from the boy to Lilly. "See, colleen. I told you."

"Told her what?"

"That you'd be a big help to us."

"Better help than she will, I wager," he mumbled, shooting a dark look her way.

"It isn't a contest, Robbie. It's a job we're working on together, and don't you forget it."

"An' how can I be forgettin' with you remindin' me every few minutes?" he complained. Then he shoved the pile of black and white he was holding at Lilly. "Here. It's your dress and apron from Miz Lagasse. She said it might be too big, but it's all she has right now."

"Thank you, Robbie," she said, taking the clothing from him.

"She sent some thread and a needle and said you could have until just before supper to work on it if you like."

"That isn't much time."

"You work on the dress, and Robbie and I will carry up our things," Cade suggested.

"Thank you." She was grateful for the help and also that her time with the theater had taught her the necessity of sewing, since the actors were responsible for their costumes for each role they played. "I'm sure it will take a while to make the adjustments."

Cade and Robbie, along with Bernard, brought up their bags and then left Lilly while they went down to learn more of their duties. It took every minute of the time allotted to take up the dress, which was too big through the midsection and needed turning up a hem's length.

She finished the handwork just in the nick of time and hurriedly prepared herself for her new position. The last thing she needed was to be late on the first day.

She washed up and smoothed her hair into a tidy bun. Then she donned the dress and the white apron that boasted a three-inch ruffle over the shoulders and around the edge. A bit frilly for her taste, but thank goodness she wasn't expected to wear any kind of cap! A quick glance in the mirror told her that she looked her part, and with a deep breath and a reminder to stay in character throughout the evening, she went downstairs.

Delicious aromas wafted through the air, with the smell of baked chicken reigning supreme.

Lamartine, who was ladling green beans and potatoes into a divided bowl, looked up as Lilly entered the kitchen. After a moment's scrutiny that raked her from head to toe, the cook gave a single nod. "You'll do. I knew the dress would be too big, but it's all I had. It looks like you're handy with a needle."

"Yes, thank you," Lilly told her. "What can I do to help?"

"Watch and listen," the older woman said. "Mrs. Fontenot has plenty of money, and she likes things done nice, but she isn't one of those uppity ladies who puts on airs and does everything all fancy-like unless there's a houseful in attendance for a meal.

"We use the Blue Willow dishes for every day, and the plain

white china for formal dinners. Do you know how to set a proper table?"

"I'm afraid not," Lilly confessed.

Lamartine got out the container that held the silverware and laid out everything the way it should be, explaining the use of the various forks and spoons as she placed them on either side of the plate, telling Lilly that they should be about an inch from the edge of the table. Next, she showed her where to place the different glasses, the salt cellars, and coffee cups.

"Mrs. Abelard has already set the table, but make sure you do it just this way, 'cause *she's* the fussy one." The pretty black woman gave a disdainful sniff. "She tries to impress the doctor," she noted. "As if anything will ever come of *that.*"

The instant Lamartine said the words, she shot a mortified look at Lilly, who feigned nonchalance and adjusted one of the glasses the slightest bit.

The awkward moment passed, and Lamartine finished her explanation. "The sherry is on the table. Mrs. Abelard will carve the meat, and the two of you will serve everything else from the sideboard. Normally, it will be just one person serving. One servant for every two people, but she wants you to learn. You Catholic?" she asked suddenly.

"Uh, not a good one, I'm afraid," Lilly fabricated.

"Well, Madam gives up meat for Lent, and during Holy Week, she only takes one meal a day, at night. Since today is Good Friday, she'll only take bread and water. Now, in the morning, she'll most likely have hot chocolate and a bite of toast. That's not considered breaking fast," Lamartine explained. "But I'm sure you already know about that, even if you're a bad Catholic."

"If Mrs. Fontenot won't eat anything, what's all this food for?"

"The doctor. He ain't no kind of religious from what I can see. And you and your family has to eat, and me and mine."

Lilly nodded.

"If we have guests, coffee is served in the parlor, and the gentlemen go to the study for their brandy and cigars, but since it's just Madam and the doctor, he'll have his coffee at the table along with his dessert. She hasn't been goin' to evening mass much since Miz Patricia's been gone, so she'll go back to her room as soon as she eats. She don't like spendin' more time with him than she has to."

Again, the cook seemed to know she had said too much to the new help.

"I take it Madam Fontenot and Dr. Ducharme aren't close," Lilly commented, making sure to use her Irish brogue. "It seems there's a bit o' that in every household."

Before Lamartine could answer, Mrs. Abelard's heavily accented voice sounded from the doorway. "What's the holdup, Lamartine? Madam and the doctor are already seated."

"I'm sorry, Mrs. Abelard," Lamartine said in a diffident voice. "I was just trying to explain to Brona how you like things done."

"I like things done at the proper time, as you well know," the housekeeper snapped. "Brona, you bring that bowl of vegetables, and I'll bring the chicken. Lamartine, you carry the gravy boat and the bread."

"Yes, ma'am," the two underlings chorused. Dishes in hand, the trio filed into the dining room, where the two household members sat, Henri Ducharme at the head of the long table and LaRee Fontenot, dressed in a gown of unrelenting black, seated at his right.

The doctor, who Lilly knew was forty-seven, was indeed a handsome man. Of medium height, he had a bladelike nose, arresting blue eyes, a dimpled chin, and a mouth that most would describe as sensual. He had no mustache, and his slightly curly dark hair had gone gray at the temples. It was easy to see how a certain type of woman might be drawn to him.

As soon as the items were placed on the sideboard, Lamartine disappeared into the kitchen and Mrs. Abelard set about carving the perfectly browned hen. "Watch carefully how I do this," she said sotto voce.

With low instructions and watching her superior, Lilly took careful note of how things were done.

As they served the meal, it was easy to see that Lamartine was right. Hedda Abelard was definitely aware of the doctor, whose every smile sent a blush rushing into the cheeks of the austere German. When the meal was served, she and Lilly stood at the ends of the sideboard, their hands folded, waiting.

"How are the preparations for Sunday's lawn party coming along?" Henri asked Madam. Even as he spoke, his gaze met the housekeeper's.

"It is my understanding that they are coming along nicely," Mrs. Fontenot said. The expression on her wrinkled face looked as if she'd taken a bite of a green persimmon. She laid aside her crust of bread. "I really wish you would call this party off, Henri."

"Now, *Grand-mère*," he said in a voice reeking with condescension.

Mrs. Fontenot's lips tightened.

"We've been through this a hundred times."

"And I have not changed my mind on the matter," the old woman told him in a sharp tone. "Not only is it Holy Week, but it's far too soon to be entertaining with Suzannah in her grave such a short time. Not to mention that your wife is locked up in an asylum."

"As you well know, I do not share your religious beliefs, so the fact that it is Holy Week is of little consequence to me," he said, eyeing a bite of chicken critically. "Mrs. Abelard, please inform Lamartine that the chicken is a bit dry. She needs to watch it more carefully the next time."

His patronizing attitude made Lilly want to walk over and slap the smugness from his face.

"Yes, Doctor."

Mrs. Fontenot pinned the doctor with a critical gaze once more. "Well, what about poor Patricia? Don't you think Sunday would be better spent in visiting her at that dreadful place you sent her?"

Lilly tried not to cringe. It was clear that the verbal jab was intentional. The little lady was courageous, she'd give her that. A sideways glance at Mrs. Abelard told her that the housekeeper was also aware of the sudden tension between the two.

Henri picked up his glass of wine, regarded the mistress of the house with a cool expression before he took a sip, and placed the glass carefully back onto the white damask cloth. "You know very well why I put her in that dreadful place, as you insist on calling it."

"I know your reasons, yes," she said. "But how do you think she will ever get better if she's locked away somewhere?"

"My dear *Grand-mère*," he said, "you know our lovely Patricia was suffering from severe melancholy as well as putting blame on others, which at times led to hostility. From what I've read and studied about these aberrations, her improvement relies upon receiving proper medications and care."

"In other words, they're drugging her into submission."

"Of course they're not," he scoffed.

"You did."

Hot color suffused the doctor's face. It seemed Mrs. Fontenot was determined to goad him into . . . what? Anger? Why? What did she want to accomplish? Or was she hoping he would confess that he'd done wrong?

"On the contrary, I put her where she could get the proper care so that she would not become dependent on the laudanum, which as you well know was the only thing that calmed her."

Lilly saw the slight slump in the woman's narrow shoulders. She'd given up. For the moment, at least.

The meal was almost over before the doctor acknowledged Lilly. She was pouring his coffee when he asked, "So, Mrs. Abelard, I see we have more new help."

"Yes, sir. This is Brona Sullivan. She'll be working with me on the household chores and Lamartine in the kitchen. Her husband, Bran, and his young brother, Robbie, will be working alongside Amos and Bernard."

Ducharme gave Lilly the full force of his smile. She tried not to reveal how uncomfortable he made her.

"Welcome, Mrs. Sullivan," he said. "I hope you'll enjoy your time with us."

"I'm sure I will, sir," she said. "Thank you."

When the meal was finished, Mrs. Abelard told Lilly that she would see to the needs of the doctor and Mrs. Fontenot the rest of the evening. Lilly was happy to let her. She wanted to think about her impressions, and she wondered if Cade or Robbie had learned anything.

The two men and the boys had joined Lamartine in the kitchen. Plates heaped with food were in front of them. Robbie was tucking into the meal as if he hadn't eaten in a week. In a matter of days, Lilly had learned that he had a hollow leg. His favorite saying seemed to be that he was so hungry he could eat the back door buttered.

"Fix yourself a plate, Brona," Lamartine offered. "I couldn't get these heathens to wait for you."

"We been working all afternoon, we have," Robbie said, talking around the food in his mouth.

Lilly pinned him with one of those "motherly" looks and tapped her closed mouth with her index finger, a reminder that he should chew with his mouth closed, as she'd been trying to teach him. Instead, he crossed his eyes and stuck out his tongue with some half-chewed food on it.

"That's enough, Robbie," Cade said in a curt tone. "Keep

your gob closed when you're eating. Now tell Brona you're sorry, and show her some respect."

"Yes, sir." He pasted that angelic face on once again and murmured, "Sorry, Brona."

Lilly knew that the agreement would last only until the next time he felt he could rub her the wrong way.

Cade gestured toward the seat next to him. "You're looking a bit tired, colleen," he said, his eyes alight with mischief. He knew there was no way she could chastise him for using the hated term in front of their new coworkers. "Sit down and tell us about your day."

Lilly's eyes narrowed, but she smiled as she took the chair. "I am a wee bit tired with the travelin' and all. A proper bed will feel wonderful tonight."

Before she knew what he was about to do, Cade leaned over, planted a kiss on her cheek, and said, "Indeed it will."

The suggestive tone caught her off guard. She felt her shoulders straighten and shot him a pointed look, which no one at the table could miss.

Cade flashed his boxer's smile at those sitting around the table. "She's still a bit miffed at me for moving her away from her family, but ya have to go where the work is, right, Amos?"

"You're right about that," Cade's coworker said. "I been real lucky. My family's been workin' for the Fontenots since I was about Robbie's age. Even before the War, they never did have any slaves. They're all good people. Fair. But things have been a lot different around here since Mr. Garrett passed and Miz Patricia married the doctor."

"He seemed pleasant enough at dinner," Lilly said with a shrug, hoping the innocence of her statement would elicit some information. "Though he and Madam seemed at odds over Sunday's lawn party."

"That's been a sore spot ever since he said he wanted to

have a party." Lamartine gave a shake of her head. "She thinks it's too soon since Miss Suzannah's passing, and she's right, but the doctor don't care a whit for customs."

"Who was Miss Suzannah?" Lilly asked, as if she had no knowledge of the family situation. She forked up a bite of potatoes.

"Miz Patricia's younger daughter," Bernard said, speaking up for the first time. "I miss her. She was always nice to me."

"She passed a little more than four months ago," Lamartine told them.

"That's too bad," Cade said. "Was she ill?"

"Weren't sick at all," Amos said. "They went to hear that Merrick woman speak about women gettin' to vote. Miss Suzie got separated from her mama and sister in the crowd. They found her a couple of days later, dead."

At a warning look from his wife, Amos left out just how Suzannah had died and what heinous things had been done to her prior to her death. That was not suppertime conversation with women and two children at the table.

"Miz Patricia was really torn up," Lamartine said. "Losing her daughter so soon after her baby bein' born dead was just too much for her mind to take, accordin' to the doctor."

"Oh, poor thing!" Lilly said, putting just the right amount of sorrow and empathy in her voice. "Bran and I know how painful losing a child can be." She reached out and placed her hand on Cade's arm in a gesture she hoped looked both tender and consoling.

He turned to her in surprise as she gave their new friends a morsel of their fabricated pasts. "We've lost a baby of our own."

She was taken aback at the pain she saw on his face. She would love to know why the mention of a child's death affected him so. The look was gone the next instant, and to her astonishment, he picked up her hand and pressed a kiss to her knuckles. He did not utter a word.

Even to Lilly, who knew it was an act, the gesture was poignant. Once again, she was amazed at his acting skills. He was quite, quite good at this. Pierce would have been proud to add him to their group of players.

"I'm sorry for that," Lamartine told them, her eyes filled with sympathy. "But it'll happen when the good Lord is ready for it to happen."

"You're right." Cade released Lilly's hand and went back to his meal.

Lamartine looked from one to the other and continued her tale. "Doctor was gonna put her in a mental hospital way out in the country somewhere, but Miz LaRee pitched a right proper fit. Said he was ashamed of her and that they'd never get to see her, so finally, the doctor put her in the city asylum, right here in N'Awlin's."

Lilly made a sympathetic sound and did her best not to let her disgust show. Troublesome female family members were often admitted to loathsome places for such nonsensical things as reading romance novels or being overly religious. She'd heard tales about the cruel and inhumane treatment common to most mental hospitals and how the difficult patients were restrained or drugged, just as Mrs. Fontenot had suggested.

"How is she doing? Patricia?"

"We haven't heard nobody say," Amos mused. "Doctor told everyone it's best if no one goes to visit, so she won't get all stirred up again."

"Well, I think he's wrong."

Everyone turned to look at Robbie, surprised the child would have an opinion one way or the other.

"It ain't right to just leave her there, is it?" He shot an irritated look at Cade. "She should have some visitors, so she'll know she ain't been forgot about, don't ya think, Bran?"

"I think," Cade said, pointing the tines of his fork at the

boy, "that this conversation is for grownups. Children should be seen and not heard—remember?"

"Well, I agree with Robbie," Lilly said.

After that, the conversation centered on all the work that would have to be accomplished the following day in order to have things ready for the Sunday lawn party. Even with temporary help coming to lend a hand, it sounded like an enormous amount to accomplish in a short time. How could she and her partners possibly do any snooping with so many tasks to complete?

Lilly stayed behind to help clean up the kitchen, and the men went out to check the horses once more before bedtime. By the time she opened the door to her room, Cade was already there, lying on his pallet in the floor, a sheet pulled to his waist. His chest was bare. The sight was disturbing, reminding her once more that her mother's willful blood ran through her veins despite her constant efforts to keep it under control.

"You aren't wearing anything . . . on top."

"No, I'm not. I'm wearing my drawers, though, so never fear."

There was no hiding the mockery in his voice or his eyes. Then, as if to underscore the words, he turned his back to her. "Go ahead and change," he said. "I won't look."

"I never thought you would."

His smile told her that he knew she was lying.

Lilly grabbed a long-sleeved gown from her bag and undressed in record time, fearful that he would not keep his word. The simple white gown had gathers that fell from a rounded yoke and was done up with tiny mother-of-pearl buttons. She was just fastening the last one when he said, "So what do you think of the Lagasses?"

Lilly settled herself in the center of the bed and pulled the covers up to her neck. "I think they're very nice and Lamartine is a hard worker."

Hearing that she was probably settled, Cade glanced over his shoulder and rolled over when he saw that she was secure in bed. "So are Amos and Bernard. Spending time with them will be good for Robbie. He needs a new path for his life. He's been on his own way too much since he was seven or so."

"What happened to his parents?" she asked, tugging the hairpins from her hair and allowing it to fall over her shoulders and past her breasts in a straight, silky swath of red.

He didn't answer for a moment as he watched her swoop the hair to one side and start to braid it. Then he cleared his throat and said, "They left him in a cemetery, told him they were going to find something to eat and never came back. He's been on his own ever since."

Hearing of Robbie's past, the child's statement concerning Patricia Ducharme made perfect sense. Without a doubt, he was comparing their situations and had seen definite similarities.

"How did the two of you meet?"

He regarded her steadily for a moment, as if he wasn't sure he wanted to share the information with her. Reaching some inner peace with the notion, he said, "For the record, I don't normally share my personal life with my coworkers, but understanding the boy's past might explain some of his actions. You might be able to give him a little more leeway when he gets . . . disrespectful."

"Perhaps it would."

He took a deep breath and began. "I sort of took Robbie under my wing more than a year ago, and we've been chums ever since. My family helps keep an eye on him." His mouth twisted into a wry smile. "It would seem from this latest escapade that he's grown a little attached to me."

Lilly was itching to know how the two met, but doubted he'd tell her if she asked. Instead, she said, "I can't imagine him fending for himself at that age. How did he survive?"

"By doing what he was doing when I spotted him on the boat. Picking pockets, stealing from the markets and begging. Going through the garbage that restaurants toss out."

The thought of a seven-year-old roaming the streets of Chicago, alone in the stench and the filth and the darkness, never knowing where he'd lay his head for the night or where his next meal would come from was unthinkable to someone who'd been loved and fed and cared for. Lilly had a new appreciation for the life Pierce and Rose had given her. There but for fortune, she could have been another Robbie . . . with even worse options open to her.

She wondered how his parents had cared so little for him that they'd abandoned him to the horrible unknowns of the city. That fact had to be a heavy burden for him to carry. It was no wonder that he had a chip on his shoulder or that he'd grabbed hold of the first person to show him any concern. She felt her heart begin to soften.

"That's terrible."

Cade shrugged. "There are a lot of lads like him out there, and whatever you do, don't let on like you know anything or change how you deal with him. He may not have any schooling, but he's smart, that boy. He can spot a phony a mile away, and he won't appreciate your pity."

Cade had been one of those boys, she thought, remembering the bit he'd told her about his past and how the nuns had helped get him on the straight and narrow.

She tied a ribbon she'd taken from her bag around the tip of her braid. "I understand." Knowing what was behind the boy's actions *would* go a long way toward dealing with him in the right way.

"So what have we learned today?" Cade asked, resting his elbow on the pillow and his head in his hand.

Lilly wasn't sure she wanted to share her thoughts with him. Still, they *were* supposed to be working together. Maybe if she gave him a crumb he'd be happy. There was no reason she should tell him everything.

"The doctor and Mrs. Fontenot don't like each other much," she told him instead. "And they quarreled during dinner over this party he insists on having."

"Amos said they've been arguing about it for weeks. I think it would behoove us to keep an eye on what happens on Sunday. He also said that Cassandra and her husband are driving in from the plantation tomorrow. They'll be here by lunchtime."

Blast! It seemed that Amos was going to be a better source of information than Lamartine. Lilly hadn't thought about Patricia's older daughter coming, which meant two more family members to keep track of. She'd planned on watching Henri with an eagle eye, weigh every move he made and find out what she could about everyone he spoke to, and now her attention would be even more scattered. Maybe William was right and this was one assignment that needed more than one set of eyes. Maybe she was a bit too eager to be off on her own after all.

CHAPTER 8

Cade dressed in the dark. He'd spent the last two hours sitting in the chair by the window, watching his pretend wife sleep and thinking about the situation.

Why had Robbie decided to chase after him when he'd been left with specific instructions about staying with Seamus and Meagan? Cade didn't want to think what might have happened to the boy as he'd followed him and Lilly halfway across the country. Cade knew his dependable brother, a Chicago copper, would be beside himself with worry, so he'd telegraphed Robbie's whereabouts to him at the same time he'd contacted William.

Cade was upset, too. He didn't need the aggravation of either of his companions, much less both of them. How was he going to keep an eye on Lilly *and* Robbie? Shadowing her in Vandalia had proved that she was apt to go off on some strange quest with the potential to land her in a heap of trouble. Without a doubt, Robbie would. It was only a matter of time.

He rested his elbows on his knees and buried his face in his hands, fighting a feeling of futility, something he'd faced time and again the past fifteen months. *Why* was a question he'd grown weary of asking and had begun to fear there were no real answers.

Forcing his mind from the past, he sifted through what he knew about the Fontenot family members—both what William had told them and what they'd learned the evening before. None of it was much help. There were a lot of "whys" to be answered about them, too, before they could consider this assignment closed.

Why had Patricia married the doctor? Love, one would suppose, but what was it about him that caught her eye out of all the men she came into contact with?

Why were LaRee Fontenot and her great-granddaughter so certain that Dr. Ducharme had deliberately misdiagnosed his wife's condition? From everything Cade knew about her actions following the deaths of her baby son and her daughter, it sounded as if the woman was as batty as Cade had first thought Lilly was.

He allowed his gaze to drift to the woman asleep in the bed. He still had no idea why she'd come running out of the decaying Illinois mansion screaming at the top of her lungs and doubted that he ever would. And he would never forget the startling splash of color she made in her long red cape against the backdrop of the snowy day. Like a cardinal in the snow.

He muttered a curse. Though he still loved his dead wife and he'd vowed to never marry again, he was still a man and as susceptible to a pretty face as the next. He could name a dozen reasons why getting involved with Lilly Long would be a disaster, the most obvious being that she was his partner, as well as still being legally tied to her husband. He could only imagine the chewing out he'd get from William if he did anything to upset the Pinkertons a second time.

Another "why" came to mind. Why that niggling attraction to Lilly?

Well, now, that's always the question, isn't it, McShane?

Knowing he would find no answers sitting there and brooding, he stood and went to light the lamp across the room. Time to get to work.

Lilly was awakened by someone shaking her shoulder. "Rise and shine," a gruff voice said. "We have mountains of work to get done today."

She rolled to her back and forced one eye open. Cade, who was illuminated by the lamp across the room, stood at the side of the bed wearing the serious, somewhat grumpy expression that had become so familiar since he'd shed the boxer's persona.

"It's dark."

"Aye, it is," he agreed. "Lamartine might forgive you for being late, but I'm not so sure about Mrs. Abelard. I imagine she's already downstairs, starch in her dress and her spine, not a hair out of place."

Groaning at the thought of dealing with the demanding housekeeper and dreading the day ahead of her, Lilly pushed herself into a sitting position. Though she'd done it often enough, rising before daylight was not her favorite time of day. "Can I have fifteen minutes to wash up and dress?" she asked in a sarcastic tone.

"You can have twenty, but not a minute more."

With that, her partner turned and left the room, taking all the energy with him and leaving behind the scent of his shaving soap. She wondered at his self-control and his ability to adapt so easily. And how could he seem so eager to get to work when he'd spent the night on the floor? Was the answer as simple as that he was, in William Pinkerton's words, a "professional"?

Would she ever reach that level of confidence and competence?

Cassandra and Preston arrived thirty minutes before lunch. A short time later, with the Blue Willow casserole dish holding the hot jambalaya in hand, Lilly entered the dining room where she found Cassandra Fontenot Easterling staring at a portrait of a woman and two young girls that hung above the sideboard: a likeness of her mother, herself, and her dead sister when they were young.

Patricia was an attractive woman with sable-brown hair, an oval face, and a wide mouth. Her most outstanding feature was her amazing green eyes. She was pretty without being a classic beauty. Suzannah had looked a lot like her. Cassandra must have taken after her father.

A quick glance and Lilly noted that the young woman was short and daintily built, just like her great-grandmother. Blond hair, tied up in a jumble of curls atop her head, made her look younger than she probably was. The swooshing sound of Lilly passing through the swinging door caused Cassandra to whirl around. An indication that her nerves were jittery?

Stop reading something into nothing, Lilly! More likely than not, there is nothing more to her edginess than that she's weary from the trip, or . . . she dreads seeing the man who confined her mother to an asylum.

"Hello," Cassandra said. "You must be the new help *Grandmère* has been expecting." Despite the haunted look in her eyes and the tenseness of her shoulders, her smile was friendly.

Uncertain how to respond to the woman's warmth, Lilly set the dish on the sideboard next to the plate of crusty French bread before turning and making a slight curtsy. "Yes, ma'am. I'm Brona Sullivan."

Cassandra clapped her hands together and laughed in true delight. "Oh, my goodness, Brona. There's no need to curtsy.

We aren't royalty here, though there are some who act as if they are. I'm Cassandra, and I'm so glad you're here to help Lamartine and Mrs. Abelard look after my precious *grand-mère*."

"Thank you, ma'am. Bran and I were proud to find the work."

They were stopped from more interaction when two men entered the room. Cassandra's husband was a good head taller than Henri, and his hair was dark and glistening with pomade. Unlike the doctor, Preston boasted a neatly trimmed mustache. Both men carried themselves in a manner that seemed to say "Look at me. I'm a cut above the rest of you."

Preston's dark gaze homed in on his pretty wife, whose face had drained of animation. Wearing a charming smile, he crossed to her and placed his hands on her shoulders and a kiss on her forehead. "How are you feeling, my dear?" he asked, all husbandly concern.

"Much better now, Preston," she said, attempting a smile. "Thank you for asking."

"Are you ill, dearest?" her great-grandmother asked from the doorway. The concern on her face could not be missed. And why wouldn't she be concerned that something was amiss? Unusual things were happening to each of her family members, one by one.

Henri looked puzzled.

"No, *Grand-mère*," Cassandra said, widening her smile the slightest bit. "Not really."

The smile looked forced to Lilly, who noticed that it didn't reach Cassandra's eyes.

Preston laughed, a hearty sound. Draping an arm around his wife's shoulders and facing the others, he said, "We'd hoped to make our announcement at the party tomorrow, but since the subject has come up, we may as well tell you our news." He drew Cassandra closer to his side. "My beautiful wife is with child."

After a round of well wishes from Henri and Cassandra's grandmother, they were all seated and Lilly served the meal. She was prevented from overhearing much of the luncheon conversation since Mrs. Fontenot announced that if they wanted more of the simple fare, they could get it from the sideboard themselves.

She smiled at Lilly. "We are not helpless, and I'm sure Lamartine can use you in the kitchen with all the party preparations."

"Thank you, ma'am," Lilly said with a slight nod.

Mrs. Fontenot looked at her great-granddaughter. "Cassandra, would you like Brona to pour you another glass of lemonade before she goes? I know it's your favorite."

"No, thank you, *Grand-mère*. Preston doesn't want me getting fat."

If Lilly expected the handsome attorney to deny the statement, she was disappointed.

"I refuse to be wed to a cow just because she's having a baby."

Lilly did not miss the annoyed look Mrs. Fontenot shot his way, but it was gone in an instant. She smiled and quipped, "Now, Preston, you know she is eating for two. There's nothing more beautiful than a woman expecting a baby who is all pretty and plump." Her gaze shifted to the doctor. "Isn't that right, Henri? How many times did I hear you say that Patricia seemed to glow when she was enceinte?"

Henri, who had appeared so self-possessed the night before seemed far less so with the younger man in the room. He actually looked dismayed at being drawn in to the conversation between the older woman and Preston.

To Lilly's surprise, he said, "*Grand-mère* is right. Some weight gain is normal, even desired."

Preston regarded the two for a moment and then laughed. He leaned toward his wife and pressed a light kiss to her cheek. "I hope you know I'm teasing, my dear. You know that I'd love you no matter how you look."

Cassandra, who still looked uncomfortable, tried to smile. "Thank you, Preston. I hope so."

As if just realizing that Lilly had heard the exchange, Mrs. Fontenot turned to her and said, "That will be all, Brona. Please tell Lamartine that she outdid herself."

"Yes, ma'am. I will."

As Lilly picked up Cassandra's dishes, she heard Mrs. Fontenot say, "Come, my dear. If you've finished, we can leave the gentlemen with their coffee and we'll go outside and take a look at the preparations for the circus."

"Circus?"

Mrs. Fontenot offered her great-granddaughter a mocking smile. "Henri's party."

Lilly turned and backed through the swinging door to the kitchen, which afforded her a pretty good look at the murderous expression in the doctor's eyes before the door swished shut behind her.

It was as if there were a pecking order in the family. Henri was cock of the walk until Preston came. Or was it simply her own biased imaginings once more, the part of her that assumed every man who crossed her path was a scoundrel—or worse? Something she could thank Timothy Warner for.

"Are you all right?" Lamartine asked as Lilly set down the dishes.

"I'm fine, but Mrs. Fontenot seemed to be pulling the tiger's tail."

Lamartine grinned. "Which tiger?"

"Both."

The cook laughed, a sound as deep and rich as Kentucky bourbon. "She's a tough old bird," she said with genuine affection.

"Have the men come in for lunch yet?"

"I sent theirs out to them," Lamartine told her. "Amos said Henri is cracking the whip and there's no time to stop for a meal. I dished us up a bowlful before I sent the pot out to them."

"Thank you."

The two women sat down to share their meal. When Lilly took her first bite, she thought she had died and gone to heaven. As she had the gumbo, she loved the spicy, flavorful concoction of meat, rice, and vegetables.

"Oh, Lamartine!" she said when she'd swallowed. "Mrs. Fontenot said to tell you that you outdid yourself. She's right. This is delicious."

Lamartine smiled. "I knew I was gonna like you the minute I saw you and that handsome man of yours."

For a heartbeat Lilly had no idea what the cook was talking about. *Cade,* she thought. *Her man.* Ha!

"There's just something about the two of you that seems down to earth. And that boy!" She laughed. "That boy is a caution, but that's just fine. Most boys are at that age, and there'd be something wrong with him if he wasn't."

At that moment, "that boy" was sitting next to Bernard, scraping the last bit of jambalaya from his bowl with a hunk of crusty bread. Like his mentor, he was always watching, always alert. He saw Henri and Preston saunter around the corner of the house, glasses of wine in hand as they strolled along, taking in the workers' progress.

He and Bernard had cut the grass earlier in the day, taking turns with the fancy mower that an Indiana man had invented several years before. Amos declared it a marvel, far easier than using a scythe. Robbie agreed for the first few minutes, then, with sweat pouring off his face, he acknowledged that it "weren't no tea party." McShane told him to buck up, that work would make him stronger, and that no one got ahead in life without putting some effort into it. One look at the muscles in the older man's forearms had made a believer of Robbie, and he'd done his fair share and more.

Around eleven, the Easterlings had arrived from River Run, and now, Robbie was surprised to see another wagon pulling up in front of the stables.

"Who's that?"

Bernard looked up from his own bowl of jambalaya. "They work for Miz Cassie and Mr. Preston. They've come to give us a hand. This party would be way too much for just us. Wait until you see this place tomorrow."

"What do you mean?"

"We'll be up at the crack of dawn, carryin' out rugs, chairs, and sofas from inside the house." He gave an all-encompassing wave. "All these tables will be covered with cloths." He shook his close-cropped head. "You won't believe how much food Mama, Vena, and Neecie will cook."

"Who are Vena and Neecie?"

Bernard pointed to a tall black woman who was being helped down from the wagon by a dark-skinned man who looked as if he'd done his fair share of work. The woman was expecting a baby.

"That's Neecie and her husband, Rollo. She's my cousin. The short one is *Tante* Vena, Neecie's mama and my mama's sister. She cooks at River Run. We'll meet the rest of them later."

Robbie stood there thinking hard about everything that was going on. He couldn't imagine bringing fancy indoor furniture outside just for a party. Rich folks were a bit odd from what he'd observed. Always hungry, what really interested him was what they'd have to eat.

"What kind of food will we have?"

"It'll be cold stuff. Sandwiches, meats, shrimp, and salads—do you like lobster salad?"

"I don't know," Robbie said. "Can't say as I've had any."

Bernard smiled, and his whole face lit up. "We'll probably have that, and jellies, ices in paper cups, and cakes and lots of fruit, plus lemonade and punch."

"Hey!" Amos called. "If you two are finished eating, stop jawing and come give us a hand with the tent."

Henri had rented a large tent, and the food tables would be set up beneath it. Robbie put down his bowl and was in the process of wiping his mouth on the back of his hand when his gaze drifted back to the two city men. Henri was standing with his hands on his hips, looking around at the men's progress with blatant satisfaction.

Preston was looking with a great deal of interest toward the servants unloading the wagon from River Run.

"C'mon, Robbie," Bernard said. "Let's start setting up these tables."

With no choice but to carry on with his duties, Robbie got back to work.

CHAPTER 9

Lilly, Lamartine, Vena, and Neecie toiled over the food preparations for a good portion of the night. Lilly liked the women who'd come from River Run to help. Vena was more of a talker than Lamartine, and they looked nothing alike except for the color of their skin. Lilly would not have known they were sisters if she hadn't been told. Neecie, who was showing with her first pregnancy, was as tall as her aunt, and just as beautiful, but she didn't have much to say either. It was almost as if she tried to keep from drawing attention to herself, but then, that's what shy people did, wasn't it?

Just before midnight, Lilly went to Bernard's room to check on the boys and found them both on their narrow cots, stripped down to their drawers. They looked as if they'd had baths, thank goodness. She'd caught glimpses of them throughout the day and was a little surprised that Robbie was pulling his weight, just as Cade had said he would. She suspected he didn't want to do anything to annoy anyone and that he was trying to impress Cade. Still, he was just a little boy, and her woman's heart was moved by the sight of him, so innocent in his sleep.

Tiptoeing across the room, she drew a sheet over him and then repeated the gesture with Bernard. Then she went back to work.

When she finally made her way up the back stairs to the room she and Cade shared, she found him sprawled crossways on the bed, snoring softly. He was fully dressed and was still wearing his work boots. She wondered if the men had finished everything Henri had demanded they do. Like the women, they'd worked late.

She didn't have the heart to wake him and ask him to move to the floor, not after the day she knew he'd had. She was bone-tired, too, but her labors hadn't been nearly as physical as his. She undressed and put on her gown, then grabbed a pillow and blanket and curled up in the large chair by the window. There weren't that many hours of the night left anyway. Her last thought was to wonder what it was about ornery little boys and irritable men that made them look so innocent in sleep . . . even when you knew they weren't?

"Lilly."

A hand gripped her shoulder and gave it a shake.

"Go away," she said, drawing away from the touch.

"I can't. Lamartine says you're to come down and get a bath and iron your uniform while the ladies are at early mass. According to her you have a mountain of work left to do."

Lilly rolled to her back and threw her forearm over her face, peeking out at Cade, who once again stood over her, his thumbs tucked into his pockets, frowning. If his unruly dark hair was any indication, he'd had his bath and was dressed in the same manner he'd adopted since taking on the role of Bran Sullivan. He looked ready to face whatever the day brought. How did he do that? she wondered, pushing herself into a sitting position.

It was only when she saw the blanket on the chair that she

realized she was in her bed. Her wide-eyed gaze moved from the chair to Cade.

"I moved you when I got up," he said, as if he could read her mind. "You were dead to the world, but you looked really uncomfortable with your head cocked over to the side."

There was no hint of anything personal in his statement or his demeanor. Satisfied that his actions were nothing more than him looking out for her well-being, but irritated because she hadn't even *known* he was touching her, she said, "I was fine where I was."

His smile was tinged with bitterness. "Ever the grateful one," he quipped, reminding her for an instant of a similar moment when he'd rescued her from the Purcells' attic. Instead of being grateful that he'd found her, she'd snapped at him. When she looked at him again, that man was gone.

"Get up, colleen. I don't have time to come back and check on ya again."

Hearing him call her by the hated name, which just happened to be the name of her husband's tart, sent her eyelids flying upward. She glared at Cade through narrowed brown eyes. His response was the familiar cocky grin that had the maddening way of making her heart stumble. "That's my girl."

Determined to stop any further verbal sparring with him, she threw the covers aside and stood. "Where's Robbie?"

Cade started for the door. "The last I saw, he and Bernard were having their breakfast and he was trying his best to pet Lucifer without losing a finger."

The image that stole into her mind made her frown in concern. "I hope he's careful. That cat is vicious."

"Aye, that he is."

"Both those boys were exhausted last night."

"Did you see him?"

She nodded. "I checked on him around midnight. He and

Bernard were both so tired they didn't move a muscle when I covered them."

"He worked like a man yesterday, I'll give him that."

"He's trying to impress you."

"What do you mean?"

"I don't know what your relationship is with him, but I do know he adores the ground you walk on, and he's working so hard because he's deathly afraid that you'll send him back to your brother."

"How do you know that?"

She shrugged. "I'm doing what Allan told me to do. Becoming an observer of people. You should have seen Robbie watching you when you went to send your telegrams. You're his hero, and he's doing everything he can to make you proud of him."

"Believe me, I'm no hero."

"You are to him. He doesn't like me being in the picture because he's jealous. He's afraid I'll take his place with you."

"As if that would ever happen."

Lilly sucked in a sharp breath as an unexpected pain shot through her heart. She wasn't sure why the comment hurt. Still, it did.

Cade scraped a hand through his black hair. "I didn't mean that the way it came out."

"It's fine. I understand." She was pleased to hear that her voice was steady.

"I doubt it," he countered. "It's nothing personal. It's just that I've no interest in forming a relationship with any woman at the moment, especially not with my partner. I've no time for a dalliance, if I wanted one. Which I don't."

Dalliance? Lilly regarded him in disbelief. "Well, for the record, I'm not interested either. I've had enough of men for a lifetime, thank you very much."

"That's settled, then, isn't it?"

He turned and left her standing near the bed, wondering how a conversation that had started out describing her duties had changed into one so very personal.

The Easter Sunday morning was sunny and bright. Madam Fontenot and Cassandra returned from mass and went outside to check on the final arrangements for the gathering, which would start midmorning. Henri and Preston had not accompanied them to Easter services, which Lamartine had predicted, telling Lilly that neither of the men had a religious bone in his body. Now, the two ladies wandered around the yard, examining the setup with a critical eye, mentally checking to see if everything that needed to be done had been completed.

As they passed near where Lilly was stacking the plates on the food table, the older woman said, "Mrs. Abelard and the girls have done a wonderful job. I didn't want this blasted party, but since it is associated with my home and my name, I didn't want the affair to discredit the family in any way."

"I'm sure there's no way that would ever happen, *Grand-mère*," Cassandra consoled.

"The whole thing is a disgrace, is what it is," Mrs. Fontenot said as they wandered toward the back door. "Suzannah barely cold in the grave and your dear sweet mama . . ."

The woman's voice trailed away and Cassandra put a comforting arm around her shoulder.

"What must everyone be saying about us behind our back? I just hope Henri doesn't do something to make himself the laughingstock of the city." The verve had returned to her voice. "The man has no tact and even less refinement."

The rest of the conversation was muted as they stepped out of hearing range. Lilly moved the plates to a better spot. The more she heard, the more certain she became that there was no love lost between the Fontenot matriarch and the doctor. Lilly was anxious to see if the day's experiences would shed any new light on the troubling situation.

By ten-thirty, Lamartine announced that she was as ready as she'd ever be, and by noon, if the number of people milling around the lawn was anything to go by, almost everyone had arrived. Most of them seemed to be having a good time and were no doubt happy that Lent had come to an end, so perhaps they were not as put off by the inappropriateness of the gathering as Mrs. Fontenot had feared. Times were changing after all.

Lilly caught glimpses of the men and the boys from time to time, as they dealt with the arriving carriages and saw that the horses were taken care of.

Henri had been in his full-fledged, lord of the manor role ever since the guests began to arrive, welcoming them with cheerful greetings and inviting them to refresh themselves with one of the fruit punches or a glass of champagne. Though he was hearty and jovial, it seemed to Lilly that whenever Preston came into his sphere, Henri's smile dimmed and his animation faded.

Mrs. Fontenot and Cassandra moved through the crowd, trying to say a few words to everyone, well-bred hostesses through and through. At the moment, they stood with the priest beneath an ancient live oak, engaged in what looked to be a serious conversation, while Henri and Armand DeMille, the attorney who had contacted the Pinkerton agency, stood away from the general gathering, as if their conversation was private.

The short, stout attorney with the gray mustache and balding head was listening to his host intently, but even from where Lilly stood, it was clear to see that the lawyer was irritated by something Henri was saying. He bore no resemblance to the comfortable, smiling man she'd seen visiting with the priest and Mrs. Fontenot just moments before. Lilly would have given anything to be a bird in the tree above them.

Just before noon, Neecie brought out a bowl of red-dyed Easter eggs, the final contribution to the splendid array of culinary offerings they'd been laboring over for the past couple of days. Since eggs were forbidden during Lent, they were often served on Easter, with the red symbolizing the joy and germinating life of spring.

⋅ Neecie make a wide berth around Preston, Henri, and a middle-aged blond fellow with a drooping mustache. Though he looked preoccupied with whatever his companion was saying, Preston's gaze followed Neecie both as she deposited the eggs and as she went back to the kitchen bearing a tray of dirty glasses.

Moments later, Preston left his companions and sauntered to the table, plucking an egg from the bowl. He cracked it against the table and began to peel it, tossing the shell carelessly onto the lawn, uncaring that one of the servants would have to clean it up.

Lilly cast a glance at Cassandra, whose eyes were dark with embarrassment. The look on Mrs. Fontenot's face gave away nothing of her thoughts. The expression on the faces of Henri and the other man would have been comical if they had not looked so horrified. Henri took a step forward, his hand outstretched.

"Preston . . ."

The plea was too late. Preston had already lifted the egg to his mouth and taken a large bite. Lilly's eyes widened at the blatant breach of etiquette, and a collective gasp rose from the guests. Henri actually looked as if he were in pain as he made a beeline for the younger man.

A wave of murmured comments began to undulate through the crowd. Clearly, Preston had made a blunder far greater than eating before a prayer of thanksgiving had been offered. A quick glance at the priest's shocked expression was further evidence that an imaginary line had been crossed. Blissfully unaware that he'd done anything wrong, Preston finished off the egg and snatched up a glass of champagne to wash it down.

Henri took his arm and ushered him away from the table while the priest excused himself from the small group and made his way toward them.

"Is there something amiss, Henri?" Preston asked, with barely concealed irritation. He made no attempt to lower his voice. "Have I done something wrong again?"

"Of course you've done something wrong. What in heaven's name were you thinking?" Henri blurted in a low voice. It was clear that while he might not have "a religious bone in his body," he'd lived in the Fontenot home long enough to pick up on the religious traditions.

"I was thinking that Lamartine was extremely slow and that I was hungry," Preston quipped before returning his attention to the priest, who mimicked Henri's gesture, taking Preston's arm and turning him away from the curious onlookers. Though he spoke softly, Lilly, who was still pretending to arrange the table, heard every word.

"You should not have eaten anything until I blessed the food. To do so means that you'll be punished by God."

"What?" Preston managed to look both surprised and amused. In fact, he laughed, a sound that carried well beyond the confines of the tent. "I'm not Catholic, Father," he explained, making no attempt to lower his voice. "How was I to know?"

"Ignorance is no excuse, I'm afraid," the priest said.

Preston gave the clergyman a dismissive pat on the shoulder. "I'll tell you what, Father. You don't worry about it, and I'll deal with God. He's been overlooking my trespasses for years now, so I don't think he'll punish me for eating an egg. Now," he said, his tone taking on a hard edge. "Will you please bless the food so that we can get the meal under way?"

Though he looked both troubled and offended, the priest

did as he was asked. When he finished, a collective breath seemed to sough from the gathering as the guests began to breathe once again. Cautiously.

"All right, everyone," Preston said in a loud voice. "Please start the buffet lines." With the announcement, the stiff, uncomfortable feeling gripping the assemblage began to gradually dissipate.

Lilly and Neecie spent the next hour replenishing the bowls and platters of food, gathering dirty dishes and cutlery, and keeping a supply of clean dishes and napkins at the ready, all while dealing with guests who were disgruntled over something or other. It was difficult to smile and be pleasant when she wanted to give them a piece of her mind. One man had given her a pat on the behind, and it was all she could do to keep from giving him a hard kick in the shins.

The last guest was gone by two p.m., and when Lilly started carrying things in, she found Lamartine and Vena already busy washing and drying the stacks of dirty plates.

"Is it true that Preston ate an Easter egg before Father Stephen blessed the food?" Vena asked, her dark eyes alight with mischief. "And did he tell Preston that God would punish him?"

"It is," Lilly told them. "And he did."

"Hope he's right," Lamartine muttered, tossing the dish rag into the soapy water. "I wish a carriage would run over him or something. For the life of me, I can't see why Miss Cassie wanted to marry him."

Playing devil's advocate, Lilly said, "Well, he's a bit brash, but he's very handsome."

Lamartine snorted in disgust. "Handsome is as handsome does."

"Me and Sister don't like the way he's always tryin' to make Miss Cassandra feel bad about herself," Vena offered.

"What do you mean?"

"He's always sayin' she's too skinny, too serious, and that she doesn't laugh enough."

"I don't understand the way men think," Lilly told them, meaning every word. "She seems to genuinely care for him and she's very sweet."

"Too sweet if you ask me."

It was clear that Lamartine disliked both Henri and Preston and was very loyal to the family she worked for, along with her husband and son, for so many years.

Three hours later, they had washed and put away all the rented dishes and glassware, and the men had loaded everything onto the wagons to be returned the following day.

When Rollo and Cade came in to take the wooden boxes of dishes to the wagon, Bernard stuck his head inside and said, "Is there anything left to eat? Me and Robbie are starving."

All four women groaned.

CHAPTER 10

It was almost an hour and a half later when Lilly dried the last dish. With the exception of Mrs. Abelard, who had taken something to nibble on to her room, the staff had all eaten and cleaned up the dishes once again. Then, with the exception of Neecie, who would stay to care for Cassandra's needs, Rollo, Vena, and the other weary River Run servants began to load up to go back to the plantation, even though it would be very late when they arrived home.

Initially, the plan had been for them to get up early and head home, but at the last minute Preston announced that he wanted them back at the plantation and everything in readiness when he and Cassandra arrived.

Though he didn't say a word, even an untried operative could see that Rollo was not happy with the change of plan. It was evident in the hard set of his lean jaw and the fury in his dark eyes. Yet there was nothing he could say or do.

With the horses hitched to the wagon and everyone loaded and ready to go, Lilly watched him take Neecie in his arms and hold her close. Everything about him said he didn't want to leave her. With their foreheads pressed together, they swayed slowly back and forth, whispering things to each other that no one could hear.

A feeling, sweet and poignant, filled Lilly's heart, bringing tears to her eyes. This, then, was love. The real thing. Then Rollo released his wife and the moment passed. Another ache, this one like sorrow settled over Lilly. Would anyone ever hold her that way? Love her that way? she wondered, as she watched everyone climb into the wagon.

When Rollo clucked to the team, Lilly saw Lamartine brush moisture from her cheeks. "I don't get to see nearly as much of my sister as I'd like, but then, that's life, isn't it?"

Thinking of how much she missed Pierce and Rose, Lilly understood perfectly. "Yes."

Lamartine pinned Cade with a mock ferocious look. "You take this woman of yours and git to bed. I'll see you both in the morning."

They wasted no time doing just that.

Lilly fell into the softness of the mattress. "I think I've died and no one will bury me."

"I know I haven't died," Cade responded, flopping down next to her. "I'm in too much pain to be dead."

Stunned by the action, Lilly grew stiff.

Cade turned his head to look at her. "Calm yourself, colleen. I only want to rest my weary back a bit. Your virtue is safe with me."

She believed him; it was her own traitorous heart that concerned her.

"Tell me about the Easter egg fiasco," he said, folding his hands across his flat belly and closing his eyes.

Lilly told him what had happened and what she'd heard both Henri and the priest say to Preston, quoting his line about the Lord overlooking his trespasses almost verbatim.

"He had absolutely no shame," Lilly said, finishing her tale.

"His kind seldom do."

"His kind?" She turned toward him and encountered a close look at his strong profile. His short, thick eyelashes looked like dark smudges beneath his eyes.

"Handsome. Self-absorbed. Looking to marry up."

Lilly recalled Simon Linedecker, the struggling young lawyer she'd hired to secure her divorce from Timothy. She remembered well how the other attorneys she'd spoken with—all from well-heeled families—had looked down their aristocratic noses and informed her that they did not handle "those sorts of cases." Simon Linedecker had not had the advantage of money to help him succeed. She wondered if he'd ever considered "marrying up."

"But he's an attorney. Aren't they usually from society?"

Cade smothered a yawn. She'd never before noticed the scars on his knuckles from his years of fighting.

"Mm. Even so, marrying into another prominent family is a feather in any young man's cap."

It all sounded rather cold-blooded to Lilly.

"Amos doesn't trust Henri," Cade said.

Lilly rolled to her side and looked at him. "Why?"

"He thinks he's a wastrel, and he says Henri has a penchant for gaming."

Lilly sat bolt upright. They already knew that Cassandra feared her stepfather would spend them into bankruptcy, but the gambling . . . well, that was new information. Her own brief experience with Timothy had shown her that gamblers could go through an inordinate amount of money in very little time. If she could find out his regular haunts, perhaps she could snoop around and learn something.

Lilly, still lost in thought, looked Cade's way. His eyes were open once more, and he was regarding her with an intent expression. "What?"

"Did you pick up on something?" he asked. "What's your opinion of him?"

Once again, Lilly debated on the wisdom of giving him the little information she'd gleaned. Then she realized that he was sharing what he'd heard, and was even asking her opinion. He was doing his part as half of their team. As much as it galled her to admit it, it would be selfish, perhaps even unethical, to withhold anything she found out.

"Lamartine is *not* fond of Henri, and that's putting it mildly. No doubt Amos has told her about his bad habits. Neither she nor Vena give a fig for Preston either, because he doesn't treat Cassandra right. After the egg incident, Lamartine even said that she wished something *would* happen to him."

"Hmm. Do you think Lamartine's and Vena's feelings are based on servant loyalty?"

"I'm sure of it. I don't know if you'd heard, but Cassandra is expecting a baby."

Cade opened his eyes and looked at her. "Really? How did you find that out?"

"I was in the dining room when she and Preston arrived yesterday, and he broke the news to Mrs. Fontenot and Henri."

Cade looked thoughtful. "I suppose that explains why he wanted Neecie to stay and help."

The expression in Lilly's eyes seemed to ask if he'd lost his mind. "I think it's all for appearances. I think he's interested in Neecie."

"That's a pretty bold accusation," he said, frowning. "What makes you think so?"

Lilly recalled the way Preston's gaze seemed to follow Neecie throughout the day. What did it mean? Nothing. Absolutely nothing. Pinkertons didn't deal with hunches. They looked for facts. She gave a shake of her head. "I don't have a thing to base it on except woman's intuition."

Cade mumbled something beneath his breath. "So what are your impressions overall?"

What did she think? She hadn't had time to really consider the scant information she'd gleaned. "I think that Henri married up as you say, and that he's very proud of himself and enjoying living high on the hog. He likes being the center of things, but . . ."

"But what?"

"I get the feeling that Preston makes him uneasy."

"Uneasy." Cade propped up on his elbow. "Uneasy as in nervous, or uneasy as in fearful?"

"Fearful? No, I don't think he's afraid of him, but something about Preston makes Henri anxious. His distress over the egg incident seemed genuine. He tried to stop Preston when he saw what he was about to do, but he was too late. Preston paid no more mind to what Henri or the priest had to say than he would have if I'd chastised him. They were both appalled."

"Preston is arrogant, then?"

She gave a lift of her russet eyebrows. "Arrogant? Oh, very. He even seemed to ruffle Mr. DeMille's feathers when I saw them speaking together."

"Well," Cade said, "it's easy to see how DeMille would take unkindly to anything coming from the man who took the position he'd held for so many years."

"Good point," she said thoughtfully. "So we're agreed that Preston may be a scoundrel."

"We are."

"There's no law against that."

"Unfortunately. Henri is the one Mrs. Fontenot feels is guilty, so regardless what Easterling may be or may not be doing, we should concentrate on the doctor."

He was right. As disgusting as the notion was that Preston might be interested in the hired help, they were not in New Orleans to keep tabs on his marriage or his morals. Rose was always saying that a man's sins would find him out. Lilly believed that. Whatever Preston's transgressions, they would catch up with him someday.

"I agree," she told him. "Have you had a chance to speak to Robbie?"

"Not alone, no."

"So what does *your* gut say?" she asked. "Do you believe anything untoward has happened here?" she asked.

"I think it's an unhappy household, but I've seen nothing to make me think Ducharme put his wife away for some nefarious reason. Still," he said, sitting up, "it's early days yet. What do you suggest we do tomorrow while we're off?"

"Mrs. Abelard informed me that we would have to help put things to rights tomorrow. We'll have Tuesday off."

Cade heaved a huge sigh. "Fine, then."

"One more thing," she said, recalling something else. "It's really nothing, but I do believe there's some truth to it." When he looked at her questioningly, she continued. "Lamartine says Mrs. Abelard is sweet on the doctor, and after watching her around him, I believe she's right."

"Hmm," Cade mused. "If Henri is interested in someone else, that could be a reason for wanting to rid himself of his wife. It's a situation worth keeping our eyes on."

"That's what I thought. I suppose on Tuesday we can look through some records. Perhaps we can find out something at the courthouse. And what about questioning Father Stephen?"

"We can't question anyone, wife," Cade said, his use of the word a subtle reminder of their status. "This isn't Vandalia, where you were a Pinkerton agent free to quiz everyone to try to find a loose thread. Pretending to be a couple of servants who know nothing about anything going on here ties our hands in a lot of ways."

Though there was no reproof in his voice or condemnation in what he said, Lilly felt the heat of embarrassment flood her cheeks. In her eagerness to find out something significant, she'd let that small, but important, fact escape her. William was right. She still had much to learn.

"I can ask Amos about Henri's gambling and perhaps even find out his usual haunts," he said. "We can check on those Tuesday."

"What if I pretend some illness and visit Henri's offices?" Lilly asked. "I can see where he went to medical school, and we can see if there's anything unsavory in his past."

"Good idea," he told her with a nod. "Very good, in fact."

On Tuesday morning, Lilly and Cade were just pulling away from the stable at the back of the house when Robbie came running up to the wagon Amos used to run errands in town. There was no way he'd have let them take the new coach out for the day.

"Where ya off to, McShane?" the boy asked, planting his hands on his narrow hips.

"We're going to check out a few places and see what we can find out about the doctor and his gambling habits."

"I'm coming with you."

"You need to stay here in case Amos needs you for something."

"Am I a part of this little family or ain't I?" the boy asked.

"Of course you are."

"Then it's my day off, too, right?"

Cade sighed. "Hop in.

Robbie was grinning from ear to ear as he climbed into the wagon. As he took a seat between Lilly and Cade he flashed her a triumphant smile.

Determined not to let him get the best of her, Lilly smiled back. "I'm glad you're coming, Robbie. I'm sure you'll be a big help. I'm hoping to persuade Cade to buy me some ice cream later on. How does that sound?"

He frowned, uncertain what to make of her friendliness. "Sure. Why not?" he replied, folding his arms across his chest. Lilly didn't miss the excitement in his brown eyes. Why shouldn't he go? He'd worked hard and deserved a day off, too.

"Lilly and I have been wonderin' if you've heard anything of interest."

"Haven't heard a thing. Saw something interestin' Sunday night, though."

Cade shot a sharp glance the boy's way. "And what was that?"

"That lawyer fella tried to corner Neecie in the hallway." He looked at Lilly to see what she made of that bit of information. "Then his Mrs. called out for Neecie, and she slipped inside the room."

Preston—the disgusting worm—had been trying to get Neecie into a corner. Lilly's intuition was more on target than she thought. "What were you doing abovestairs?" Lilly asked.

"Working, the same as you."

Cade cast a baleful glance her way. "You probably don't want to know."

No doubt he was right.

During the ride, she thought of what Robbie had told them. She hoped Preston burned in a fiery hell for even thinking of being unfaithful to his pregnant wife . . . with a woman who was expecting her own child no less! Of course, it didn't surprise her, but still . . .

Another memory from Sunday slipped into her mind: Neecie carrying the eggs from the kitchen and carefully skirting Preston and the group he'd been talking to. At the time it hadn't seemed important, and perhaps it meant nothing at all, but hearing about his inappropriate advances toward her caused Lilly to wonder. With a little growl and a shake of her head, she banished the troubling thoughts, reminding herself that it had no bearing on their reason for being there. Still, the thoughts wouldn't quite leave her alone.

It wasn't long before Cade pulled to a stop in front of the building Amos had told him housed Henri Ducharme's medical practice. "We'll wait for you," he told her.

"It may take a while."

"There's no way I'm goin' off and leavin' you in a strange town. Just get a gander at the license and come on back. We'll wait, colleen."

Lilly glared at him, but inside she was pleased that he cared enough to be concerned for her safety.

Ducharme's offices were located on the second floor. When Lilly entered the outer room, she noticed that the furnishings were plain, basic. Three other patients sat waiting for their turn to see the doctor. They looked up curiously. A prim matronly woman dressed all in white sat behind a table and smiled when she entered. "May I help you?"

"I'm here to see Dr. Ducharme," Lilly told her. "I've been having a bit of dyspepsia and thought perhaps he could give me something for it."

The woman looked at the book on the table that served as a desk, and said, "As a matter of fact, he can see you after he sees these patients. Please have a seat, Miss . . ."

"Warner," Lilly said without a second's hesitation. No one here would connect Mrs. Lilly Warner with Mrs. Brona Sullivan. "Mrs. Lilly Warner, and I'm in a bit of a hurry."

"I'm sorry, ma'am, but to be fair we have to take the patients in turn. I'm sure you understand." She gave Lilly a tight smile, and she thought she saw a hint of irritation in the woman's eyes. "Now, have you had the upset stomach long?"

"The past few mornings," Lilly lied.

The woman smirked, as if she already knew the cause of the ailment. Good heavens! Lilly thought. The matronly lady assumed she was with child, but she'd learned a couple of weeks ago that she was not carrying Tim Warner's baby, thank goodness!

A voice Lilly recognized as Henri's called out from the hallway, and with a murmured apology the woman disappeared through a doorway. Lilly shook off the irritation that accompanied the very thought of Timothy and took the opportunity to wander around the room and examine the various framed medical illustrations hanging on the wall as well as the prominently displayed diploma.

It seemed that Henri had received his medical training in Ohio. That was interesting. His speech and his name suggested that he was Louisiana born and bred, but one never knew. She'd have to ask Lamartine if she knew anything about his past. At least they had something to check on.

With no intention of waiting for the woman's return, Lilly left the office and headed downstairs. There was no sense keeping Cade and Robbie waiting since she had the information she'd gone for, and she had no intention of letting Henri examine her just to glean a morsel of information. The very thought sent a shudder through her.

Seeing her step through the outer door, Cade hopped down from the wagon. "That didn't take long," he said, giving her a hand up.

Lilly explained what had transpired between her and the nurse. "When Henri called for her, I got a look at the certificate and left. I certainly had no intention of meeting him face-to-face."

"So where did he go to medical school?" Cade asked.

"Cincinnati."

"Hmm. Let's go check out Henri's gambling haunts and then we'll stop by the telegraph office so you can ask William to look into Ducharme's medical records."

Lilly felt a rush of pleasure that Cade was allowing her to do her part in the investigation. Perhaps teamwork wasn't such a drudge after all.

Armed with a list of places Amos claimed were favorite haunts of Henri's, they headed toward an area where disreputable taverns were a dime a dozen. This time it was Lilly and Robbie who sat and waited while Cade went inside to find out what he could about Henri's habits. She had no idea why Cade cared what Henri did when he left the house at night or where he did it. Wasn't it enough that they knew he gambled heavily? How could knowing where he lost money be of any use to their investigation?

Their first stop was a small grog shop near the docks called The Wharf.

"Well, isn't this a proper dump?" Robbie said, regarding the exterior of the building in disgust. "I hope McShane don't get to feeling too much at home in there."

The comment took Lilly off guard. She curled one hand around his chin and forced him to look at her. Regret lingered in his eyes. The boy had no notion how much his offhand comment had revealed. "What does that mean?"

"It don't mean nothin," he mumbled, jerking free of her touch. "I was just runnin' off at the mouth."

"Jenks . . ." she began, knowing before she spoke that he would offer no explanation. "If there are things you know that would help me to better understand Cade, things that might help me be a better partner, I'd like you to tell me."

"You've asked me before, *sister dear,*" he said in that mocking tone that made her want to give him a good shaking. "And I'm tellin' you again that I don't snitch on my friends. And it's not Jenks anymore, it's Robbie, and don't ya be fergettin' it, *Brona.*"

★ ★ ★

As Cade strode through the fleapit toward the bar, he, like Lilly, wondered what on earth would bring a man of Henri's social standing to such a place. *And aren't you the one to be disgusted by such a dive?*

There had been a time, not too long ago, when he'd spent most of his waking hours in places like this, or lying in front of them, too drunk to stand. A cold sweat broke out across his forehead, and he wiped it away with a quick swipe of the handkerchief he drew from his rear pocket.

"What'll it be?"

"Beer. Dark." While the barman drew the brew, Cade examined the reflection in the hazy mirror. All taverns were basically the same, yet some were fancier and frequented by a higher class of patrons. This was a workingman's bar. Hard used. Smokey. Filled with men who had no money to spare for such things. Men who used the rent money in search of the forgetfulness at the bottom of a glass and women trying to scratch out a meager living with the only commodity they had left to sell.

At ten in the morning, the room was relatively smoke-free, though the smell lingered, no doubt having penetrated into the very walls. The piano stood silent. The girls were upstairs sleeping, preparing for another night. Only two men sat at one of the scarred tables, and they were dressed as if they belonged in a gentleman's club.

The server slammed the foamy mug of beer onto the bar. Cade stared at it for long seconds before picking up the mug and cradling it in his palms. Lifting the thick glass to his nose, he drew in a deep lungful of the yeasty hops-filled scent and closed his eyes. Then he set it back onto the bar.

"Slow day?"

"About normal," the bartender said.

Cade jerked his head toward the two men. "I mean no of-fense, but what brings a couple of gents like them to a place like this?"

"None taken. I'm not sure about those two, but sometimes the upper crust comes here to meet someone they don't want to be seen with in public, if you know what I mean."

He did. Like a mistress. Or someone in cahoots on a shady deal. Oh, yes, he knew well.

"Many of them come to gamble?" Cade pushed his drink back.

"Not so much. The locals have a game every now and again, but most everyone comes to drink, or enjoy the girls when they can scrape up the cash. There's a swell comes in every now and again to meet up with some of his rich friends and they play."

"Really? Do you know his name?"

"No." The barkeep frowned. "Why are you asking?"

"There's a guy who owes me some money from a long time ago," Cade lied. "Can you describe this fella?" He slid a coin across the bar to the man, who looked at it curiously and then, never losing eye contact, slipped it into his pocket before describing a man who fit the bill for Henri. Cade knew the description could match a dozen others, but it would be worth it to explore a little more.

"He was in a few nights ago," the bartender offered before Cade could delve further into the unknown man. "In fact, he lost big to some Yankee hotshot. He wasn't none too happy over it, and said the man was cheating . . . only not saying it to his face."

"What about you? Do you think he was cheating?"

"Mister, I serve drinks. Unless a fight breaks out over something, I don't pay any attention to what goes on in the games. All I can say is that when the Yankee scraped up his winnings and left, all the other swells agreed that he was at least a professional, if not a downright cheat."

"Thanks for the information." Cade stood and pulled some money from his pocket.

The bartender frowned. "Something wrong with the draft?"

"Nothing. I don't drink. You enjoy." He placed money for the beer on the counter, stood, pulled his cap from his back pocket, and plopped it onto his head. The man behind the bar stared after him with a curious expression on his face.

"So what do we do with this information?" Lilly asked when Cade told her and Robbie what he'd learned.

"I'd like to see just how heavily he loses and how often, who he meets and so on. I'll tag along next time he goes out for the night. Robbie, you ought to come, too. I'm sure you can pick up a lot of information hanging around on the street."

"Well, that's big of you, McShane," Robbie drawled, his Irish brogue as thick as the humid air. "I thought per'aps ya'd forgotten I'm part of this team, don't ya know."

"You will not go," Lilly said, giving Robbie a look that said she meant business, a look that had been programmed into women since God fashioned Eve from Adam's rib. She turned to Cade. "Perhaps, McShane, it has escaped your notice that he's a child. He has no business staying out all hours and hanging around taverns. He needs to be at home in bed having someone reading him a bedtime story."

Robbie burst out laughing. "Well, ain't that rich? Brona's worried about little Robbie." The last was spoken in a pitiful sing-song tone that scorned the notion that anyone could care for him.

Weary of his disrespect and unprovoked dislike, Lilly snapped, "Yes, Brona does worry about little Robbie, though she cannot imagine why, when he obviously doesn't give a fig about himself."

The boy looked taken aback by the statement and the vehemence behind it and opened his mouth to reply, but Cade stayed him with a curt, "Fine. I won't take him. Let's find some ice cream and cool off." The look he gave them both told them he meant that in more ways than one. "After that, we'll go to the telegraph station and you can send the agency a note about Henri's diploma."

Lilly did her best to calm her irritation. She knew she should not have reacted to the child's antagonism with exasperation, but he really did have a way of getting under her skin . . . just like Cade. The truth was that she was in over her head, both with the case and with dealing with her two male counterparts.

Even though she had no desire for a partner, especially one who seemed to dislike her so intently, the longer this case went on, the more she realized that she could have never worked through all the angles if she'd been on her own. Not only was her time too limited, with one day off a week, but she would never have thought of some of the avenues to explore that McShane had brought up. Experience.

It was hard working so closely with a virtual stranger, obliged to share your observations and thoughts with him when you were more or less feeling your way through each day and were trying hard not to look the fool. But she couldn't fault him for his willingness to throw himself wholeheartedly into his work for the agency or the Fontenots, or even Robbie for that matter. She was fast learning that Cadence McShane was one of those people who gave one hundred percent to whatever task he undertook, and she saw him working to impress those values on Robbie.

Sharing a room with her partner was a whole different source of conflict and distress. Just knowing that he was there was disturbing. She was sensitive to his every move, conscious of every breath he took. Every rustling movement of his body.

She told herself it was simply that he was an attractive man and she was a woman who had tasted the sweetest fruits love had to offer. Then she would remind herself that her feelings were nothing but her mother's foolishness coming out in her, and she had sworn she would not behave as imprudently as Kate. It was a vow she meant to keep no matter how often thoughts of Cadence McShane entered her mind. She'd learned hard lessons from Timothy Warner, and she refused to be so easily led astray a second time.

CHAPTER 11

Tensions among the trio eased somewhat as they sat outside in the April sunshine enjoying a dish of ice cream. Though Robbie was quiet, she and Cade tried to lighten the mood by making a game of watching the people passing by and trying to guess who they were and where they were headed just by their clothing and manner. To her surprise, he actually smiled a time or two at her outrageous guesses. Allan Pinkerton had been right. A lot could be learned from observing people and learning to read their actions. Isn't that what she did to prepare for her onstage roles?

"We should go and visit Missus Patricia."

The suggestion came from the boy, who was focused on scraping the last drop of melted ice cream from his bowl.

"The doctor doesn't want her having visitors," Lilly told him. "He doesn't want reminders of home to upset her more than she already is."

His fearless brown gaze met hers. "Did we come here to do what the doctor says or to find out if the missus is batty?"

"Robbie, that isn't very nice."

The boy shrugged and swiped his tongue along the edge of his bowl.

A twinkle of amusement flickered in Cade's. "He has a point. We do need to figure out how to get into the asylum and see her. There's no other way to gauge her mental condition."

Lilly recalled challenging the sheriff of Vandalia with a similar statement about doing her job. "B-But you're always saying that we don't need to rush into things, that we need to plan our strategy. We've barely arrived, and we don't know much about anything yet. Why don't we wait until a day that we can come dressed a bit better and tell them that we'd like to check out the hospital because we're looking for a place to put my poor *grand-père*."

He shrugged. "There are advantages to surprise attacks, too."

She didn't know if she was afraid of what they would find, or uncertain of their ability to make any headway by rushing into this crazy plan. "I don't know. . . . What will we tell them?"

"How about we buy a sweet of some kind and you and Robbie go in and say you worked for Patricia and you've brought her a treat from the girls in the kitchen and would like to give it to her."

For a spur-of-the-moment plan, it was a good one. "Not bad, Mr. Sullivan," Lilly said with a sigh of agreement. She turned to Robbie. "Are you willing to go in with me?"

His shrug was offhand, but she saw the interest in his eyes. "Ain't I here to help?"

"All right, then. Listen to me, Robbie. You keep your mouth shut and let Lilly do the talking, right?" Cade ordered.

He gave another unconcerned shrug. "Sure."

"Mouth closed, eyes wide open."

"No need to draw me a picture, McShane," the boy said in a testy tone.

Cade frowned, but that twinkle in his eyes was back. Good grief! Lilly thought. He was as bad as the boy.

In less than thirty minutes, the rig was sitting in front of the hospital. From where they sat, it did not look like a happy place. Lilly and Robbie climbed down and started toward the door. Robbie carried the pralines they'd purchased.

There was no one to greet them when they entered, and Lilly paused, uncertain how to proceed. Robbie had no such compunction and headed down a long corridor to places unknown. Lilly whispered his name loudly, but he didn't respond, and she had no choice but to follow. She caught up with him at the doorway of a large room where several of the patients milled around like lost souls looking for . . . what?

A woman was marching around the edge of the room, her back ramrod straight, singing "Dixie" in an off-key alto and waving a small Rebel flag above her head. Another sat rocking in a battered rocker, knitting needles flashing and clicking, and muttering about "finishing by Christmas." The muffler she was working on had to have been twelve feet long, and still she knitted with furious intensity.

"Ain't this a bl—" He glanced up at Lilly and changed the word he was about to say for another, knowing she would chastise him if he didn't. "Blasted mess?" He jerked his head toward a huge man who was headed their way, a fanatical look in his eyes.

"Hey! You there!" he said, pointing to Robbie.

"What do you think he wants with me?" the child asked, genuine alarm in his dark eyes.

"I have no idea," Lilly said, adding, "and I have no intention of finding out." She placed a hand on his shoulder and propelled him away from the wild-looking man. As she did so, she saw a woman sitting across the room in another rocker. Unlike the unkempt creatures around her, she was dressed simply, but nicely, in a plain green morning dress with the merest hint of lace at the cuffs. The woman's hair was drawn sleekly back and tied with a ribbon at her nape. Her hands curled around the curved portion of the armrests and she was rocking slowly, staring straight ahead. There was absolutely no emotion in her eyes that Lilly could see. Having seen the portrait in the dining room, Lilly had no doubt that she was looking at Patricia Ducharme. "There she is."

Robbie's head swiveled to the right and he gave a sharp nod. "That's her all right." He tipped his head back and looked up at Lilly. "What do we do now?"

"I'm not sure. Try to talk to her?"

Robbie nodded and they started across the room. Before they took more than half a dozen steps, a harsh voice stopped them. "You there! Stop!"

Lilly and Robbie froze and turned slowly. A large woman wearing a white apron over a dark dress and a white cap on her graying hair bore down upon them with a purposeful stride.

"What are you doing here?" she demanded, stopping in front of them and crossing her arms across her ample bosom. "Visitors are required to check in at the desk and are absolutely *not* allowed in the common room."

Reminding herself that she was an actress by trade, Lilly donned a timid smile and called up her best Irish accent. "I'm so sorry, ma'am. I've never been here before, so I didn't know. I'm Mrs. Bran Sullivan, and this my young brother-in-law, Robbie. We work for Dr. Ducharme and Mrs. Fontenot, and we've brought Mrs. Patricia a treat from the girls in the kitchen. Would it be possible for us to see her?"

The woman's features and tone softened somewhat. "I'm afraid that's impossible, Mrs. Sullivan. Mrs. Ducharme has had a hard time settling in here."

"Oh, but we won't stay long," Lilly pressed. "Just long enough to say hello and let her know we're all thinking about her."

The matron shook her head. "I'm very sorry, but both Dr. Ducharme and Dr. Ballantine feel it would be in her best interest not to have any unnecessary reminders from the past to hinder her progress, at least until her evaluation is completed."

"Oh!" Lilly let her disappointment and sorrow show in her face. "We didn't know. Perhaps later, then. When she's more settled." Determined to get as much information as possible, she asked, "Is Dr. Ballantine overseeing her care, then?"

"As the city physician, he is the one doing the evaluation, yes."

While they were talking, Robbie had wandered away from them several feet, almost as if he were trying to catch Patricia's eye. "Come back here, young man. I've said you're not allowed to be in here."

"Robbie!" Lilly said sternly. "Come back here and do as you're told."

He turned, the expression on his face so wide-eyed and innocent it would have made an angel look guilty. "I'm sorry, ma'am, Aunt Brona. I meant no harm. It's just that I was curious. I've not ever seen crazy folks before."

Part of Lilly wanted to sink through the floor at his irreverence for a serious condition; the other part wanted to give him a kiss. She had the feeling that most boys his age would respond in much the same way. He walked back to Lilly, and the woman turned her attention back as well.

"Do you have any news I can take back to her family? Is she doing all right?"

"I'm not at liberty to give out any information about the patients to anyone other than family members." When Lilly pasted an even sadder expression on her face, the woman huffed a sigh, almost of resignation. "She's well. She eats. She wants to go home and is confused about where she is. That's the best I can do."

"I understand. Thank you for your time." Lilly turned to go, but the woman's next words stopped her.

"Would you like to leave the treat for her?"

"Oh, of course," Lilly said, holding out the pralines. "Thank you."

She and Robbie turned and started back down the hallway toward the door. From the corner of her eye, she saw him turn and glance back.

"Well, if that don't beat the Dutch!" he growled.

"What are you talking about?"

"I'll bet you this week's wages that Missus Patricia never sees that candy."

"Why would you say that?"

"Green as grass, ya are?" he told her in a long-suffering tone. "That ol' bag was eyen' that sweetie like it were a piece o' gold, she was. It'll be gone before we get to the wagon."

"Well, she seemed very helpful to me."

He gave her another pained look. "People are what they need to be at any given time of the day," he told her, sounding very mature and certain of his statement. In truth, it sounded like something she might have heard from the man waiting for them in the wagon. Or even Allan Pinkerton himself. Cade was right. The boy was sharp. But then, he'd had to be.

She was pondering the validity of Robbie's comment when he spread his arms wide and added, "Just look at us, sister dear."

After she told Cade what the matron had said, and Robbie took great delight in describing the patients milling around, Cade drove Lilly to the telegraph office, where she sent William a short message telling him simply the name of the medical school in Ohio. He would know what to do.

As she stood thinking about their inability to get into the

asylum and have any sort of conversation with Patricia to gauge her sanity . . . or lack thereof, an idea leaped full-blown into her mind. Without stopping to think it through or consult her partner, she dashed off a cryptic message to Pierce.

> *Consulting alienist needed as soon as*
> *possible for assessment. Situation serious.*

When she left the telegraph office, she was feeling quite pleased with herself. The mood lasted until she caught sight of Cade, who was wearing his usual frown. Good heavens! What had she been thinking? He would be furious with her if she told him what she'd done.

Don't tell him.

Deciding that the inner voice was one she should heed, she made no mention of the second telegram. Surely Pierce would arrive within the next two weeks. There wasn't much Cade could say about it when he arrived . . . was there?

It was almost dusk by the time he pulled the wagon into the stable. The eventful day had taken its toll on them all. She and Cade hardly spoke on the ride home, and despite Robbie's defiance and cockiness, he was only a little boy. Halfway to the house, she'd felt him leaning against her shoulder and saw that he was sound asleep. Being careful not to wake him, she'd eased his head into her lap and spent the remainder of the ride running her fingers through his tousled hair without even re-alizing what she was doing.

Now she looked down at him, gauging the changes in him since he'd been discovered on the paddle-wheeler. Though he would probably always be thin, he'd gained weight and no longer looked like a half-starved waif. He was clean. Taken care of. He was still mouthy, irreverent, and brash, but he'd proven himself to be loyal to Cade and was doing his part in their roles as the Sullivan family. Not a bad improvement for such a short time. All he needed was the security of knowing someone loved him, and that he had someone to catch him when he fell.

Something they all needed.

She sighed and glanced over at Cade, who hadn't said a word. His gaze was focused on the tender touch of her hands. When he looked up at her, there was an expression in his eyes she couldn't read, a softness she didn't recall seeing before, and his mouth, that amazing mouth beneath his heavy mustache, was curved into the barest hint of a bittersweet smile.

Her return smile was as effortless as drawing her next breath. For a split second there seemed to be a moment when they were in complete union in thought and feeling, and all the barriers they'd erected in their lives and hearts had fallen away and there was nothing between them but the purity of that moment.

"I'll take him."

The sound of the simple statement shattered the feeling. Lilly wondered if it had been her imagination, some fanciful daydream. She nodded, and Cade lifted the boy from the wagon seat, which, of course, woke him.

"Put me down, McShane!" he grumbled, wiggling and trying to get free. "I'm no baby to be carried around and coddled."

Cade set him none too gently to the ground. "Never thought you were, lad. Just trying to let you sleep."

"I wasn't asleep."

Lilly and Cade shared another amused look over his head.

"Come on, Robbie, let's see if Lamartine has anything left over from supper."

By the time they ate and she'd helped Lamartine clean up, Lilly was worn out, but recalling the moment with Robbie's head in her lap, she was determined to do one more thing.

Seeing the condition and scarcity of his clothes, Lamartine had given Lilly a couple pairs of pants and three shirts Bernard had outgrown, and she'd been working in the evenings to alter them for him. She'd finished the day before, but still needed to press them, which she did even though Lamartine told her they could wait another day.

Since Lilly was insistent, Lamartine kept her company while she ironed.

"Did you all have a good day?"

"It was fine. We looked around, and Bran brought us ice cream. I thought of stopping by Dr. Ducharme's office to get something for my upset stomach, but felt better after a bit."

The semi-truthful comment brought a considering light to Lamartine's eyes. Then she frowned and said, "I'd be careful of takin' anything that man prescribed."

Lilly didn't have to feign her surprise. "Really? Why?"

"He's not much of a medical man in my opinion. He never did seem to help Miz Patricia a whole lot when she was expectin', and my natural remedies seem to do more for Miz Fontenot than whatever it is he gives her."

Well, Lilly thought. That was one more thing to add to their scant pile of information about the family. "Well, it's a good thing I started feeling better, isn't it? It's probably nothing more than all the spicy food I've been eating."

Lamartine placed her hands on her slender hips. "Did you ever stop and think that you might be enceinte?"

Expecting a baby? Thank goodness Lilly knew better than that.

"Would that I were," she replied, concentrating on her ironing so that her friend wouldn't see her face. "But I'm not."

"One of these days . . ."

Lilly decided to change topics. "We tried to visit Mrs. Ducharme, but they wouldn't let us see her."

"That was nice of you."

"We thought she might like to hear what was happening here, but evidently they haven't finished evaluating her yet . . . whatever that means."

"Hard to say, but it was nice of you to try, since you've never met her."

"It seems to me that any sick person or shut-in would like some company, and Robbie insisted we try."

Again, the truth.

The talk turned to tomorrow's duties, and it wasn't long before Lilly had finished the clothes. She hoped he liked them. Laying the pants and shirts over her arm, she bade Lamartine good night and went upstairs.

Neither of the boys answered when she knocked. Figuring they were outside catching lightning bugs or doing whatever else boys did, she let herself in and laid the clothes on Robbie's bed, arranging and smoothing them so that they were displayed to their full advantage. Then, with a sigh, she turned and went to her own room.

After watering the horses for the final time that night, Robbie followed Bernard into the room they shared. The first thing he saw were the clothes on his bed. Two pairs of denim trousers and three shirts were spread on the quilt.

"Where'd these come from?" he asked, wide-eyed.

"That's some of my things that I outgrew. I've been seein' Miz Brona busy with her scissors and needle the past few days."

Brona. So *that's* why she'd wanted to get his measurements, Robbie thought. He touched the clothing almost reverently. He'd never had more than an extra shirt and pants before. He looked up at Bernard. "I wonder why she'd do such a thing?"

The older boy looked at him in disbelief. "Because you need them?" he said, turning the statement into a question. "Besides, it's what mamas do."

"She ain't my mum," Robbie snapped.

"Maybe not, but she's the closest thing you got."

Lilly had washed up and was in bed rereading one of her favorite dime novels when Cade came in. He was much later than usual, and she couldn't help wondering where he'd been and what he'd been doing. His wet hair and collar told her that he'd done his washing up outside, but what else had kept him? Without a word, he took the folded blankets from the end of the bed and spread his pallet on the floor.

"I've been thinking about today," he told her, sitting down on the edge of the bed. "I can easily go to the taverns and check on Ducharme's activities, but we really need to get into the asylum if we hope to get any real sense of Patricia's mental state. Do you have any ideas?"

Her heart plummeted. She let her gaze drop to the book that lay in her lap, but the words were nothing but a blur. She never imagined that she'd be caught out so soon.

"What?" he asked.

"Ummm."

Without warning, she felt his calloused fingers gripping her chin, forcing her to look at him. His expression was both questioning and angry, as if some inner sense told him he would not like what she had to say. "What have you done now, lass?"

"What makes you think I've done something I shouldn't have?"

His mouth twisted into the semblance of a smile. "I didn't say you'd done something you shouldn't have." His voice was terrifyingly soft. "Did you?"

Lilly heaved a deep sigh, knowing she had no choice but to acknowledge her actions. She pretended a calm she was far from feeling and forced herself to meet his cool blue gaze. "I thought about that very thing earlier, so while I was at the telegraph station I sent Pierce a message telling him to come as soon as possible to act as an alienist at the asylum."

"You did what?" Cade thundered, shoving to his feet.

Lilly's startled gaze flew to the doorway. Amos and Lamartine were just across the hall.

"Sh," she said in a harsh tone. "Someone will hear."

"Do ya think I care?" he said as heatedly as before. "What on earth were ya thinkin'?"

Lilly noticed that his Irish brogue was more pronounced when he was angry. "The same thing you were, obviously," she shot back in a loud whisper.

"Without talking with me about it first."

Thank goodness his statement was delivered in a much lower tone. She lifted one shoulder in a half shrug. "Well, I thought it was an excellent idea, and we were at the telegraph office, so it seemed like the ideal time to do something."

"When did you plan to tell me? When your friend showed up?"

Lilly stared down at her hands. "Probably."

"You seem to forget that we're partners. A team. That means we work together, and that you have no right and certainly no authority to make that sort of decision without discussing it with me."

A memory from her brief marriage surfaced: Timothy telling her that her keeping tabs on every cent he spent was demeaning. This was not at all the same thing, but Cade's tone was so reminiscent of Tim's that Lilly felt that same sense of condemnation, that she'd done something wrong. Why were men so good at doing that?

"Did ya stop and think that by telling yer friend to come and get involved you might be jeopardizing our assignment, or that he could be in danger simply by being connected to us?" Cade asked, pressing home his point.

Of course she hadn't thought of that. Her irritation faded in the face of the dangers he'd pointed out to her. It had never occurred to her that involving Pierce could do anything but help. Once again, she had not thought things through. She'd acted on impulse, just as she had when she'd taken it upon herself to visit one of Tim's favorite Chicago drinking establishments alone, in the dead of night with a head injury. *Not prudent at all, Lilly.*

Once more, she was faced with the realization that she had much to learn before she became the operative she wanted to be. Blast it! She owed McShane an apology. And her loyalty. But oh, did it gall her to admit it!

"I'm sorry."

Cade placed his hands on his hips and lifted his gaze to the ceiling as if he were looking for patience from above. When he looked back at her, skepticism filled his eyes. "Sorry? Well, that's easy enough to say, isn't it, colleen?"

Something told her he'd called her by the dreaded name on purpose, and at the moment, she was in no position to call him out over it. She gritted her teeth and swallowed her ire and her pride. "I admit that I didn't think things through, and I promise not to do anything like that again. I'll discuss any ideas I have with you and share anything I hear that may be important."

"Prettily said, but do ya mean it?"

"Of course I do!" she snapped, meeting his reservations with irritation. "I know I have a lot to learn, but I've always been the impulsive sort and have a tendency to act before I think."

"Tell me something I don't know," he snapped.

She drew in a deep breath. "I . . . I know that even though you are a man and have more experience, you have no intention of undermining my work in any way. From here on out,

I'll share everything with you, and I expect the same courtesy. The thing is, McShane, sooner or later, I intend to make it on my own."

"Oh, I've no doubt of it." He regarded her for long seconds. "Of course I'll reciprocate. I have been."

There was no sound in the room for a few moments while he spread his bed onto the floor. Then he turned suddenly and regarded her with his hands on his hips.

"For the record, I like a woman with ambition and guts, so long as she doesn't forget she's a woman." He gave a slow shake of his head. "It would be a real shame if that happened to you, Lilly Long. Maybe one day you'll tell me who it was who made you so bitter toward men."

Forget she was a woman? What did that mean? She was not likely to forget that, since it was that very fact that had motivated her to spend the rest of her life trying to help other women. As for what man had made her so bitter . . . it would take a list to enumerate them, starting with those who had paraded through her mother's bedroom and ending with Timothy.

"And maybe one day you'll tell me about the circumstances that led you to meet up with Robbie."

He offered her a cynical smile. "Possible but doubtful." He tossed a pillow onto the floor. "By the way, he said to tell you thank you for fixing the clothes."

Lilly's first thought was surprise that the boy had mentioned it. That was progress, wasn't it? "You spoke to him?"

"I . . . was with him and Bernard earlier." He shot her a derisive smile. "I went to talk to him about how he's liking it here . . . that sort of thing. Robbie asked me to tell Bernard about grogochs."

"Grogochs. Isn't that what you called him that day on the boat just before he'd had a bath and a haircut?"

"Aye, I've always called him that."

"And what is a grogoch, exactly?"

"Basically, he's a fairy who looks like an old man, but untidy and covered with hair. They're the most companionable of all the fairies and sometimes attach themselves to one person."

"The way Robbie has to you."

Lilly was fascinated by the tale, but even more interested by the fact that Cade had taken the time to check on the boy to see how he was faring. To all intents and purposes he had tucked him in for the night. Was he taking his responsibility for the child more seriously?

Cade shrugged. "They can go for long periods without rest or food, and are said to be invisible." This time his smile was reminiscent of the boxer's cocky grin. "If that isn't Robbie, I don't know what is. I've never seen anyone who can get into the places he goes and never be seen."

There was no arguing that. "And you believe in fairies."

It was as much a statement as a question.

Cade smiled again. "I'm Irish, aren't I?"

Lilly placed her book on the small table next to the bed and blew out the light.

Cade undressed in the darkness and stretched out on his makeshift bed. What he wouldn't give to spend a night on a nice soft feather tick!

Folding his hands beneath his head, he stared into the darkness and listened to Lilly roll and toss. He hoped she was strangling on guilt for going behind his back and setting up something that had the potential to destroy their whole operation. On the other hand, she was pretty clever for coming up with the idea.

She was the proverbial thorn in his side. And having Robbie around was just one more thing he had to think about when he should be focused on the assignment, but there was nothing he could do about either complication, so he'd have to make the best of it. So far, Robbie hadn't slipped anything of value into his pocket and set the whole house into an uproar.

That, he supposed, was progress.

CHAPTER 12

Despite the fact that Amos drove Henri somewhere almost every night to gamble and Cade followed in the old wagon, they'd learned nothing except that Henri was a terrible card player.

Housebound by their daily chores, there was no opportunity to look at legal records that might tell them something about the doctor's past, and so far there had been no word from William about the validity of Henri's medical schooling. Lilly was beginning to think they would never make any headway in finding out whether or not Patricia was sane, or if her husband was perpetrating some elaborate scheme to gain the Fontenot fortune.

On Thursday, two days after their visit to the asylum, Bernard came to breakfast and announced that Robbie was gone and that most of the radishes had been pulled up. Lilly could have cared less about the radishes, but she went tearing up the stairs to the room the boys shared, as if her arrival would somehow make him magically appear.

Robbie's top blanket was rumpled, but the covers had not

been pulled back for sleep, which hinted at the possibility that he had intended to leave the moment Bernard fell asleep. Where had he gone? she wondered, gazing around the room. The same sort of panic she'd felt when Tim abandoned her coiled inside her like a rattler about to strike. She felt it ease somewhat when she saw that Robbie's meager belongings were still in the room.

With Bernard following, she ran down the stairs and out to the stables, where she found Cade and Amos mucking out the stalls. The odor of manure and horse assaulted her when she stepped from the bright spring morning into the dim shadows of the barn. Dust motes dappled the sunlight slanting through the cracks between the boards. She paused, waiting for her eyes to adjust to the semidarkness.

"Ca—" In the nick of time, she stopped herself from using Cade's name and ruining everything. "Bran!" she called, aware of the alarm in her voice.

He stepped out of one of the stalls, and before she realized her intent, she threw herself at him. His arms closed around her without hesitation, and her distress eased immediately. He would know what to do. He was used to dealing with the boy and his peculiar ways.

Cade untangled her arms from around his neck and held her at arm's length. "What is it?"

"Robbie's gone."

"What do you mean, gone?" Cade circled her wrist with his fingers and drew her back outside, where they could have some privacy from Amos's sharp ears.

Lilly told him about Bernard's discovery and confirmed that Robbie was nowhere to be found, adding that it didn't look as if he'd slept in his bed, but his things were all there. "Where do you suppose he's gone?"

"Heaven only knows," Cade said, rubbing a splayed hand back and forth through his hair. "I imagine he had some notion that came to mind and went to see what he could find out without telling me. The two of you have that in common." The statement held a note of irony, but she heard no rancor in his tone.

"What should we do?"

He shrugged. "Nothing. He'll come back when he's good and ready."

Lilly recalled the terrifying night she'd spent searching for Timothy in Chicago, where people disappeared by the dozens. From what she'd seen of New Orleans, it wasn't any different. "Aren't you worried about him?"

"Of course I'm worried about him," Cade said, his irritation making a comeback. "But he's tough and he knows the streets, and he's the best at slipping around without anyone noticing. He does this sort of thing all the time. He'll be fine, and he'll be back. Go on inside and we'll just sit tight awhile before we start worrying too much."

Lilly nodded, unconvinced. Her shoulders slumped in despair, she headed back to the house.

"Everything all right?" Amos's disembodied voice echoed through the shadows of the barn when Cade went back inside.

"Not exactly. Robbie's run off."

"Shouldn't we go look for him?"

"No," Cade said. "It's not the first time. Ever since Ma died, and he came to be with me and Brona, he gets a notion to be by himself," he fibbed. "He'll be back."

Amos appeared in the stall doorway. "He's pretty young to be roamin' the streets all by hisself."

Cade sighed. "I know. If he isn't back by dark, we'll go looking for him."

Robbie returned around suppertime, his usual swagger in place and whistling some jaunty tune. The relief that rushed through Lilly left her weak in the knees. Her first thought was to throttle him.

Cade and Amos, who were just coming in to eat, saw him headed toward the kitchen. Cade stopped where he was, his hands on his hips, his head cocked to the side as he contemplated how to handle the matter.

"Where on earth have you been, Robert Sullivan?" Lilly cried. "We've been worried sick."

He just gave her one of his looks and turned toward Cade, who motioned for him to join him near the barn. Robbie lost some of his bluster, but headed after Cade. Not wanting to miss anything, Lilly followed.

When they stopped in front of him, Cade asked, "Where've you been?"

"Went to the asylum, didn't I?"

"The asylum? Why on earth would you do something like that all by yourself?" Lilly asked.

"I got tired of waitin' for you and McShane to figure out something."

Cade sighed. "I'm sorry we're not working fast enough to suit you, but these things take time," he said in a sarcastic tone. "Sometimes more time than we'd like. Did you find out anything useful?"

"I saw the missus, I did."

"Mrs. Ducharme?"

"Aye, Patricia. We had a nice little chat."

"How did you manage that?" Lilly asked, amazed. "How on earth did you sneak in without anyone seeing you and tossing you out? What did she say?" Lilly spat the questions out in rapid fire.

Robbie pinned her with a withering look. "Patience, Brona, patience. These things take time, ya know." He shot a smile at Cade. "So, when I got there, I went around back in a sort of yard, and I saw this old man walkin' around the fence.

He was a right mess. Dirty and slobberin' and such. Told me he was the watchman." He rolled his eyes heavenward. "Crazy as a bessie bug, he was. When I saw he couldn't hardly talk, I went lookin' fer the kitchen help. Sold 'em some radishes."

Lilly fixed him with a narrow-eyed gaze. "So that's where the missing radishes went."

"I had to have some reason to talk to them, didn't I, and I made a bit o' change, too."

Lilly shook her head in dismay. Now was not the time to tackle the issue of it being dishonest to sell things that had been stolen.

"One of the ladies working in the herb garden said everyone got to go outside for a while on nice days, so I just looked busy and waited until they brought her out." Almost as an afterthought, he added, "She likes outside."

"How do you know?"

"Because she turned her face up to the sun and smiled. She's terrible pale and scrawny," he added. "I think she was having a hard time staying awake. She sounded a bit tipsy."

Lilly had thought as much the day they'd snuck into the common room. She looked at Cade.

"Medication," he told her. "What did the two of you talk about?" he asked the boy.

Robbie paused and looked from one to the other of his keepers. "I gave her a little bouquet of flowers I picked from some gardens along the way, and she thanked me and told me I was delightful." He grimaced at that.

"What else?"

"Well, she said she had two daughters, but that they were all grown up and one of them died, and that she'd had a baby boy, but he died, too. She got really sad fer a bit and I thought she was goin' to cry, but then she asked me if I knew that flowers and plants had special meanings. I didn't know anything about that. What was she talking about, McShane?"

"Rosemary for remembrance," Cade said thoughtfully. When Lilly gave him a questioning look, he offered, "One of my sisters is a bit of a healer and knows a great deal about plant properties, especially those that can be used for medicinal purposes. Just about every plant represents some feeling or emotion. There's a whole language of flowers the English used in their courting."

Once again, Lilly was surprised and impressed by his knowledge.

"Yeah, that's what she was telling me, but I didn't know what she was talking about."

"Anything else?"

"No, one of the men watching over them saw me and knew I wasn't supposed to be there, so I lit out over the fence."

"That's my boy," Cade said, grinning and riffling the boy's hair. Lilly glared at him. How would she ever teach Robbie to be an upstanding young man if Cade continued to encourage him in his wayward behavior?

On Friday evening, Cade came into the room freshly bathed, shaved, and wearing clean clothes. After spending so much time with him, she should have been familiar with the little hitch in her breathing whenever he walked into a room, but the sight of him in his brown twill trousers and white collarless shirt set her heart to racing nonetheless. Which made her furious.

"I'm going out for a while."

She ached to ask him where he was going and if he was leaving to attend to something related to the case or for personal reasons. If it were the latter, it was none of her concern. Who was she to question his comings and goings?

"Are you taking Robbie with you?" Even though she'd told him letting the child tag along was a bad idea, she found herself hoping he was.

"I'm not planning on it." He looked into the small mirror and raked a hand through his damp hair, trying to scrape an unruly lock into place.

"Good."

Satisfied that he was presentable, he turned to her with his usual frown. "I won't be late."

And with that, he left her standing in the middle of the room, feeling more miserable than she had since finding out her husband was a liar and a cheat and an adulterer.

Cade paused outside the doors of the drinking establishment, the fourth he'd visited in as many hours. He was waiting for Robbie to catch up. "I hope you know that Lilly will skin you alive if she finds out you followed me here."

"Ain't none a her business, now, is it?" the boy asked in a cranky tone.

"Believe it or not, she cares what happens to you."

"I'm not lookin' fer pity."

"And she isn't lookin' for your sass. You might try being nicer to her."

"I might. Do ya think he's gonna be here?"

Cade had explained that he hoped to find the gambler who'd fleeced Henri and see if he could possibly learn more about the doctor's habits. All he had was a vague description of a young, good-looking man with dark hair who dressed a bit dandified.

"You stay out of the way and watch for anything that doesn't look right," Cade ordered. Robbie gave a little salute and then slipped inside the bar to some unobtrusive corner, where he could see and not be seen.

Cade found a group of laborers and one merchant type playing poker and joined the game. He wondered which, if any, of these players was the double-dealer. They played for perhaps an hour without anything untoward happening. Then one of the gents said he'd best head home or his wife would lock him out of the bedroom.

He had just gathered his winnings when another man sauntered up to the table. He was taller than Cade, but slender, and too pretty to be a man in Cade's estimation. His smile was as artificial as the diamond stickpin in his cravat.

"Tim Warner," the man said, shaking hands all around. Friendly and jovial though he seemed, Cade was not inclined to like the newcomer. The fellow's grasp was as limp as a shirt with too little starch, and Cade had a theory about men and their handshakes. In his mind, this fancy man's grip said much about what he was not. His gut, which was seldom wrong, told him he'd found his swindler.

They were into the third hand when he knew he was right. This might not be the man who'd taken Henri's cash, but he was no casual player. Warner bet larger sums than were comfortable for the others, and more often than not won the hand. Like his flaccid handshake, his nonchalance and indifference to the consternation of the other players spoke volumes about his character. It was official. Cade did not like him.

They played another hand. Seeing the frown on one player's face and the drops of perspiration on another's, there was no doubt that the friendly poker game had taken a turn for the worse. Finding himself tight on funds after a couple of losses, Cade, who'd been sitting next to the newcomer, had dropped out of the game earlier.

During a break where more drinks were dispensed, one of the girls whispered to Cade that he was wanted outside. Thanking her, he excused himself and stepped onto the street, wondering who was looking for him.

"Psst." Robbie stood in the shadows to Cade's right.

"What is it?"

"I been watchin' the game. Don't exactly have a ringside seat, and I wouldn't bet my life on it, mind you, but I'd keep an eye on the peacock in the saffron vest if I was you. I don't like the looks of him. He's too slick by far, and I'll wager he's got one up his sleeve or something of that nature." He gave a slight shrug. "He acts like a crook."

Cade stifled a smile. Took one to know one, he supposed. "I'll do that." He threw a harmless punch toward the boy, who dodged it easily. "Now get on out of here. Go home and get some sleep."

Robbie mumbled something about not needin' a keeper and slunk through the shadows, presumably to do as he was told.

Cade went back inside. With Robbie's warning fresh in his mind, it was easy to spot Warner deal a card from the bottom of the deck. Cade was stunned that he hadn't noticed before. He had not grown up on the ruthless streets of Chicago without learning a thing or two about con games, thievery of every kind, and sleight of hand. It was hard to believe that he hadn't noticed earlier that Warner was cheating. Cade realized he'd grown soft during the months he'd been away from his work. But now that he'd seen the truth with his own eyes, he couldn't be silent.

"Sir," he said, deciding that the man would not resort to violence with so many people about. "It appeared to me that you dealt that card from the bottom."

The good humor vanished from Warner's eyes and his nostrils flared in anger. He shoved back his chair with so much force that it turned over. He stood, trembling with fury. Whether it was feigned or real was hard to say. "Are you calling me a cheat?"

Cade rose to his feet with slow deliberation, his gaze focused on the violator's hands on the off chance he tried to reach for a weapon. "I'm telling you that I saw you take a card from the bottom and give it to Mr. Jeffers."

"No one calls me a cheat, you blasted Irishman!" Warner grated, following the hateful words with a swing toward Cade's head.

The closeness of their bodies made protecting himself hard, but he managed to get one arm up in time to ward off the brunt of the blow, which grazed his cheekbone. Then taking a step back, he swung a solid left to Warner's solar plexus and followed with an uppercut that laid him on the floor.

He did not get up.

Cade stared at him, silently cursing his stupidity and knowing that if William Pinkerton got ahold of this bit of information, his days with the agency would be good and over. There would be no third chance. A hearty back slap jolted him from his thoughts.

"Good job, Sullivan!" the merchant, Jeffers, said. "I'd figured out the man was a professional, and I thought I'd seen him dealing from the bottom, but I wasn't certain. Quite frankly I wouldn't have had the guts to confront him the way you did. That's quite a right you have!"

The man's words eased Cade's mind somewhat, but he knew he'd have to make a full report of his actions to William Pinkerton.

The owner came out from the back, demanding a full accounting. Everyone's version of the story made Cade out to be a hero and Warner to be a cheat. Satisfied that things had come aright, the owner had two burly patrons heave the gambler to his feet and shove him out the door into the street.

Sick with worry even though the heartfelt thanks of his fellow poker players still rang in his ears, Cade broke his promise to himself and ordered a beer.

Lilly had left the lamp turned low and was just drifting off to sleep when she heard Cade coming down the hallway.

When he opened the door he found her propped up on one elbow, waiting for him.

"I thought you weren't going to be late," she said, and could have bitten off her tongue. She sounded like a shrewish wife.

"Things got interesting," he said, sitting on the edge of the bed and unlacing his boots.

She was about to ask what he meant by that when a whiff of smoke and cheap perfume clarified everything. Memories of Timothy came rushing back, and along with them, a memory of Colleen strutting around MacGregor's in her satin robe, telling Lilly in a self-satisfied voice that Timothy owed her for three nights.

"You've been to a tavern."

Cade drew the shirt over his head. The lamplight glistened on his chest and shoulders. "What?"

"You've been to a tavern," she repeated.

"Wrong."

"I can smell the smoke, and . . . and perfume."

"I haven't been to one tavern, lass. I've been to several."

"And you're drunk."

He smiled a crooked smile. "I am not drunk. Believe me, I've learned my lesson about that. My friends bought me a single brew after I flattened a cheater."

She gave a little gasp. "You've been fighting?"

He frowned. "And if I have? What's it to you? Why are you actin' like a jealous wife when ye've got no claim on me? You're not even sharin' my bed."

"And I never will!"

He leaned toward her, so close she could feel the disturbing warmth radiating from his bare torso.

"Never say never, lass," he warned as he had once before. "Life has a way of makin' ya eat yer words."

He straightened suddenly and began to toss his bedding to

the floor, all banter gone. He was the prickly, sour, and serious agent once again as he stripped off his trousers and tossed them to the foot of the bed. Though he wore thigh-length undergarments, Lilly did her best to keep her gaze averted.

"I went around to some of Henri's favorite haunts tonight, looking to find a game. I hoped to get a better sense of what he's like away from his day-to-day routine."

"That shouldn't have been hard."

"No, but I was hopin' to find a particular game with a particular player." When she frowned, he explained. "Bernard told Robbie that he'd overheard his da tellin' his ma that Henri lost a lot of money to a cardsharp on Wednesday night."

Cade stretched out on his pallet and folded his hands behind his head. Lilly leaned over the edge of the bed. "And did you find him?"

"I found someone. I'm not sure it's the man Henri played with, but he was definitely a cheat."

Even in the semidarkness Lilly noted the discoloration on Cade's face. "Did he do that to your cheek?"

He reached up and rubbed his fingers over his cheekbone, a rueful expression in his eyes. "I suppose he did."

"What will William say if he finds out?" she asked, suddenly worried about this new complication.

"He'll find out, because I intend to tell him."

"You'd tell him, even though you know it may be the end of your career?" she asked, aghast at the notion.

Cade shrugged. "I shouldn't have hit the pretty boy."

"Did he take the first swing?"

"Yes, but that's beside the point."

"Surely the Pinkertons won't penalize you for standing up for yourself. And you were working at the time, not carousing."

He offered her a strained smile. "I appreciate your loyalty, wife. We'll know soon enough, won't we?"

She was too troubled to be upset by his sarcasm. "Tell me what happened."

He sighed and stared up at the ceiling, as if he could see the entire evening playing out in the shadows. "I'd been to some other bars, and this was the last of Henri's haunts I planned to check. I joined a friendly game of poker, and we'd been playing awhile when this peacock asked if he could sit in."

"Peacock?"

"Yes, a fancy-dressed fella who gave me a real bad feeling."

"In what way?"

Cade's forehead puckered in thought. "He seemed too . . . slick. It wasn't long before he started mopping up, and I started figuring him for a professional, and a cheat to boot. Robbie called me outside and told me the gent was dealing off the bottom of the deck."

"Robbie!" Lilly cried. "You told me he wasn't going with you!"

"Don't take off my head, colleen. I wasn't planning on it, and I didn't ask him. He followed me. So when I called the man out on it, he took a swing at me."

Well, at least Cade had had provocation, Lilly thought. Surely the agency would take that into consideration. And now that she'd been talking to him for a while, she could tell that he was not drunk at all. "What did you do?"

He shrugged. "Coldcocked him. The owner came, and the other players backed up my story. Timmy boy was thrown out, and I doubt he'll be welcome there again."

Lilly felt the blood drain from her face. "Timmy? The gambler's name was Tim?"

"Aye," Cade said, frowning up at her. "Tim Warner. Why?"

Suddenly feeling light-headed, Lilly put a hand to her brow and moaned, a terrible sound that seemed to come from her very soul.

"Are you all right?" Cade's voice sounded far, far away. A part of her recognized that he was regarding her with an expression of concern, while another part of her was trying to make sense of her disbelief. What were the chances that something like this could happen? *Had* happened? Timothy was here, in New Orleans. Cade had played poker with him. What were the odds, really?

"Lilly?"

She gave her head a shake to clear her thoughts and forced herself to rein in her emotions. "I'm fine," she said in a no-nonsense voice. "Just a bit . . . taken aback for a moment."

"You're not fine. What is it? Do you know him?"

"Not as well as I thought I did," she said, meeting his gaze squarely. "Tim Warner is my husband."

CHAPTER 13

Although not many things fazed Cade anymore, he wondered if her announcement left his mouth hanging open in shock. "Your husband?"

"Yes," Lilly said tartly. "I assumed the Pinkertons gave you some background on me when they decided we should work together."

"Aye, they did. I knew you were married and the chap took your savings and left, but they didn't give me a name. Why don't you go by Warner instead of Long?"

"I'm using my maiden name because I started divorce proceedings before I left Chicago, and I want my former name back. The sooner I can be rid of anything connected to Tim Warner the better."

Cade propped his head in his palm, his elbow on the pillow. "D'ya want to tell me about him?"

Lilly thought about that a moment. She had no desire to tell Cadence McShane her deepest, darkest secrets, but now that this had happened, it made sense that she should at least give him a sketchy idea of what had happened with Timothy, on the off chance that something like this cropped up again.

"Not particularly," she confessed with a weary shake of her head, "but maybe you should know." Her voice was sad and low-pitched as she started with how she'd met Timothy at the train station, how he'd swept her off her feet, and how they were married in a month's time. She told him of Tim's gambling, his manipulation, their constant arguing, and finally, how he'd physically attacked her and Rose the day he'd stolen her savings.

"I went to one of his favorite taverns, but he wasn't there and hadn't been in more than a week," she told him. "It seemed I wasn't the only one trying to find him."

Cade arched a quizzical brow.

"The police had been in earlier looking for him, and not only did he owe another customer money from a poker game, but he owed one of the tarts for services rendered." She met his gaze in defiance. "Her name was Colleen."

Lilly could see by Cade's expression that he now understood why she was so adamantly against being called Colleen.

Lilly flung her legs over the side of the bed. "Now, I want you to take me to this place so I can confront him."

"He isn't there. He left before I did," Cade said. "In fact, after I hit him, a couple of guys threw him into the street. He must have come around, though, because he was gone when I left about twenty minutes later."

The indignation drained from her. "I should have known it was too good to be true."

"I'll go back tomorrow and see if I can find any trace of him anywhere."

"I want to go with you."

"Lilly. Lass, ya have to stop acting without thinking things through. D'ya really think it's wise to go off on your own business in the middle of an assignment? I may already be in hot water over what happened tonight, so if the agency pulls me from the case, you need to be here to finish up. Besides, it's best if you stay out of things and let the lawmen do their job."

The fact that he wanted her to be able to stay on the case eased her fears that he would try to take over and gain all the glory when it was solved. It seemed McShane was a professional after all. But none of that changed how she felt about confronting Tim.

"I want to talk to him."

"Why?" Cade challenged. "What would you say to him if you saw him?" He shook his head. "It would serve no good purpose."

She gave his questions and conclusion serious consideration. "You're right. I've always been impulsive, which is the only reason I had the courage to interview with the Pinkertons," she admitted. "Impulsive and hardheaded. Pierce and Rose have warned me about these faults of mine for years."

He felt the corner of his mouth lift in a half smile. He identified with her more than she might think. "It's been my experience that thinking things through is crucial in our line of work. Unfortunately, it's one of those traits that develop with age, and you're very young yet."

"And are you so ancient?"

"It depends on what day it is."

She chewed on her lower lip, and he saw the hint of worry in her dark eyes. "Will you really tell William what happened, then?"

"I have to." With that, he lay back down and turned away from her, indicating that the conversation was over. A few seconds later, she blew out the lamp.

When the room was quiet, Lilly lay still, listening to Cade's slow, even breathing and trying to ease the tension binding her. She thought if someone touched her she might shatter. Tim. In New Orleans. Or maybe by now he was already headed for some other distant place.

It seemed her soon-to-be ex-husband's approach to life was to find a new town, someone he could sucker in a card game, and, just possibly, a woman naïve enough to influence with his considerable charm. Then when he'd cleaned her out or she started getting wise to him, he moved on.

Oh, how she'd like to meet Tim face-to-face one more time, but deep inside, she knew Cade was right. She needed to leave it alone and let the police do their jobs. She would report him to the authorities on her next trip to town. Or maybe Cade would find him first.

She heard Cade snore softly, and her heart dropped at the thought of the agency's reaction to him getting into another barroom fight. Would they fire him a second time? For good? As much as she'd complained about being paired with him, the thought of not having him around was upsetting. There was something to be said about having a partner working different aspects of a case, watching out for you when things got unpredictable, and just knowing you had a backup if you needed one.

Hardly a day passed that she wasn't reminded how illequipped she was for the job she'd finagled her way into. William and Robert Pinkerton, Pierce, and Cade all said she was too untried by life. She knew she was too reckless, too apt to act on a hunch or a whim instead of waiting to see what the facts might be.

And she was a woman.

When she'd answered the Pinkerton ad in Chicago, she'd been spurred by righteous indignation, impulse, and hurt feelings. As much as she hated admitting it, William was right in forcing her to work with Cade until she became more experienced. There were days she felt as if all the cards were stacked against her, but despite feeling out of her depth most of the time, she loved what she was doing, even though there was certainly nothing glamorous about it. Cade was shoveling manure and she was working in a hot kitchen and doing housework.

She reminded herself that she was doing something worthwhile. Every time she saw Henri and heard the condescension in his voice, she felt in her bones that there was more to him than what he presented to the world. The validity of his medical license would prove her feelings one way or the other. Whatever happened, she hoped Cade was around to help finish the investigation.

When Cade awoke the following morning, it was too early to rouse Lilly. He dressed as quietly as possible and left the room. His mind was filled with her confession about her past and her connection to Tim Warner. Maybe someday she'd go into more detail, but at least now he understood why she'd sought a position with the agency and why she was so bitter toward men.

Cade had trouble picturing Warner and Lilly as a couple. He supposed women would think the gambler was handsome, but he was too smooth by half. On the other hand, while Lilly's fiery red hair and pretty brown eyes were certainly enough to draw the interest of most men, there was that sharp tongue for a man to deal with. Cade didn't see her as the type to appeal to the gambler. He wondered if Warner had even been aware of the gentle heart she protected with those sharp barbs. The softness was something she seldom allowed to show, but he saw it whenever she looked at Robbie or pitched in to help Lamartine without being asked.

He suppressed a smile at how she bristled every time he called her colleen. After hearing her story, it was no wonder she hated the name. He supposed he had no choice but to refrain from calling her that in the future, but he would miss seeing the anger blaze in her eyes.

However, recognizing and even admiring her good qualities didn't make him any happier about being saddled with her, but after watching her in Vandalia and working with her here, he'd be the first to say that she needed someone to guide her. She was as green as grass when it came to detecting, but she gave it everything she had. Sometimes she gave it too much. Like when she'd taken it upon herself to put a plan into motion without talking it over with him first, like contacting her longtime friend.

He admitted to being curious about this Wainwright fellow, who'd been both father and mentor to Lilly. If he was even half what she claimed him to be, he'd be a good one to have poking around the hospital to see what he could learn. They needed something to take them in a new direction. Some thread to start unraveling this whole unseemly mess.

After a week, they had little to go on. There was not one shred of evidence to prove that Henri had deliberately sent his wife to the insane asylum to get his hands on the Fontenot money. Suspicions would not hold up in court, or bring Patricia home.

Lilly suspected that Mrs. Abelard was interested in the doctor. Robbie confirmed that he had seen her coming from Henri's room in the dead of night, and once he'd peeked into Patricia's room and saw that Mrs. Abelard had dressed in her mistress's clothing, parading around the room and acting as if she owned the place.

So Hedda Abelard appeared to be sleeping with the doctor. Had she agreed to an affair believing that if Henri were rid of his wife he would offer her something more than the housekeeper's position? Had she helped him to get rid of Pa-

tricia in some way? It was a common enough tale, and certainly provided a motive, but there was nothing so far to
solidly bring to court.

Besides, Cade couldn't see Ducharme tying himself to
Hedda Abelard if he *did* wind up with all the Fontenot money.
Henri would not rid himself of a wife with long-standing ties
to society just to take up with the housekeeper, especially
when she was willing to dally with him on the side. His gut told
him there was something else at play here, and so far money
was the only viable motive for the doctor's behavior.

Always, in the end, everything came to money.

When Lilly went to Mrs. Fontenot's room the following
morning, the overwhelming stench of gastric upset assaulted
her the instant she opened the door. The old woman's small
frame was curled into a fetal position, and she was making
sounds of distress.

"Madam! What is it?" she asked, rushing to the bedside
and placing a palm on her employer's forehead. She felt clammy
and cold.

"I seem to have eaten something that does not agree with
me," she replied. "I've been up half the night with vomiting
and . . . other gastric problems."

"Shall I fetch Dr. Ducharme?"

"Absolutely not. The last time this happened, he gave me
some medicines that didn't help me a whit. I would rather die
on the spot than have that man treat me."

Well, Lilly thought, that was a rather staunch stand. "You've
had these symptoms before?"

"Yes, shortly before Patricia was . . . sent away." She sighed
and tried to smile. "I'm just getting old, Brona. When you get
old you find that you often can't eat the things you've always
enjoyed without suffering for it later. I'll be fine soon enough."

Lilly wasn't so sure of that. The older woman looked terrible. "Let me get everything cleaned up, and I'll see if Lamartine has any idea what to do."

Lamartine literally wrung her hands and paced the kitchen when Lilly told her of their mistress's dreadful night. The cook whirled suddenly and pinned Lilly with an unwavering look. "It wasn't anything she ate, Brona. Not in this house. Ever since she got sick before, I've been careful to see that whatever she eats goes straight from this kitchen to the table and her mouth."

Lilly couldn't help the widening of her eyes at the statement. "Why would you do that?"

Lamartine placed her hands on her slender hips and looked at Lilly as if she didn't have a lick of sense. "Too many things been happenin' to the women in this house for my likin'. I aim to make sure that nothing happens to Miz Fontenot if I can help it."

So, the suspicion that there was something nefarious going on was shared by the help as well as Mrs. Fontenot and Cassandra. Wasn't that interesting? "Could it have been something from Sunday?"

Lamartine shook her head, and the jeweled pin on her tignon glistened in the sunlight streaming through the window. "If it was something she ate, it wouldn't take this long to make her sick."

"What do you think it is, then?"

"I don't know, but I don't intend for it to happen again. You throw out all that medicine the doctor gave her. I'm sending up a pitcher of water. She needs to drink as much of it as she can. Oh! And a glass of milk. That seemed to help her last time. Soothed her stomach and all."

Lilly nodded. If Lamartine was so certain that the things the elderly woman had ingested were not the culprit, what else could it be? *Mrs. Fontenot is most likely right. It's probably nothing more than she's just an old woman with gastric upset.*

Possibly. But Pierce had always said he didn't believe in co-incidence, and the more she dealt with crime, the more in-clined she was to agree. There were too many unanswered questions surrounding the legitimacy of Patricia's so-called in-sanity, especially coming on the heels of the unexpected and unusual death of her daughter at a suffragist rally.

On the other hand, the human mind was at once fragile and incredibly strong. Lilly had firsthand knowledge of what amazing things it did to protect one from situations too painful to dwell on. The events surrounding her mother's murder had been blocked from her memory until an incident during her previous assignment had caused all the hateful images to come flooding back.

It was possible that Patricia Ducharme had gone mad after the loss of her infant son and her daughter in such a short time. Possible. But Lilly's gut and what she'd learned since coming to New Orleans told her that Patricia was made of sterner stuff than her husband claimed.

The following morning, Robbie sat next to Mrs. Fonte-not's bed, watching her sleep. Lucifer lay curled up next to her, his one good eye regarding Robbie warily. Robbie had spent so much time with Mrs. Fontenot and brought the cat so many tidbits to eat that Lucifer now took the morsels from the palm of his hand on the days he was feeling charitable.

They'd reached a truce of sorts, but Robbie was too smart to believe he'd won the vicious feline over. He had yet to touch the cat in any way, but knew the day would come. Pa-tience was a trait worth developing when you lived on the street.

He sat there watching the old woman breathing, wishing

he knew how to pray and hoping she would wake up so she could see that he was worried about her. She had improved steadily the day before under the care of Lamartine, Lilly, and Mrs. Abelard. The doctor left her medicines, which the women who were caring for her put in the bottom of a drawer.

Robbie wanted her to get better. He'd never had a grandmother, but if he had, he hoped she would be just like Mrs. Fontenot.

She seemed content to take care of the business decisions that came her way, sit in her garden, and read. Robbie and Bernard joined her sometimes if they got their work done, fascinated with the stories she told of her childhood on the plantation.

He looked around, taking pleasure from his surroundings. He liked this room. It was bright with sunshine and light colors. The paintings on the walls were scenery instead of boring pictures of people, many of them painted by Suzannah Fontenot, the girl who had been killed while out with her family.

Though he'd never admit it, that bothered him. He'd been on the streets for so long, so confident in his own wits and skills, it had never occurred to him that anything could happen to him. He wasn't stupid. He knew people died in shadowy alleyways every day, but hearing that a wealthy woman had been separated from her family and later found dead was scary. He didn't understand how bad things happened to rich people.

Someone had picked a bouquet of flowers from the garden. Bored, he picked up the vase and smelled each flower in turn, wrinkling his nose when he encountered one whose scent was not nearly as pleasing as it looked.

Then he took up the book that sat next to a small pitcher of water. He looked at the words printed on the pages but had no idea what they said. Maybe he should learn to read now that he was becoming all respectable and everything.

Spying Mrs. Fontenot's gold snuffbox near a letter opener, he picked it up and ran his fingers over the raised scrollwork, marveling that anyone could make something so fancy. He held the trinket in his fist and hefted its slight weight, wondering what it had cost . . . and how much someone would pay for it.

He opened the small box and examined the contents. It was a brown powder. Though she didn't use it every day, Mrs. Fontenot loved a pinch of snuff now and again. He'd had a few puffs of a cigar once a couple of years ago and shared a chaw of tobacco with the kid in the boxcar with him. The cigar had choked him and made him dizzy, and the chewing tobacco had made him sick to his stomach.

What would snuff be like?

He glanced over at Mrs. Fontenot and saw that she was still sleeping. Quietly, he stood and slipped the snuffbox into his pocket; then he tiptoed out of the room and down the back stairs.

Two days later, Mrs. Fontenot was well enough to come downstairs for breakfast.

"I've decided to go and spend a few days with Cassandra at River Run," she declared.

Henri regarded her with a concerned expression as he slathered a piece of toast with some fresh-churned butter. "I must object, *Grand-mère*. You've been very ill, and I'm not sure you're up to that long drive. What's brought this on anyway? Cassandra and Preston have barely had time to get home."

The old woman sighed. "I'm well aware of that, Henri, and the truth is that I'm feeling my age. My common sense tells me that it won't be too many years before I'm unable to travel, so I might as well do it while I can." She smiled, a trifle sadly it seemed to Lilly. "Besides, it's lonely here without Patricia and Suzannah. I miss them dreadfully, as I'm sure you do."

"Well, of course I do," he said, managing a look of affront. "Despite what you may think, I haven't forgotten that I lost a son and a stepdaughter or that Patricia is still my wife. I suppose their absence doesn't weigh so heavily on me since I have my practice to take my mind off things."

Lilly sensed that his indignation was nothing but a sop to the old woman's grief.

"I was simply referring to the fact that Cassandra and Preston just left, and since she is expecting she may not be up to having visitors."

"You're right of course," she conceded, "but I thought that since she is feeling so poorly with the pregnancy and seldom gets out these days that I might be some company for her. She confessed to feeling quite neglected since Preston spends all week in the city in order to take care of his law practice."

Lilly could only imagine that a woman alone on a plantation with no one around but the help for company could get very lonesome.

"Well, she's a married woman now. They're expecting a child. That is a huge responsibility. Perhaps she should grow up and realize that a man must do whatever he has to in order to take care of his family."

"You're right, Henri, but she's young," Madam Fontenot said in a gentle voice. Lilly noticed that she kept her gaze fixed on her plate.

"Of course, of course. You have a point," the doctor said. "And I know you well enough to know that when you make up your mind, there is no changing it. When will you be leaving?"

"By midmorning." She glanced at Lilly. "If it won't be difficult to get things together, will it, Brona?"

"Not at all," Lilly assured her. "I'll let Mrs. Abelard know so that she can pack for you."

Wearing an expression that Lilly could not quite fathom, Henri looked up from the piece of ham he was cutting.

"I'm sorry, my dear. I didn't make myself clear," Mrs. Fortenot said. "I'd like for you to come with me instead of Mrs. Abelard. She gets all atwitter if she has to leave here for longer than a day."

"Yes," Henri added with a little smile. "She thinks this place will fall down around us if she isn't here to oversee things."

Mrs. Fontenot gave Lilly an apologetic smile. "I hate to drag you away from your handsome husband, and there was a time I'd have happily made the trip alone, but I'm afraid I'm still a bit weak."

"Certainly, Madam Fontenot," Lilly was quick to say. "I'll tell Bran as soon as we finish with breakfast."

Lilly was almost to the hall door when Mrs. Fontenot's voice stopped her. "Oh! Will you ask Mrs. Abelard if she's seen my snuffbox? I seem to have misplaced it."

When Lilly went to the barn to tell Cade of this newest development, he slid an arm around her shoulders and led her out into the spring sunlight. "I don't like it."

She turned to face him, escaping his disturbing touch. "Why? Maybe I can learn something from the servants while I'm there. There was no time to do much talking at Easter."

"You may be right, but I don't like the idea of us being separated. I haven't found out enough about either of these men to have any idea what they might be capable of."

"I understand, but I don't see that we have a choice. Mrs. Fontenot wants me to go. Besides, I think you're borrowing trouble. I thought we'd decided that at worst, Preston is a good-for-nothing, and Henri, who we think is the real culprit, will be here for you to keep an eye on."

"You're right, but I don't have to like it."

"I'm actually not crazy about the notion either. Oh. By the way, would you let Robbie know that Mrs. Fontenot's snuff-box is missing and see how he reacts?"

Cade looked horrified. "You don't think he took it, do you?"

"I'm just telling you the facts. I would hate for us to get the sack because he couldn't resist a pretty trinket."

Three hours later, Amos, Bernard, and Robbie had loaded the family brougham and Cade helped Mrs. Fontenot up. To Lilly's surprise, before he handed Lilly inside, he took both her hands in his, leaned forward, and brushed his lips to hers in the briefest of kisses. She might have been angry if she weren't so shocked.

"Have a safe trip, wife," he murmured in a low voice.

Only then did she realize the kiss was meant for show. Knowing she had to play her role, she smiled up at him and then went over to Robbie, leaned down, and gave him a hug. She felt him stiffen, and for a moment she thought he might break away and give her what for, but instead, he hugged her back for the briefest second.

She met his gaze squarely. "Take care of your brother, Robbie," she said for the benefit of the servants who were watching.

"Oh, you can be sure of it."

"Good. Stay out of trouble." She leaned closer and whispered into his ear. "And put Mrs. Fontenot's snuffbox back where you got it before she returns."

The first directive was the words that any adult might charge a child with upon leaving, but the second caught him by surprise. He met her gaze squarely. Wearing the angelic look that never failed to amaze her, he only smiled.

With a final wave of farewell, Lilly allowed Cade to help her into the carriage. When she was settled next to her employer, Amos guided the horses toward the street. Lilly kept her head turned toward the open window until they rode onto Rampart Street and she lost sight of him. With a sigh of disappointment she really didn't understand, she looked at her employer, who offered her an indulgent smile.

CHAPTER 14

It was midafternoon when the brougham turned down a shaded lane leading to the plantation house. Trees with feather-like foliage dripped Spanish moss, their knobby knees poking up out of the marsh on either side of the road. Mrs. Fontenot pointed, and Lilly saw a huge alligator slither from the bank into the murky water, barely marring the smooth surface. A grayish bird her employer called a blue heron waded along the shallow shoreline, looking for a midafternoon bite. The shimmer and dazzle of dragonfly wings sparkled in the sunlight. A kingfisher darted from an overhanging branch and swooped low to nab an unsuspecting victim.

The river had been visible in the distance for some time, so when the plantation house came into view, Lilly was surprised to see that the waterway was nowhere in sight. Instead the house was located a distance away from a small lake.

"Where's the river?" she asked Mrs. Fontenot.

"The river has a way of changing course through the years. It also has a tendency to eat away at the outer edges of a bend and deposit the soil on the other side. The lake you see is the course it probably took a hundred years ago when the house was first built. What's left is called an oxbow pond. The river itself is just beyond those trees."

Before she could explain further, Amos pulled up the circle drive in the front lawn of a French Colonial–style house. A steeply pitched, hipped roof extended over the upper and lower galleries that spanned the entire length of the house. Square posts supported the second-story porch that boasted a railing. The wide staircase that led to the upper floor was centered in the structure.

Huge trees, already green with leaves, dotted the lawn surrounding the house. A vine with tiny yellow blossoms scrambled among the branches of smaller trees, and a sweet floral scent permeated the air, mingling with the marshy odor of the wetlands. River Run was a simple house, a fine representation of the style, but it was a far cry from the opulent homes Lilly had seen along the way.

The upper front door opened and Cassandra, accompanied by Preston, stepped out onto the upper gallery and waved. Mrs. Fontenot waved back, a happy smile on her face. By the time Amos stopped the carriage, Rollo had appeared to help the ladies alight and to unload the luggage. Amos would start the return trip as soon as he had a bite to eat.

Cassandra, Preston, and her great-grandmother were soon ensconced in the upstairs parlor with cups of hot tea in hand and a delicious-looking array of cookies on a china plate awaiting them.

Neecie showed Lilly to a small room off the kitchen, where she would sleep while she was visiting.

Lilly set her carpetbag on the narrow bed. "It seems you and Cassandra made the Easter trip just fine."

"We did," the pregnant woman said in the soft, lilting patois so common in the area. "But she's right glad that her *grand-mère* decided to come and stay a few days. It's lonesome for her when Mister is away in town."

"Why is he here in the middle of the week?" Lilly asked. "Someone said he stays in town for work and comes home on the weekend."

"He does, but some bigwig came to visit from Baton Rouge, and he didn't leave until this morning." Neecie shot Lilly a quick smile. "I'm hopin' he leaves out in the morning. The rest of us like when he's gone."

Lilly glanced at her over her shoulder. "He does seem a bit . . . high-handed," she stated, hoping that offering her own opinion would open up the conversation. "But then I haven't been around him much."

"High-handed." Neecie's mouth seemed to taste the word. If the expression on her face was any indication, she didn't like its flavor. "I'd say that's a fair picture of him." She took the extra uniform Lilly handed her and hung it on a nearby nail. "I was surprised to hear you traveled with *Grand-mère*. Not that it isn't good to see you."

"I was surprised she asked me to come, but she's had a gastric upset and didn't want to make the trip alone. Since Mrs. Abelard doesn't like being away from the city house, she asked me to come with her."

Neecie actually chuckled. "No, I'm guessin' Miss Hedda likes it just fine when everyone is away. She's got pretty attached to that house and everything in it."

Lilly didn't see the humor in that, but the young servant added no further explanation.

"How do you and your family like working with Mrs. Fontenot?" Neecie asked.

"So far, it's been good. Ca—" Lilly broke off the word she

was about to say with a series of coughs. She'd almost called Cade by his true name. "Can't complain," she substituted. "Lamartine is a joy to work with, and Bernard is a blessing. It's good for Robbie to have some structure to his life. I'm afraid he was too often left to his own devices before coming to live with us." Well, that was the truth. "Having Bernard around has been good for him. I believe he's a steadying influence."

"He's a good boy."

"Speaking of boys . . . are you and Rollo hoping for a boy or a girl?"

Neecie turned away and placed a stack of Lilly's undergarments in an open drawer. "*Maman* and Aunt Lamartine both say it's not a good idea to get too attached to the idea of having a baby when there are so many things that can go wrong, so I just take it a day at a time."

Lilly stood in the quiet of the room and reflected on the matter-of-fact statement. What a strange way of looking at things. She'd always assumed that when a woman carried a child inside her, that she would be overjoyed at the thought that her love for another person had culminated in such a miracle . . . unless, of course, that child had been conceived out of wedlock as she and her dead sibling had been.

Or one is told over and over that something might go awry, as Henri had done to Patricia. Lilly doubted there had been any joy during her confinement.

"Oh, Brona, I'm so sorry for reminding you," Neecie said when the silence in the room stretched out uncomfortably.

The statement jolted Lilly from her morbid thoughts. "What?"

"I'd forgotten that you and Bran lost a baby."

Lilly drew in a breath. She, too, had forgotten the lie she'd told everyone. That was the problem with lies. They were hard to remember, and the more you told, the harder it was to keep them straight. She schooled her features into what she hoped was a suitable expression and said, "It's all right, Neecie. If the Lord is willing, we'll have a child of our own. If not, we have Robbie."

Lilly was happy to hear that she sounded sincere. "Now, since I'm sure Mrs. Fontenot will be spending most of her time with Cassandra, what on earth am I going to do to fill my days?"

Neecie laughed again. "Don't worry. I'm sure *Maman* will think of something."

"I'm ready."

Cade was using a hoof pick to clean one of the horse's feet when Henri's voice preceded him into the shadowy interior of the carriage house. The ladies had been gone barely fifteen minutes, but Cade had already hitched up the buggy so that he could drive his employer to his office in Amos's absence.

He dropped the gelding's hoof. "Yes, sir. Is it all right if Robbie comes along? I need to pick him up a pair of boots on the way back." Amos had clued Cade in on the fact that Ducharme was not too much of a stickler about the help making stops on the way home as long as everything was up to snuff in the yard and carriage house.

"I won't be going to the office today," Ducharme said with a jovial smile, "but the boy is welcome to ride along in the turnout seat." The small seat in the back was a common addition to the popular buggy style in the South. "I'll tell Amos when he gets back that you have permission to take the wagon tomorrow and make your purchase."

Despite what anyone thought he'd done, and whether or not it was all for show, Ducharme was usually pleasant, but Cade didn't recall seeing him in such good humor. It made him curious as to where they might be headed.

"Thank you, sir. And I'm sure he'll enjoy the outing," Cade said, though he knew Robbie had been looking forward to new footwear. His toes threatened to poke out the front of the boots he was wearing now.

The boy must have been watching for their employer, because he came sauntering around the corner of the house, munching on a breakfast biscuit. He seemed always to be eating something. Cade figured there was more food available to him here than he'd ever seen in his life.

Bernard looked a little despondent when Robbie climbed into the small rear seat of the buggy, but Cade brought back his smile by telling him that he could accompany him and Robbie the next day when they went looking for shoes.

Cade sat next to Ducharme, who only spoke to him when he told him where and when to turn in order to reach their destination. When his instructions took them out of the city, Cade grew more curious. Where on earth were they headed?

After another hour, the buggy started down a long lane. Sugarcane fields bordered either side of the narrow road, which soon ended in front of a small frame house with a slight overhang above the door. The only saving grace was the large trees shading the bungalow. The small dwelling with its flaking paint did not look like the sort of place the fastidious doctor would frequent.

Cade pulled the horses to a halt. "Is this the place, sir?" he asked, turning to his employer with a questioning look.

"It is. You and Robbie wait out here. Water the horses. Do whatever you can find to do. I'll be a couple of hours."

As he pondered Henri's reasons for coming to this out-of-the-way spot, the door flew open and a woman stepped out onto the poor excuse for a porch, a wide smile on her face.

She was blond, perhaps in her early thirties. Slender and of medium height, the unknown woman wore a plain black skirt and patterned shirtwaist. That she was happy to see Henri was evident by her broad smile. For a moment, Cade expected her to throw herself into the doctor's arms, but she did not. Then they disappeared into the house and shut the door.

Cade guided the buggy to a shady spot, set the brake, and looped the reins around the right-hand lantern. If they were going to be sitting and waiting for two hours, he didn't plan to bake in the sun.

Robbie hopped down from the back seat and came around to confront Cade. There was a gleam of cheekiness in his whiskey-colored eyes. "What do you think this is all about, McShane?"

He gave a slow shake of his head. "I haven't a clue, lad."

Robbie snorted a little laugh. "If ya don't, yer not as smart as you think you are. Here's a hint. He's a man and she's a woman mighty glad to see him."

The boy might make an agent yet, if he could be kept on the straight and narrow the next dozen years. Though Cade suspected the same thing, he was acutely aware that Robbie Jenkins knew far more about the facts of life and the sordidness of the world than any ten-year-old ought. Why, the child thought no more about slipping into a tavern than he would a church. Truth to tell, he'd be far more at home in a pub.

Cade lifted his eyebrows in question, but the twinkle of mischief in his eyes said they were in agreement. "Are you suggesting that there's something goin' on between them?" he asked in a scandalized whisper. "That the doctor is not only being unfaithful to his poor wife with Mrs. Abelard, but this woman as well?"

Realizing that he was being played, Robbie grinned his impudent grin. "It would seem so, you buffoon, and I intend to find out."

Without waiting for consent or denial, he turned and ran

toward the bungalow, slipping through the trees until he disappeared behind the residence. Cade opened his mouth to call the boy back but didn't want to take a chance on alerting Ducharme or the woman. As usual with Robbie, it was best to just sit back, try not to worry too much, and see what happened.

While he waited for the child's return or for all hell to break loose, Cade paced back and forth from the buggy to a small barn a distance away. On the third trip, he decided to have a look around the structure, on the off chance that the decrepit building held some clue to their investigation. He found nothing but an ancient nag, an old buggy with a folding top, some leather harness that needed some care, and a grain box filled with oats. A pile of hay rested in one corner.

He went to the doorway of the barn, folded his arms across his chest, and leaned against the doorframe, regarding the house. Did the unknown woman live here alone? *Was* her relationship to Ducharme the obvious one? If so, how many women was the doctor stringing along? Could their theory be right? Was it his carnal appetite for one of these women behind him needing to rid himself of his wife? If so, could he possibly be willing to trade the beautiful, accomplished Patricia for either of the two women who seemed in the running? And just how much further would he take his scheme to gain control of the Fontenot fortune?

One thing was certain. They'd know sooner or later.

His gaze shifted to the road and he found himself wondering if Mrs. Fontenot and Lilly had arrived at River Run. Would she find that one crucial bit of information that would lead them to the culprit in this investigation . . . if indeed there was one? He shook his head to rid himself of thoughts of the case that kept circling round and round in his head.

For some obscure reason the memory of Lilly asking him to teach her how to defend herself came to mind. Why hadn't he taken the time to do it before now? It would have been easy enough to find someplace where no prying eyes could see them, if it was just in the barn after everyone had gone to bed. What if she needed some way to protect herself while she was gone?

"What's the matter, *Bran?*" Robbie quipped, ducking into the barn. "Missin' Brona?"

"I wouldn't call it missing her," he corrected, surprised that the boy could read him so well. "More concerned about not being around in case she needs me."

"I been watching her, and she keeps her eyes open," Robbie offered.

That was good to know. It was also good to know that even though his feelings for her were ambivalent at best, Robbie was looking out for her, too, though he'd deny it if asked. "Did you see anything?"

"Found a nice shrub where I could see in the parlor window, I did. Saw the doctor playing with a baby."

"A baby?"

Hearing that Ducharme was inside playing with a baby was the absolute last thing Cade expected to hear. What in blazes was the doctor up to? And who on earth were the woman and child? She looked too young to be his lover, but then when it came to some men, were they ever too young? Was she a daughter from his previous marriage and the baby a grandchild?

"Looked to be a boy, but I didn't see the goods, if you know what I mean, and I'm no expert on the matter."

Cade fought to suppress a smile. "What else?"

"I watched them awhile, and then the woman dished up some soup or stew or something, so I found me an open window, climbed in, and had me a look around." The announcement was accompanied by a roguish smile.

"You went *into* the house?" Cade could not hide his astonishment at the boy's audacity. "What if they'd heard you?"

"Well, that would've been a fine mess, wouldn't it? But they didn't, so that's a moat point."

"Moat?"

"Unimportant."

It was Cade's turn to smile. "Moot, lad. It's a moot point."

Robbie shrugged.

"Did you find out anything of importance during your little break-in?"

"I didn't break into anything. The window was wide open. And whatever they were eatin' smelled really good, and I'm starving."

"You had breakfast and a biscuit on the way. You can't be hungry."

"I'm a growin' boy," Robbie said in all seriousness. "Lamartine says I have a hollow leg."

"Well, you'll just have to be hungry for a while. The doctor didn't say anything about us being gone for dinner, and I didn't bring anything."

"Won't be the first time I went without a meal," Robbie said philosophically. "Probably won't be the last."

Cade ignored his dramatic tone. "Let me rephrase my question. Did you find out anything of importance to the case?

"I looked in the drawers, and—"

"You didn't help yourself to anything, did you?"

Robbie somehow managed to look both guilty and insulted.

"I'll have you know, McShane, that I have turned over a new leaf. As you keep reminding me, I'm part of a Pinkerton team, and they do not suffer their agents behaving in a disgraceful way. You, of all people, should know that," he pointed out. "All that's in my past."

"D'ya have your fingers crossed behind yer back?" Cade

asked, only half teasing. "It seemed a legitimate question, since you've the skills of a light-fingered monk."

"I was rather good at it, wasn't I?" Robbie said with a satisfied nod. "There wasn't much in there. Some letters, and a little book with writing in it. A Bible."

"What did the letters say?"

"How would I know?"

Cade had forgotten that Robbie had received little to no schooling and couldn't read. "Well, that will have to be remedied. Lilly can teach you. We can't be having a Pinkerton who can't read. Why didn't you bring me one of the letters?"

The boy made a sound of disgust and gave Cade an offended look. "Make up your mind about my thieving, McShane."

Cade admitted the kid had a point, though he'd have given a week's wages to see the name on the letters and what was written inside them. Nevertheless, the chance was gone. Even if he weren't trying to lead Robbie down the straight and narrow, he couldn't send him back to get the letters long enough to read them and then go back a third time to return them. Could he?

No, it was far too risky. Henri might walk out the door at any moment and announce that he was ready to go, or he and the woman might retire for an hour's rendezvous in the bedroom. Either scenario and young Robbie would be in a pickle.

Besides, even though Lilly was always spouting Allan Pinkerton's motto about the ends justifying the means, he could imagine the tongue-lashing she'd give him for putting the boy in harm's way. He'd almost forgotten how hard it was to stay on the right side of that woman.

He released a deep breath. "Right. No stealing. Was there anything else?"

"Some men's clothes hanging on some nails on the wall. Just a couple of extra outfits."

"Were they the doctor's size?"

Robbie folded his skinny arms over his chest and cocked his head to the side in disbelief. "I don't know, McShane. I didn't ask him to try them on."

"That's it, then?"

"Not quite."

"What do you mean?"

"There was some pretty paper in the drawer and a pencil and I copied what was on the outside of the envelope the best I could."

For a second Cade wondered if he'd heard right. "You what?"

Grinning, Robbie pulled a small piece of paper from his shirt pocket and handed it to Cade, who gathered the child into a tight hug and spun him around, Robbie complaining every second.

"Good work, lad." Setting the boy to the ground, he unfolded the paper and tried to decipher the poorly formed letters. After much scrutiny, he said, "Delia Breaux."

"The same thing was written on the outside of all the envelopes. I guess that's her name, but who is she?"

"Good question." Who was Delia Breaux? Just another woman the good doctor was sleeping with? Where was her husband and the father of the child? Was it possible he was out in the cane fields working while she dallied with a rich man . . . or a man who would someday be rich . . . if something happened to the Fontenot women?

Cade reached out and cuffed the boy's shoulder. "You did right well. I don't know who this woman is, but when we learn more about the doctor, all the pieces of the puzzle will start to come together and make sense. We'll have to see what Lilly makes of it."

The minute he said the words, Cade grew irritated with himself. Just because he was forced to work with her on the case and share their clues didn't mean he needed her to piece them together. He'd done just fine working alone all these years, and he didn't plan on getting close to another woman, not even in a working capacity. When you allowed yourself to care about someone in any meaningful way and something happened to that person, it was bad. Really bad. He half regretted the closeness he felt to Robbie Jenkins.

"So," Robbie said, cutting short Cade's train of thought, "if there's nothing to eat, what do we do while we wait?"

Cade pulled a worn deck of playing cards from his pocket. The nuns who'd done their best to shape him into an upright person would have a fit if they knew he was corrupting the boy by teaching him to watch for dirty tricks while playing cards, but Cade figured the boy could learn far worse things.

"What say we sit in the buggy and play a few hands while we're waiting?"

"Sure. Bet I can beat you without cheating."

"If you cheat, I'll see it."

"You didn't notice that swell dealing from the bottom the other night."

The swell. Timothy Warner. Lilly's husband. But not for long. So she said. He'd told her that he'd go back to the tavern and see if he was there, or had been around since their set-to. He'd take care of that tonight.

Cade and Robbie played several hands of poker while waiting for the doctor, and shortly before Ducharme came out of the cabin, Robbie started complaining that his stomach wasn't feeling so good. Hoping he wasn't taking what Mrs. Fontenot had, Cade told him he was probably just hungry and had him lie down in the seat until time to go. Finally, there was a commotion at the front door of the house.

The woman exited with Henri. The sight of him carrying

the baby took Cade aback. The couple embraced, the baby between them, and Henri gave the woman a lingering kiss. Cade
wasn't surprised to see him flaunt the affair in front of him and
Robbie.

It was a well-known fact that servants knew everything
that goes on in a household.

CHAPTER 15

After tea with her great-granddaughter, Mrs. Fontenot asked Lilly to accompany her to her room so that she could rest a couple of hours before supper. Lilly was about to leave when the old woman said, "Stay and visit a minute, Brona."

Lilly's initial response was panic. The last thing she wanted—or needed—was to be questioned by her employer and run the risk of saying something that would lead her to realize that she and Cade were not who they pretended to be. Forcing calm she didn't feel into her body and her voice, she turned and met her boss's gaze. "Is something wrong, Madam?"

LaRee Fontenot's smile pushed the wrinkled apples of her cheeks upward. "Not at all. On the contrary, all is quite well. I believe I feel a bit better breathing the country air, and I actually think I might be able to eat a bite at suppertime."

"I'm glad, ma'am," Lilly said, "but what I meant is, is everything all right with my work?"

"Stop worrying, child," the older woman chided. "From everything I've seen and heard, you and your husband are doing an excellent job."

"Thank you, ma'am."

The diminutive woman gestured toward the chair sitting by the bed. "Indulge an old woman and sit for a moment. One of the things I hate about growing old is that family and friends leave one by one. It gets lonely."

Lilly saw the sorrow reflected in the old woman's eyes. "I can only imagine how hard it has been to lose Miss Suzannah and Miss Patricia, and in a sense, even Miss Cassandra," Lilly said, taking the seat and folding her hands in her lap.

"It's been . . . terrible. Young people like Suzannah are not supposed to go before us old ones, and"—her voice broke—"she should never, ever have to suffer the atrocities she did before she died."

Though Lilly knew exactly what had happened to Suzannah, she looked inquiringly at Mrs. Fontenot, who gave a shake of her head. "Forgive me. I shouldn't have brought it up. It's my sorrow to bear, not yours. Cassandra is a wonderful, caring woman and I love her very much, but I do miss Suzannah. She was so full of life! Always smiling, laughing, and into things. To be truthful, your Robbie reminds me of her in many ways." She smiled. "I'm actually glad he came with you and Bran. I'm enjoying watching him flitting about."

Lilly attempted a smile. If only she knew. Lilly was almost one hundred percent certain the boy had taken the missing snuffbox. "It's been good for us as well, and I hope he isn't doing anything he shouldn't be."

"Not to my knowledge. Both he and Bernard are very inquisitive and eager to learn."

Lilly had noticed that when he was with Cade. "He can be quite taxing from time to time."

Mrs. Fontenot laughed. "Oh, that's quite obvious. He is, as my mother used to say about me, and we said about Suzi, 'full of himself.' "

"That he is, ma'am."

"Do you know what I saw him doing the other day?"

Lilly felt her heart take a sickening dip. "I confess I am almost afraid to ask."

"He was trying to make friends with Lucifer."

"I know," she said with a sigh of relief. "Bran and I have cautioned him about the cat, so if he gets scratched or bitten, he's been warned."

Lilly had seen him trying to tempt the cat to take a scrap from his hand. Cade had told him that if he didn't stop he was apt to come up missing a finger, but Robbie only smiled and said the wicked feline no longer hissed and swiped at him, and had even taken a bite from his palm a time or two, so he was making progress.

"It's the strangest thing," Mrs. Fontenot said. "I've seen them stare at each other for moments on end, almost as if they're trying to take each other's measure. When I mentioned as much to Robbie, he just smiled that impish grin of his and told me they understand each other perfectly, and that they are two of a kind, which I thought was a strange thing to say. I hadn't a notion of what he meant."

"With Robbie it's hard to say. How did you get Lucifer?" she asked, trying to find a neutral topic for the conversation.

"He was just a young thing, probably just a few months old, when Amos found him in the ,carriage house. He'd been in a fight, and was hurt badly. Bite marks and scratches all over, and that one ear almost gone and his eye put out. When he wouldn't allow Amos to touch him, Amos came and got me, since I've always been a cat lover.

"With patience and a little food, I was able to win him over in a few days. For obvious reasons, I decided to call him Lucifer. To this day he won't tolerate anyone but me touching him." She gave a rusty laugh. "I have a feeling young Robbie is about to change all that."

"If you'd rather him not bother the cat, I'll tell him," Lilly said. After hearing of Lucifer's background, she thought she knew exactly what Robbie meant by the two of them understanding one another. They'd both been abandoned and left to survive by any means available. And, fortunately for them both, they'd each found a rescuer.

"Oh, heavens! I don't mind at all. I'm no spring chicken, and as I've learned the past year or so, something could happen to me at any time. I rather like knowing that if it did, Lucifer would have a friend."

Lilly smiled. "All right, then. As long as he isn't causing any trouble."

"None at all." Mrs. Fontenot sighed and smiled. "Well, my eyes are getting heavy and I've kept you long enough. Thank you for indulging an old woman in a moment's loneliness."

"Anytime, ma'am." Lilly stood and went to the door, where she turned. "Have a good rest. I'll be up in time to get you ready for dinner."

"Thank you."

Back in the kitchen, Lilly found both Vena and Neecie in a state of agitation. "Is something wrong?"

"We just talked to Mr. Easterling and he told us that since Miz Fontenot is visiting he'll be staying at home to help entertain her," Vena said.

She glanced at Neecie, who stood chewing on her thumbnail, her striking face a study in misery. "We thought he'd go back to the city in the morning."

"I don't understand." Pretending ignorance, Lilly hoped the statement would lead to more information. "Is there a problem? I'll be here to help with any extra work. I came to see to Madam's needs."

"It isn't the work." Vena threw her hands into the air in a gesture of helplessness. "I'm sorry, Brona. We shouldn't have mentioned it, but when he's around everyone is more . . . frazzled, I guess you could say."

With that, Neecie stormed out of the kitchen.

"Is she all right?"

"As well as can be expected under the circumstances, I s'pose. Will you wash some of those new potatoes? Mr. Easterling likes them with the skin on them in a cream sauce with his ham."

CHAPTER 16

Mrs. Fontenot seemed to feel much better in the country—the nausea and dizzy spells had departed—and Lilly was glad for that, but time felt like it dragged.

She'd been accustomed to a rigorous schedule of practice and performing when she was onstage, and even on her first assignment, she'd been busy from daylight till dark. Under Vena's deft hand, she and Neecie kept the household running smoothly, and there was little for Lilly to do. Inactivity did not suit her.

In an effort to break the monotony, Preston, who himself complained of boredom, had planned a small dinner party on Monday evening in honor of Mrs. Fontenot and invited three couples who'd known her when she and her husband made the plantation their home. That had been the night before last.

To pass the time when she finished her chores, she'd been spending several hours a day thumbing through the magazines in the library, with Mrs. Fontenot's approval, of course.

When she'd asked the matriarch's permission, the old woman pinned her with a curious expression. "Certainly, Brona. I always like to see someone who wants to gain more knowledge. Do you have any favorites?"

"Actually, ma'am, my taste is varied. I am quite a fan of dime novels, but I adore Shakespeare."

Mrs. Fontenot smiled. "That is quite a difference. If you're like the other young women I know, I imagine you like the ladies' magazines, too."

"Actually, I prefer *Harper's Monthly* and *Puck*."

As soon as she'd answered the innocent question, Lilly felt her heart lurch in dismay. Once again, she'd acted without thinking. She should have lied about her answers instead of speaking the truth. No doubt Mrs. Fontenot would find it strange that a mere servant girl liked Shakespeare and preferred magazines that featured essays, biographies, and social topics rather than clothing, home, and family.

Thank goodness her employer made no comment about her reading preferences.

"Well, feel free to enjoy what we have to offer while you're here."

"Thank you, ma'am."

Thursday dawned bright and hot and humid. Another day to get through. With her chores all completed, Lilly was headed to the library once more. Thankfully her employer had announced at breakfast that they would be heading back to the city Sunday morning, saying that she knew Brona must be anxious to get back to her little family.

Though it was hard to believe she'd said it, much less meant it, Lilly admitted that she did miss them.

She was dusting the library when she saw a collection of Lord Byron's poems. Laying aside the duster, she began to thumb through the book. She was thinking that she should get back to her work, when she caught a movement through the partially open window that looked out over the rose garden.

Preston had hold of Neecie's upper arm and was propelling her along beside him. That Neecie was resisting was obvious from the expression on her face and the way her body was angled away from him.

Pressing against the back of the sofa, as if she could hide from any eyes that happened to look into the room, Lilly prayed that neither would turn and see her. As she watched, Preston, who was facing the window, jerked the girl close and tried to kiss her. Neecie's head whipped back and forth as she tried to evade him, and it was obvious that she was trying to push against his shoulders, but she was no match for the man, who was so intent on getting what he wanted.

Once again, an innocent woman was being taken advantage of by a ruthless, selfish man. A married man whose wife was expecting a child.

Fury flared in Lilly's heart and began a slow burn as an image of Timothy kissing Colleen McKenna came to mind. She wondered for perhaps the hundredth time if Cade had been able to find Tim, and if so, what had happened.

"Neeeecie!"

The sound of Vena's voice drifted through the window, jolting Lilly from her troubled thoughts. The couple surrounded by budding rosebushes froze. Reluctantly, it seemed, Preston lifted his head. When he did, he looked straight into the library, his narrowed gaze unerringly finding Lilly, who sat wide-eyed and immovable. Then Preston released his hold on the young woman's arms and took a step backward.

Neecie lost no time in darting around him and heading for the security of the kitchen, scrubbing her fingertips over her lips as she went. After smoothing his dark hair with his palms and straightening his cravat, Preston once again sought Lilly's gaze. He smiled at her, a smug, confident sort of smile that told her that he knew he need not fear her telling anyone what she'd seen. And then he followed the servant.

Lilly wasn't completely innocent. She'd heard how, in the past, plantation owners had often taken advantage of their slaves, but Neecie was not a slave. She was free, working for a wage, just as Lilly was. She was also married and expecting a baby.

In and of itself, adultery was appalling, but using social status and masculine strength to compel an unwilling victim, an unwilling *pregnant* victim, was nothing short of detestable. And any way you looked at it, it was rape.

Suzannah had been violated before she was murdered.

The sudden realization that the unspeakable act could happen to anyone sent Lilly surging to her feet. Her book fell to the floor. With her heart racing, she picked up the slim volume and replaced it on the shelf. She needed to make herself scarce, just in case he took it upon himself to come and confront her about what she'd seen.

Her mind filled with images of what she'd witnessed, Lilly hurried down the hall toward the kitchen stairs. She rounded the corner and literally bumped into someone coming up.

Hands grasped her shoulders to keep her from falling. "Careful there."

She looked up to see Preston Easterling standing in front of her. *What on earth was he doing coming up the servants' stairs?* "I'm so sorry, Mr. Easterling," she told him. "I was in too much of a hurry to watch where I was going."

The hands grasping her upper arms gentled and he actually had the audacity to run his palms up and down her arms.

"That's quite all right." He smiled his too-perfect smile. "You're a pretty thing, Brona."

"Please, don't do that." Her stomach churned with nausea at his blatant lack of respect and memories of what she'd so recently witnessed. Suppressing a shudder, she shrugged free.

"I'm your employer."

"My employer is Mrs. Fontenot," she corrected. "Not you."

In response, he gripped her chin so hard she flinched, forcing her to meet his cold gaze.

"A mere technicality. I can still make life difficult for you. Don't forget that I saw you in the library earlier, shirking your duties."

Lilly knew it would do no good to tell him she had Mrs. Fontenot's permission to use the room when she could. She refused to drop her gaze or show him any kind of alarm at his threat. Instead, she countered, "I saw you, too."

The statement lay there between them. Acknowledgment that she knew exactly what he was up to with Neecie. Stalemate.

He released her chin, and she had to force herself not to rub at her throbbing skin. She hoped she wouldn't bruise.

"As I said, I can make things difficult for you." Without another word, he stepped past her and sauntered down the hall as if he hadn't a care in the world.

The longer she worked as a Pinkerton the more she realized what a monumental task finding justice was. Pierce and Robert Pinkerton were right: She was an innocent when it came to the ruthless ways of the world, yet she was learning quickly. One betrayal after another eroded her naïveté and opened her innocent eyes.

She felt a rush of tears as a sudden longing for Pierce and Rose swamped her. Her life in the troupe had been one of consistency, of knowing what to expect each day from the people around her and from her own efforts. Now she was floundering in a sea of ignorance and uncertainty, trying to decide what to do next, making decisions she had no business making . . . trying to repair the damage done to the lives of others when she was still dealing with her own wounds.

Stop feeling sorry for yourself, Lilly Long. You've never been a crybaby. Where is your spunk? Your backbone? That hardheadedness Pierce is always fussing about?

She swiped angrily at her eyes. William Pinkerton had assigned her to this case because he'd known it was one she would identify with and pursue with her best efforts. He trusted her and Cade to solve it. Mrs. Fontenot was expecting someone to find out the truth of Patricia's mental state and whether or not Henri was scheming to do away with his new wife to gain the family fortune. She deserved an honest assessment, whatever it might be.

Whether or not Henri was dallying with Mrs. Abelard was of no consequence to the case, unless, of course, the liaison could be part of his scheme in some way. Could the housekeeper be privy to information that might be gained by some means of cunning on Lilly's or Cade's part? It was an avenue they'd overlooked.

At the moment, she had no way of knowing if Henri was up to something wicked or not. She did know that both he and Preston were despicable and immoral, though Preston's character—or lack thereof—had nothing to do with the assignment. Nevertheless, it was enough incentive to stir up Lilly's moral outrage. Ill-equipped for the job or not, she was not a quitter. People were counting on her, and as she'd done in Vandalia, she vowed she would not let them down.

Cade pulled off his boots at the bottom of the stairs and tiptoed up the steps. He was dog-tired and looking forward to sleeping in the bed he'd taken over during Lilly's absence.

"Did ya find out anything?"

Robbie's low question came out of the darkness. Cade strained to see where the voice was coming from and spied the dark outline of the boy leaning against the door to the room he shared with Lilly.

"What're you doing up at this ungodly hour? You've been throwing up your toenails. You should be in bed."

"I started feeling a wee bit better after drinking that foul stuff Lamartine gave me. I wanted to make sure you got in okay."

"I'm a grown man, Robbie."

"Don't mean something can't happen to you."

Cade was torn between the urge to laugh and a rush of tenderness. Was the boy so concerned about his welfare that he'd left his sick bed to wait up for him? Or was he sitting here to see for himself whether or not Cade had fallen off the wagon while hoping for a glimpse of Tim Warner. Either way, it was a sad testimony to their past and their current relationship.

"I haven't been drinking, Robbie. Now go to bed."

"Not until you tell me if you found ol' Tim. Why are you lookin' fer him anyways?"

"He's Lilly's husband."

Robbie's eyes grew wide with disbelief. "Yer joshin' me."

"No, he knocked her upside the head and stole all her money."

"Surely she don't think he'll give it back."

"No, but she'd like to see him in jail."

"Can't say's I blame her."

"Well, it won't be happening anytime soon. I checked the tavern where the card game took place, and no one's seen hide nor hair of him since the night I knocked him out and he was tossed into the street."

Lilly dreamed strange dreams on Thursday night, dreams of being chased through the streets of Chicago, while someone in the shadows cried and moaned as if their heart was breaking. When she woke, she felt the wetness of tears on her cheeks and wondered if they were tears of fear for the threat she'd felt during her dream, or sorrow for the anguish in the sobbing sounds she'd heard in the darkness.

The first thing she did after checking on Mrs. Fontenot and finding that she was still asleep, was go to the kitchen where Vena and Neecie were in the middle of preparing breakfast. The two women said little beyond "Good morning."

"Is everything all right?" Lilly asked after a while.

"'Bout like always," Vena said without glancing up from the ham she was slicing. Neecie's gaze was fixed on the biscuits she was mixing. "If you don't mind, I'd like for you to serve breakfast this morning. Neecie's feeling poorly."

"Of course. I don't mind at all." Lilly didn't know what was going on, but something was.

An hour later, she helped Mrs. Fontenot get dressed and down the stairs. Preston was already ensconced at the head of the gleaming cherrywood table. Cassandra, looking pale and red-eyed, sat at his right. If Lilly had to guess, she'd wager that the mistress of the house had spent a considerable portion of the night crying. Hmm. With her mind spinning with all sorts of possibilities, she settled Mrs. Fontenot across from her great-granddaughter.

"Are you well, Cassandra?" Mrs. Fontenot asked with a concerned frown.

Cassandra pasted a smile on her delicate features. "I'm fine, *Grand-mère*. I just didn't sleep well last night."

LaRee Fontenot offered an indulgent smile. "With a *petite bébé* on the way, your nights of good sleep will soon be few."

"So they say." Cassandra placed a crisp white napkin in her lap and Lilly began serving the morning meal.

"Where's Neecie?" Preston's displeasure showed in his tone and his scowl. Lilly found his manner interesting considering the scene she'd witnessed the day before.

"She's feeling a bit under the weather this morning, sir," Lilly told him, casting a surreptitious glance at Cassandra. The young woman's face had lost its color.

"Well, it's early days in her confinement. No doubt she'll soon feel better." Mrs. Fontenot offered the comment with the certainty of one who'd experienced the same complaints.

"No doubt," Preston mumbled.

The conversation turned to Mrs. Fontenot's departure the following day and the meal continued without further incident beyond Cassandra expressing her dismay at losing her grandmother's company.

Lilly performed her duties by rote, thinking of the earlier conversation. Was it possible that the crying she'd thought was part of her dream had been Cassandra weeping? If so, why?

That's easy enough to guess, Lilly.

Considering the situation, it did not take a genius to figure out that something had transpired between Preston and Neecie. Something that Cassandra was aware of. It did not take a mastermind to figure out what that might be either.

It was all Lilly could do to keep her features schooled to blankness when she wanted nothing more than to slap the smug, superior expression from Preston's face and tell him what she thought of his dreadful treatment of his wife . . . and his servant.

Did the heartbroken Cassandra ask herself what she was lacking, as Lilly had after learning of Tim's infidelity? Did she wonder why she wasn't enough? As innocently as the Fontenot girls had likely been reared, she doubted if Cassandra had any inkling of a fact Pierce had imparted to Lilly: Some people were never satisfied with one lover; they needed variety in their lives.

And what of Rollo? Did he know what was going on? How could he not? Of course he knew, but he also knew better than to make any show of retaliation. Did he cry? Doubtful. Recalling his brawny build and the intensity that radiated from him, Lilly could envision him lying in bed, his fists clenched, imagining heinous punishment on his employer . . . perhaps even plotting various means of securing his death, just as Lilly had done with Tim.

"*Oh, the tangled web we weave . . .*"

Lilly forced herself back to the present and her duties.

"I've been feeling so much better since I've been here," Mrs. Fontenot was saying. "I believe the country air has cleared my head and my thoughts. The house on Rampart Street is so filled with memories that it's hard to break free of them. Here . . . well, everything seems clearer."

"What do you mean, *Grand-mère?*" Cassandra asked.

"I mean that no matter what Henri says about how my going to see your mother would upset her, I intend to do just that as soon as I rest up from the trip. I fail to understand how a visit from someone who loves her can make her worse, and I don't want her feeling as if we've abandoned her, which I'm sure she does. Even young Robbie agrees. He said he thought she would like to see familiar faces."

Preston rubbed his lower lip with his thumb and regarded her with a thoughtful expression. "And how do you think Henri will feel about that?"

"Frankly, Preston, I don't give a fig what he thinks."

CHAPTER 17

That evening, the supper dishes were done and darkness had yet to settle when Lilly decided to brave the ferocity of the mosquitoes and take a walk through the gardens, which Rollo kept in exquisite condition. She was just going around the corner of the house when she saw the flash of something disappearing into the trees. She was reminded of how she'd been so frightened of the woodland creatures during her first assignment. She'd grown marginally wiser since then and figured that what she'd seen was nothing more than a fox or a deer.

With her hands clasped behind her back, she strolled to the edge of the lake, wondering what it would have been like having the river running so near the house and if it had ever escaped its banks and flooded everything.

She was about to turn around and go back to her room when she imagined she heard the faintest, rhythmic beating of a drum. Ridiculous! There was no reason for drums to be in the middle of the forest.

Nonetheless, she stood quietly, her head cocked to the side, listening. . . . There it was again! This time she thought she heard some sort of singing. Were Vena and the other workers having some sort of get-together?

Goaded by curiosity, Lilly headed into the forest, following a narrow but distinct footpath through the clinging vines and over the fallen trees blocking the trail. The stagnant air grew even denser as she went deeper into the undergrowth. Breathing became a chore.

The farther she went, the murkier it grew. The thickening shadows and the humid air made her increasingly aware of the dangers hiding in the gloom, an unwelcome reminder of the fear she'd experienced as she'd walked the hazardous streets of Chicago a few weeks ago.

The sinister silence was broken only by the unfamiliar sounds of the woodland. Rustling. The cracking of twigs and branches as unknown creatures slithered and slunk through the fetid leaves and rotting vegetation. The rat-a-tat of a hungry woodpecker searching for his supper far-off in the distance. And underlying it all, like the restless beating of a primordial heart, the hypnotic, increasingly quickening tempo of the drums. Spellbound, Lilly followed the sound until she saw a clearing beyond the trees. She stopped and peered around a huge oak, afraid of being discovered, yet compelled to stay and watch.

Several people were gathered in the open space near a table laden with food. Lilly recognized some of the field hands who'd come to the kitchen for one thing or another. At first glance she thought they'd gathered for some sort of feast, but an inborn sense told her that they had not come into the forest to break bread.

At another, smaller table, a few flowers from the garden were stuck haphazardly into a tin can next to a glass of water, a white candle, and a picture of someone. A small doll lay next to the picture.

The drum grew quiet.

A tall, thin woman dressed all in white stepped through a

break in the trees on the opposite side of the clearing, carrying a small coop with a couple of young chickens. Lilly recognized her as the woman Vena called Dahlia. She placed the pullets next to a stump where the head of a bloody hatchet was buried. Then she straightened, lit the candle, and stood with her chin lifted to a regal angle, waiting. . . .

At that Lilly realized what she'd stumbled onto.

Voodoo!

What she knew about the pagan practice could be put into a thimble with plenty of room left over, but she did know that despite it being forbidden, the slaves who'd claimed conversion to Christianity had often continued in the old ways, blending the two beliefs and substituting the names of saints for that of their loas, the spirits who served as protectors, helpers, and guides.

She should leave.

They would not take kindly to an outsider encroaching on their private ceremony. Before she could do more than push away from the rough bark of the tree, the music began again, and a couple appeared from the trees.

Rollo and Neecie. Completely naked. Lilly's eyes widened with surprise; then she squeezed them shut, thinking she must be mistaken. But when she opened them again, nothing had changed.

Dahlia raised her arms above her head and began to speak, words that sounded like a prayer, asking Papa Legba for permission for Neecie to communicate with Damballa Wedo, her personal loa. After a while, Neecie took up the doll on the table and began to speak to it. Her words sounded harsh, accusatory. Angry.

Lilly watched the unfolding ceremony, transfixed. Fascinated. Revolted. There was singing. Dancing. Praying. Dahlia took the chickens one at a time and chopped off their heads. Lilly covered her mouth to keep from crying out. When the birds began to flop around on the ground, she swallowed back her nausea. After a while, Neecie seemed to go into a trance, swaying to the ancient rhythm. Rollo moved with her, their bodies moving in perfect, erotic synchronization.

Enough!

This was no place for her, Lilly thought. These were not things she should be witnessing. The whole thing was too disturbing . . . in many ways.

She whirled around, intent on heading back to the house, but when she did, she once again ran headlong into a warm, chambray-covered wall. Her heart leaped in fear and her gaze flew upward.

Cade. Eyes wide with surprise, she opened her mouth to ask him what he was doing there. Shaking his head, he placed a rough finger over her lips to silence her. She felt the heat of his body through his shirt and his thighs pressing against hers. With the images of Neecie and Rollo seared into her mind, reminding her of her nights in Timothy's arms, and the sensual rhythm of the music pulsing through her body, the touch— though innocent and impersonal—was nonetheless disturbing.

Her breathing quickened as he stared into her eyes. Then his gaze drifted beyond her to the swaying couple. When he looked at her again, his blue eyes had darkened with an emotion she recognized all too well, one she had seen many nights on the face of her husband. She held her breath.

He stared at her for long seconds; then he smiled, a smile tinged with the barest hint of regret. Stepping away from her, he took her hand and pulled her behind him, back toward the house.

"What are you doing here?" she asked when they stepped into the clearing near the house. "Where's Amos?"

"Feeling poorly," Cade told her. "He sent me to bring you back. Bernard came along to show me the way."

"What about Robbie?"

Cade shook his head. "Robbie's been sick. He's fine now," he assured her, seeing the look on her face. "It was a rough couple of days, though. It looks like the same thing Mrs. Fontenot had. He said he'd rather stay there and check out a few things."

Then, as any husband who'd missed his wife might do, he slid his arm around Lilly's shoulders and drew her close, pressing a kiss to her forehead. When she stood stiffly before him, he whispered, "You really ought to act as if you're glad to see me, colleen, just in case anyone is watching."

Her eyes narrowed at the hated name, but she stepped closer and reached up to touch his cheek with her fingertips. His arms went around her. She stroked the thick mustache draping his upper lip and gave it a sharp tug. "Don't call me that," she warned in a low growl as she smiled up at him.

"I forgot." And then he drew her closer still and touched her lips with his.

The kiss was brief, light. Nothing but a peck. The merest brush of his mouth to hers. A simple kiss of welcome that any man might give his wife after not seeing her for a week. So why did it feel as if the earth was falling away beneath her?

She felt his hands tighten on her waist and then he was pushing her away. Lilly let her hand fall to her side and looked up with a bemused expression. His face gave nothing away. Without another word, he turned and started across the lawn.

As she struggled to keep up with him, Cade was busy calling himself ten kinds of fool. It was easy to convince himself that their happy husband and wife scene was a necessary part of their charade, but the truth was that when he'd come upon her in the woods and seen the latent desire in her eyes, he'd wanted very badly to kiss her. In fact, he'd wanted to kiss her for a while now. Wanted to see if those lips of hers that were so good at blunt comments, tart replies, and saucy comebacks held any sweetness at all.

He'd found they did.

Unfortunately.

He was not looking for a wife, real or pretend. Was not even looking for a woman with whom to have a casual fling, but this woman had managed to burrow her way into his life in a dozen different, unexpected ways. Her kindness to Robbie. Her willingness to take on whatever the case demanded. Her intelligence.

Blast it all!

The best thing he could do was solve this case as soon as possible and move on to the next one, where hopefully, they would not be in such close proximity to one another.

"What do you think that was back there in the woods?"

It took him a few seconds to gather his thoughts. "A voodoo ritual of some sort would be my guess."

"That's what I thought. Do you know anything about voodoo?"

"Not much."

"I'm almost a hundred percent certain that Preston is sleeping with Neecie and that Cassandra knows."

Cade stopped abruptly. "Neecie and Preston? That seems strange. She seems so crazy about Rollo."

"I believe she is, but it isn't her choice." She proceeded to tell him about the things she'd seen and heard since she'd been at River Run.

Cade shook his head. "There appears to be a lot of that going around."

"What?"

"Infidelity." He told her about the day trip he and Robbie had made with Henri to the cottage and the homey setup they'd found. Her eyes widened when he mentioned the name Robbie had discovered on the envelope.

"Who do you think she is?"

"I have no idea, but I thought it would be a good thing to check into."

"I agree. Cade, do you think that baby boy you saw is Henri's?"

"I'd say it's either a grandchild or his and the woman's."

"If it's the latter, it certainly gives him a reason to get rid of Patricia, doesn't it?"

"It does."

He started to walk away and Lilly reached out and placed a hand on his arm. "There's something else."

He turned. "What?"

"I think the odds are pretty good that Neecie's baby could just as easily be Preston's as Rollo's, and she really doesn't want to know."

Lilly rose early, but Cade was already dressed and gone, no doubt getting the rig ready to leave as soon as breakfast was over. It had felt good to have him in the room with her again. There was something comforting about hearing his soft snoring.

She went to help prepare breakfast. When she saw that Neecie was already there, peeling potatoes, memories from the night before came flooding back. What had happened when she'd left the clearing?

"*Vena! Neecie! Get yourselves into the dining room right this minute! And send someone to fetch Rollo and that wretched boy of Lamartine's!*" The words were accompanied by feet pounding down the stairs.

Preston.

A very angry Preston.

Vena dropped the butcher knife she was using to slice the slab of bacon. There seemed to be a question in her gaze as she looked at her daughter, but nothing showed on Neecie's face. No surprise. No fear. No guilt. Nothing but calm. It almost seemed as if she'd been expecting something like this to happen and had prepared herself mentally for it.

Finding no satisfaction in her daughter's attitude, Vena set the hot skillet to the back of the stove and calmly wiped her hands on her apron.

"Should I come?"

"No, Brona. This has nothing to do with you. You just see to it that Madam Fontenot is all packed and ready to leave when the time comes."

"Should I finish breakfast?"

"No," Vena said. "Run and get Rollo and Bernard. This is gonna be an ugly mess."

Lilly raced through the back door and down to the stables, where she knew she would find all the men, calling for Rollo as she went.

"Whoa there, lass!" Cade said, stepping out of one of the stalls as she ran into the dim barn.

"Brona? What is it?" Rollo asked as he came around the corner with a bag of grain balanced on his shoulder.

"Mr. Easterling is on a rampage about something," she said, breathing hard. "He called for Neecie and Vena to go to the dining room and wanted you and Bernard, too. Vena told me to come get you."

"What do you think it's all about?" Cade asked his friend.

Rollo set the bag onto the ground. "It's hard to say. Bernard! Come on, boy. We need to go see what's got Mr. Preston so upset."

"What's he want me for?" the young man asked, leaning his pitchfork against the wall. "I didn't do anything."

"I guess we'll find out."

The quartet hurried to the house. Lilly and Cade stayed in the kitchen and watched as Rollo and Bernard pushed through the door to the dining room. Lilly opened the swinging door the barest crack in an attempt to see what was going on.

Vena and Neecie stood as still and erect as statues in a garden, their hands folded together in front of them. Bernard looked scared to death. Rollo went straight to his wife's side and offered her a slight smile of encouragement.

Preston, partially dressed for the day, stood inside the pocket doors that divided the dining room from the winding staircase that swept upward from the polished floor of the foyer.

His face was mottled with fury, and his dark eyes were narrowed and filled with accusation. His finely chiseled mouth was pressed into a straight line of wrath. He'd donned his black trousers, but had thrown a silk paisley robe over them. It hung open, revealing the fact that he hadn't yet put on his shirt.

"I found this in my shirt drawer." He stretched out his arm and Lilly saw that he held something in his hand that looked like a doll clad in black. It reminded her of the doll she'd seen at the ceremony.

"I don't suppose any of you have any idea how it came to be there."

The four people standing in front of their employer looked from him to one another in confusion.

Lilly turned to look up at Cade. "Voodoo doll," he whispered in her ear.

Voodoo doll? She'd heard of them of course. As he'd schooled her, she and Pierce had spent considerable time talking over various newsworthy topics and things of interest she wanted to learn more about. He'd explained how the dolls were supposed to work, but she had never believed any of the far-fetched tales about something dire happening to the person the doll represented, yet many swore the dolls could drive a victim mad or send them to their deaths.

The ceremony she'd witnessed the night before began to make sense. Clearly, it had been for the sole purpose of bringing calamity to Preston. Most likely for the things he'd done and continued to do to Neecie.

The law could do nothing about his actions. Wouldn't. He was an attorney whose wife was from one of the most respected families in New Orleans. Rich. A woman of color, Neecie had little recourse but to seek justice and revenge in the only way available to her.

"Vena?" Preston snapped. "Did you put this abomination in my room?"

"No, sir, Mr. Easterling. I don't have no truck with voodoo. I'm a Baptist, just like my sister."

His mouth twisted into an ugly smile. "Neecie?"

Lilly thought she saw the Negro woman's fingers tighten on each other, but her voice was steady. "No, sir. It wasn't me."

Preston reached out and took her chin in a hard grasp, forcing her to meet his gaze and reminding Lilly of their confrontation the day before. It seemed as if the place his fingers had gripped her chin throbbed in sympathy.

His chuckle lacked any warmth or humor. "I wonder why I don't believe you?" Rollo's hands curled into fists. Preston released Neecie so abruptly that she staggered against her husband, who slipped a steadying arm around her waist.

"I suppose you know nothing about it either, Rollo."

"No, sir, Mr. Easterling, sir, I don't, and Bernard would have no reason to do such a thing."

Lilly would have given anything to see Rollo's face. How he could remain so calm considering the situation was beyond her comprehension.

"What's going on, Preston?"

The question came from Cassandra, who entered the room arm in arm with her grandmother. Cassandra, who was dressed in the palest of greens, looked very much the lady of the manor. Mrs. Fontenot wore her usual black. She had a thoughtful expression on her face.

"I found this in my shirt drawer," Preston said, holding the doll out for her inspection.

It was then that Lilly saw the pin stuck into the doll's forehead.

"It didn't get there on its own, and I want the person responsible to pay."

To Lilly's surprise, Cassandra began to laugh. The sound seemed to infuriate her husband even more. "Oh, Preston!" she said when her giggles subsided. "I thought you were more sophisticated than to believe in those silly folktales."

If possible, Easterling's face grew even redder. "I've heard they can drive a person mad if that's the intent."

Cassandra helped her grandmother into her chair and circled the table to place a hand on her husband's arm. "My dear," she said gently, "if you go into any voodoo shop in town, you'll find that they can be used for good as well as evil. You've been having those terrible headaches lately, so perhaps you should look at it in a different light."

Recalling the anger she'd seen Neecie directing at the effigy the evening before, Lilly had serious doubts that the doll was intended for benign purposes. Still, she admired Cassandra's skill in diverting a volatile situation into one of humor.

Cassandra lifted her narrow shoulders in a careless shrug. "And for your information, the practice of voodoo did not come from Africa as everyone has been led to believe, but Britain."

Lilly was as impressed by her command of the situation as she was her knowledge. After seeing her cowed and despondent, Lilly would never have imagined the young Mrs. Easterling would be so composed.

Preston looked positively flummoxed. "And just how do you know all that?"

She gave his arm a maternal pat and sashayed toward her place at the table. "I read, husband. There is little enough to do here, so I read."

"Well, no matter where the blasted thing originated, I doubt it was meant for good, and since none of these people will own up to putting it in my room, I'm firing them all. As of this minute."

"No, you are not."

The statement came from Mrs. Fontenot, who was calmly placing her napkin in her lap.

"You have no say in this, *Grand-mère,*" he told her.

She finished smoothing the linen square and rested her elbows on the table and her chin on the backs of her laced fingers. A magnificent amethyst glistened in the morning sunlight.

"But of course I do, Preston," she informed him with supreme authority. "Until I die, this is my house, and these are my employees. The family has served me well for many years, and they will remain in my employ until Cassandra takes over ownership of the plantation upon my death. At that time she can do as she wishes. You are only living here by my good graces."

Preston's lips tightened. He was not accustomed to being spoken to like a naughty child, and he certainly did not like being put in his place in front of the servants he had only moments before been shouting at.

Mrs. Fontenot gave a flick of her fingers, the small gesture dismissing the whole unsavory incident. "Now run along and finish dressing," she told him. "I'm quite hungry. Vena, will you ask Brona to bring in the juice please?"

"Yes, ma'am."

"Thank you. You're all free to go."

Lilly marveled at the way the Fontenot matriarch had taken control of a situation. For the first time since arriving in New Orleans, she'd seen the strong woman who'd been described in the letter William Pinkerton had read to her and Cade.

Now, they stepped away from the door as the servants filed back into the kitchen. Wide smiles blossomed on their faces. Vena and Lilly clasped forearms and danced a silent jig around the kitchen, while Cade shook hands with Rollo and Bernard.

Then, donning her Brona persona, Lilly picked up a small pitcher of orange juice. Smiling at her coworkers, she pushed through the swinging door. Another two hours and she would be away from this hateful place and could start working on the investigation again.

CHAPTER 18

During the drive back to the city, Mrs. Fontenot allowed Lilly to sit with "her husband" on the outside seat, where they whiled away the four-hour trip telling each other everything that they'd seen and heard while they were apart.

Lilly wasn't happy that Cade had found no sign of Timothy, but she wasn't surprised either. She told him about the incident between Preston and Neecie the afternoon before they'd happened upon the voodoo ceremony in the woods. She didn't mention her own run-in with him after seeing them together.

Cade told her that he'd heard from William, who said that there was no record of Henri Ducharme having attended any medical school in Ohio.

"Are you saying he attended somewhere else."

"No."

Lilly thought about that. "So, he isn't a doctor at all?"

"It seems not."

"That's not only morally wrong, but criminal. How many people have gone to him for help and been given wrong treatments?"

"I know. The repercussions of his actions could very well—and probably have been—lethal in some cases."

The full weight of the announcement sunk in. "That's frightening."

"William also found out that Henri was married to one Angela Markham years ago." Cade glanced at Lilly. "I'm betting she's the one he called his angel. She did die in childbirth, so that part of what Armand DeMille told William in his query letter was true. What we didn't know is that Angela Markham Ducharme had two daughters from a previous marriage, Corinne and Delia. He hasn't located either of them yet."

"So you and I can try to track them down."

Cade shrugged and gave a slight smile. "Sometimes fortune smiles on you and evidence seems to fall from the heavens."

After that ambiguous statement, he began to tell her about the trip he and Robbie had made with Henri to the sugar plantation the day she and Mrs. Fontenot had traveled to River Run.

"I'm sure it was interesting," Lilly said in exasperation. "But what about the evidence that fell from heaven?"

"Patience, my impulsive partner. You must learn patience."

With Lilly fuming at his side, he explained about the woman and the baby at the cottage and about Robbie sneaking into the cabin.

"You *let* Robbie go into someone's house without their knowing it?" she asked in a loud whisper. "Did it ever occur to you that he could have been in danger, not to mention that it's against the law?"

"You don't know the little hellion the way I do," Cade said. "You don't *let* Robbie do anything. Robbie does what he wants and the devil be hanged."

"Well, you should have more control over him."

Cade frowned at her over his shoulder. "Oh, yes. Of course. It's easy for you to say, and once again, since you're his 'aunt,' feel free to step in and help with his rearing anytime the notion strikes you."

"Thank you. I will."

They sat in silence for a moment, and when it became clear that Cade had no intention of talking to her about what Robbie had discovered, Lilly finally said, "Well?"

"Well, what?"

The cool expression in his eyes drove her mad. "Ooh! You know what I mean. What did he learn of importance?"

"Something pretty interesting as a matter of fact." He told her about the envelopes in the drawer addressed to Delia Breaux, who was no doubt Delia Markham.

Lilly processed the unbelievable information for a moment. "As in Angela Markham's daughter Delia?"

"It would be hard to believe she was anyone else."

Excitement rippled through her. This was the first concrete break they'd received since starting this case. "Did Robbie tell you what the letters said?"

"Unfortunately, the boy doesn't read or write."

"I beg your pardon?"

He met her disbelieving gaze. "You heard correctly. Teaching him would be a fine undertaking for you, Brona."

Disbelief and anger momentarily overshadowed her elation. "And one that I'll be sure to undertake," she said in a tart tone. "It is positively unbelievable that anyone in this day and age should be without basic reading and writing skills."

"I agree."

She drew a deep breath and brought her attention back to the investigation. "Did you send William this new information?"

"No," Cade said, "I thought we would try to find Corinne on Monday. We can let him know what we've learned after that."

"Excellent."

Lilly was beyond ready to do something meaningful to-ward solving this case. Until now, things had been more or less at a standstill. All they'd really known before finding out about Henri's medical background and the shadowy Delia was that he and Preston were miserable, wretched men who cheated on their wives. Sinful, surely, but not against the law.

Lamartine enveloped Lilly in a warm embrace when she went to the kitchen in the late afternoon.

"I'm so glad you and Mrs. Fontenot are back, Brona. It's been too quiet here with just the doctor."

"I hope you got a bit of a rest. How's Robbie?"

"Oh, he seems fine, but he was a sick little boy for a day or two."

"What about Amos? They must have taken whatever it was that Mrs. Fontenot had."

"I don't think so," Lamartine said, as she dredged some pork in flour. "Robbie and the missus had the same symptoms, but Amos just had a bad headache."

"Hmm."

Lamartine turned to look over her shoulder. "Oh! I almost forgot. Your uncle Patrick came by yesterday and said he would stop by again this evening."

For a second or two, Lilly didn't have a clue whom she was talking about. Then she realized that Pierce must have finally arrived. She smiled and gave a sigh of relief.

"Oh, good!" she said, clapping her hands together. "He said he might try to see us while he was in the area."

"What does he do?" Lamartine asked, reaching for a lid to cover the rice pot.

Oh, dear! What did *Uncle Patrick do?* She and Cade hadn't discussed it. In fact, they hadn't talked about Pierce since the day they'd argued about her asking him to come without discussing it first. Would he be upset that Pierce had actually come? Would the two very strong-willed men clash?

Of course they would.

"Well, it's a rather strange occupation, but he is a seamstress or tailor or whatever who travels with theater troupes and sews their costumes."

As lies went, it was simple enough. Even more important, it was easy to remember, since it was at least partly true.

"Hmm," Lamartine said. "That's interesting. I bet he's been a lot of places."

"Indeed he has." Anxious to dodge any more questions, Lilly said, "If you don't need me, I'll go and let Bran know to expect my uncle."

"Go on, child."

As she neared the barn, she heard voices. Cade and . . . was it possible? Was Pierce already here?

Lilly picked up her faded blue skirt and her pace, running into the shadow-shrouded barn. Pierce was dressed in the same trousers, shirt, and cap that Cade wore, the costume that seemed essential for Irish immigrants. She would have known him anywhere.

They heard her coming and both men turned. Lilly flung herself into the arms of the man who was most likely her father and hugged him tight.

"I can't believe you're here!" she said, leaning back and looking up at him.

Pierce smiled down at her, his gray eyes crinkling at the corners. "I told you I'd come if you needed me, didn't I?"

"You did." Lilly noted that, like her and Cade, Pierce had adopted an Irish brogue for his role as her uncle. She stepped away from him and turned to Cade, who was watching the reunion with great interest.

"I was coming to tell . . . Bran that you'd be stopping by," she said, "but I see the two of you have already met."

The two men stared at each other like two dogs sizing each other up before jumping on a meaty bone. After the fiasco with Timothy, Pierce would be eager to see if she'd done the unthinkable yet again and was falling for her partner, and he would want to know just what kind of man that partner was.

Cade would be sizing up Pierce to see if, like Robbie, the older man was just another person he had to deal with while they were working on the assignment.

"Have you seen Robbie?"

"Briefly," Pierce said with a smile. "It seems he and Bernard had important things to do before supper." He gave a little shake of his head and shot a wry smile toward Cade. "He's quite a lad."

Cade didn't return the smile. "He is that."

"I've only just met him, but there's something about him that reminds me a bit of, uh . . . Brona here when she was a lass."

"Really?"

"Enough about my naughtiness when I was a girl," Lilly said, grabbing both of Pierce's hands. "Come inside. I'm sure Lamartine has some lemonade to cool you off, and dinner will be ready in less than an hour."

Lilly had to give it to the two men. Though she was aware of the undercurrent of wariness between them, they did a fine job of loosening up for the benefit of their small audience, and supper was not the ordeal she'd expected it to be.

Robbie and Bernard listened with rapt attention as Pierce regaled them with actual tales of things that had happened during his years with various theater troupes, careful to leave Lilly out of the picture. Though his time was spent in managing the troupe these days, she'd always known he was a superb actor, and he did not disappoint, giving a perfect portrayal of a beloved uncle who lived a wonderful and adventurous single life, only having occasional contact with his few family members.

The Lagasses listened in delight as he talked about theater life and working with often egotistical actors. He made direct eye contact with Lilly when he mentioned that. She was so happy to see him that she didn't even care. The fact that she had not strayed far from his actual profession lent an air of authenticity to his stories that a made-up occupation would not have.

After a couple of hours of talk, Lilly and Cade accompanied him to the street, where he would find his way to his boardinghouse. They spoke for the first time of the plan for Pierce to finagle his way into the asylum where Patricia was locked away.

"I made it a point to contact William before I came," Pierce said.

"Pinkerton?"

Lilly's heart sank knowing William knew she was pursuing the investigation in an unorthodox way and using people who had not been vetted by the agency. Would Pierce's innate honesty ruin her chances of keeping her job as an operative? Would Cade be in trouble because of what she'd done? She cast him an apologetic look that he returned with cool disdain. Once again, her impulsiveness may have landed her in hot water.

"Who else?" Pierce was saying. "I thought it was important that he know what was going on, and I hoped he'd learned something we didn't know."

"Was he angry?"

"Did he?"

Lilly and Cade spoke as one.

"Not for long, and yes, he did," Pierce said, answering both questions. "After he settled down and I explained your pen-

chant for leaping before you look, I was told you should tem-
per your enthusiasm in the future and to work with your partner as a team."

"We've already had that discussion." Cade's voice was sharp
and to the point. "My partner has agreed."

Pierce looked at him with a thoughtful expression. Without dwelling on the subject, he continued. "You know about
Ducharme's medical diploma being a fake and about his marriage to Angela Markham and that she had two daughters from
that marriage."

Both Lilly and Cade nodded.

"William still hasn't located Delia, but he's traced Corinne
to Baton Rouge."

"Actually, we're one step ahead of the agency on this,"
Cade said.

"Meaning?"

"Meaning I know exactly where Delia Markham is." For
the second time, Cade recounted his and Robbie's trip with
Henri to the little house in the heart of sugarcane country.

"That's grand," Pierce said. "It will save some footwork."

"Cade and I had planned on looking for Corinne on
Monday. Now we'll know more specifically where to look."

"It looks to be a busy day," Pierce said. "William also checked
deeper into Mrs. Markham's and Dr. Ducharme's pasts. Not
only had Angela been married before, it seems Henri had a
wife before meeting *her*."

"What?" This was getting more and more complicated,
but Lilly knew that if they found the correct string to pull, the
whole confused situation would start to unravel.

Pierce offered them an ironic smile. "With the exception
of Angela, whom he looks to have married for love, the good
doctor has always used his marriages to help him climb the social ladder, choosing his wives with an eye toward the bottom
line. *Their* bottom line."

No surprise, really. As Timothy had done, Ducharme chose his women with careful deliberation and then began to weave his web of lies and deceit. If she and Cade could find evidence that he had benefitted financially from his marriages, they would have much more reason to believe he was trying to rid himself of Patricia.

Lilly needed no more proof. Her heart, or woman's intuition, or some natural instinct, told her that Ducharme was guilty. It was a feeling she was learning to trust, and she was more determined than ever to help the poor woman living her life in the hell hole that was the City Insane Asylum.

"So who was his first wife?" Cade asked.

"Judge Ethan Roswell's widowed and rather unmanageable daughter, Sophia."

"I'm guessing the judge is someone of note."

"He wields a good bit of power not only in Baton Rouge, but the entire state."

"If she was a widow when she and Henri met, what happened to her first husband?" Lilly asked.

"I've no idea," Pierce told them with one of his graceful shrugs. "And there is no record of Sophia ever marrying again after Henri. Interestingly, and rather conveniently, several years of public records were stored in the basement of the courthouse and were ruined during a flood."

Cade swore. "More likely the judge used that clout of his to determine where they were stored, hoping something of that nature would happen."

Pierce cocked a quizzical eyebrow. "A bit cynical, are you, Bran?"

It was Cade's turn to shrug. There was no stylishness in the lifting of his wide shoulders, only pure, raw power. "I like to think of it as being realistic."

"For what it's worth, that was my thinking, too. I've never been much of a believer in coincidence," the older man said.

"Using one's influence to make life easier . . . or someone else's hell . . . is one of the perks of power."

"Always has been," Cade agreed. "Well, Lilly and I can take a train to the capital and see if we can find Corinne, and maybe we'll look up the Roswells, too."

That settled, they talked over plans for the following day, finally agreeing on a scenario they believed would work. Since it would be Sunday, they all agreed that it was unlikely the regular hospital administrator would be working, making it a perfect day for Pierce to present himself as the "renowned" alienist Henri had called in from St. Louis to give his opinion on Patricia's mental state.

Lilly insisted the case was hers and Cade's and that they should go along. At first Pierce argued that it would be difficult to explain who they were to whomever was left in charge and that the last thing they wanted to do was raise any suspicions or be refused entry.

"He's got a point," Cade told Lilly. The he turned to Pierce. "Why couldn't I come along as an apprentice who's training under you?"

After a moment's thought, Pierce nodded. "Do you think you can get tomorrow off?"

"Probably. There's not much happening around here on Sundays."

"Excellent. Then you will come along as my assistant, newly arrived from Edinburgh for more training."

"I'm going too."

"Lil—"

"I'm going," she said again. "There's no need to try to talk me out of it. Times are changing. Women can become doctors."

Cade and Pierce exchanged irritated looks, but finally nodded.

"Fine, then. Come if you must. But you'll be quiet, since you're training under me. I'll play my part of trying to assess the treatment and medications Patricia is taking, and you can help me observe what's going on in that place. We'll try to get some private time with her, to evaluate her condition for ourselves. I'm no doctor, but I have some medical knowledge."

"That's what Lilly told me. I know a fair bit about street drugs and their effects."

"Good. Surely the three of us are intelligent enough to have some feeling whether her mental state is one of sorrow or drug-induced lethargy."

They would meet up here again on Sunday evening to discuss what they'd learned, and Cade and Lilly would make their trip to search for Corinne and the Roswells on Monday as planned. Lilly was satisfied that she would be able to participate in their charade to the mental facility, even though she would be little more than a watcher. At least she'd be of some help.

CHAPTER 19

The Sunday morning was fresh and relatively cool. The sun had not yet reached its zenith and started to suck the moisture from the ground, and the air was still breathable. Dr. Anton Pierce strolled toward the entrance of the asylum, his assistants beside him.

Pierce wore a two-piece suit of fine wool with pearl-gray pinstripe trousers and a double-breasted coat with darker gray velvet collar and cuffs. A matching bowler, walking cane, medical bag, and fancy shoes with contrasting toe caps completed his attire.

Cade, playing a young student doctor from Scotland, was dressed with far less style; after all, he wouldn't yet be able to afford the finery of the expert he accompanied. Instead, he'd chosen to wear brown tweed trousers and a solid single-breasted coat with a waist seam and leather-covered buttons. Lilly said that with his unruly hair and a pair of tortoise shell spectacles Pierce had the foresight to bring, Cade looked every inch the studious young alienist-to-be.

Lilly wore the infamous Mrs. Partridge costume—her green

skirt, white blouse, and wire spectacles. She added a fitted vest and scraped her hair back into a no-nonsense bun, leaving the gray wig behind.

As they walked up the sidewalk, Cade admitted he was concerned about how to play his part, since he knew little to nothing about the workings of the brain or mind. Lilly felt the same way, but hadn't spoken of her fears. Pierce instructed them to just look intelligent, interested, and thoughtful unless they noticed something out of the ordinary, and to take notes, lots of notes, as if they were inordinately fascinated with the case.

They followed Pierce into the shadowy entryway. A middle-aged man wearing white trousers and shirt was seated behind a scarred desk, reading a tattered copy of *Good Health* magazine. He set the periodical aside and stood, pushing his wire-rimmed glasses up with his forefinger as he did so.

"May I help you?" he asked, glancing from one visitor to the other.

Looking around with cool disdain, Pierce held out his hand. "Dr. Anton Pierce, my assistant, Dr. Bran Mahoney, and a student, Brona McGill."

Lilly shot him a sharp glance that Pierce ignored. So Cade was an associate and she a mere student! Cade caught the look and she could tell it was taking every bit of his willpower not to crack a smile at her indignation.

"We're here at the request of Dr. Henri Ducharme, who asked me to consult with Dr. Ballantine about a patient in his care," Pierce explained.

"Oh!" The young man looked a bit flustered as he shook hands all around. "Dr. Ballantine never comes in on the week-ends, but Dr. Wesley is here. He's in charge."

Intimidated by the self-confident man standing before him, he gestured toward a couple of straight-backed chairs. "If you'd care to be seated, I'll fetch him for you."

"Thank you. We'll just stand." Pierce pulled a pristine white handkerchief from his pocket and proceeded to wipe his hand as if it had been contaminated by the mere touch of the other man.

"Oh! Do you mind giving me the patient's name?"

"Not at all," Pierce said with a condescending smile. "He asked me to have a look at his wife, Patricia Ducharme."

"Oh, of course. Mrs. Ducharme. Lovely lady. Just lovely. It's hard to believe she's gone crazy."

Pierce gave the underling a cold smile. Good grief, the man was a consummate performer!

"As a profession, we're trying to stop those who work with mentally impaired people from using such derogatory terms," Pierce stated. "They are human after all, and you know what they say. There but for fortune . . ." He let his voice trail away.

Understanding that he'd just been reprimanded in a roundabout way, the man smiled, the merest twitch of his lips. "Of course, sir. Of course. I'll just go and find Dr. Wesley."

In a matter of moments, the weekend supervisor stepped into the corridor from a door down the hall. He was shrugging into his coat. Buttoning it over a definite paunch, he straightened his tie, smoothed his hair, and forced a smile to his ruddy face.

Lilly had seen the signs often enough. She'd wager a week's pay that the man left in charge for the weekend had been sleeping off a night of drinking.

"Welcome, Dr. Pierce" he said, extending a plump white hand. "I'm Dr. Trevor Wesley, the weekend administrator."

He and Pierce shook hands and he once again introduced Cade and Lilly.

"Dr. Mahoney," the man said, shaking Cade's hand as well. Then, with the conventions satisfied, he looked from Cade to Pierce and asked, "How can I be of assistance this morning?"

"Dr. Ducharme and I met years ago when we were both in

medical school, but we lost contact when we went into different fields."

Pierce spoke the lie with amazing believability. Dr. Wesley nodded, accepting every word as truth.

"When his wife's loss of her son and her daughter threatened to consume her, he contacted me and asked that I come and meet with her at my earliest convenience, to spend some time with her, so that I could give him my opinion of her mental state and, if possible, a prognosis. He is hoping she can return home as soon as possible." He gestured toward Cade. "My associates will be observing and passing on their thoughts as well."

Wesley looked confused but nodded. "Certainly. Please." He made a sweeping gesture with his arm. "Come into my office, where we can be more comfortable."

Without a word, the trio followed the man down the hallway and into a small room. While not extravagant by any standards, the interior of the small private sanctuary was head and shoulders above what little bit Cade had seen of the asylum proper.

The doctor settled into a chair behind a large oak desk and Pierce, Lilly, and Cade took two worn leather chairs across from him. Pierce's "associates" withdrew small tablets and pencils, as if they were seriously jotting down important information.

"I quite understand why Dr. Ducharme asked you to come," Dr. Wesley told them. "He is the kind of man who would want the very best for his wife, and I'm sure you're well aware that the Fontenots have been pillars of New Orleans business and society for as long as anyone can remember."

"So I understand." Pierce offered another superficial smile. "May I ask about her mental state when she was admitted?"

"As I recall, she was calm, even somewhat lethargic. I know

because Dr. Ducharme brought her on a Sunday afternoon, and I admitted her."

"I see. And what sort of behavior made the doctor suspect mental frailty?"

"As I understand, it was just what you mentioned. She lost her infant son at birth and then a short while ago, her daughter was kidnapped and murdered while on an outing with her and her other daughter, Cassandra."

"So she was despondent over her losses."

"Yes, naturally so."

"And her diagnosis?"

"Dr. Ducharme felt she was suffering from melancholy insanity," Wesley said.

Cade scribbled something in his notebook.

"And Dr. Ballantine? Did he agree with Dr. Ducharme's assessment? He is, after all, the professional in these matters, while my old colleague is simply a medical doctor."

The shock in the supervisor's eyes would have been comical had it not been so pathetic. "Well, I . . . I can't say with any certainty."

"He *did* do his own evaluation, didn't he?" Pierce's voice held a note of accusation.

"Oh, yes!" the man said with a vehement nod. "That is, I'm sure he did. He must have. We do that. Always. In fact, Dr. Ballantine and I have consulted about Mrs. Ducharme at length. We have meetings once a week about the state of all of our patients and their progress," he offered, as if the practice was innovative in some way.

The man protesteth too much, Lilly thought, willfully butchering the line from Shakespeare.

"And you, Dr. Wesley, what was your diagnosis?" Cade asked, joining the conversation for the first time.

The man straightened, realizing that he was dealing with

two men who took their jobs seriously. He seemed to gather his thoughts as well as his dignity.

"I concurred with Dr. Ballantine's evaluation."

Lilly glanced over to see Cade jotting more nonsense in his tablet. She noted he was having trouble keeping the disgust from his face. They all realized that chances were slim to none that Patricia Ducharme had been analyzed once she was deposited at the asylum.

"So she was sorrowful and grief filled," Pierce pressed.

"Yes."

"Tell me, Doctor, have you ever lost a loved one?"

"Of course," he said. "Who hasn't?"

"And weren't you filled with grief and sad over the loss?"

"Certainly."

"Wouldn't you agree, then, that Mrs. Ducharme's sadness was and is a natural occurrence?"

Wesley realized he'd stepped right into Pierce's trap. "Of course it is, but—"

"And," Cade added, "Mrs. Ducharme lost *two* loved ones in a year and a half, so wouldn't her melancholy be a natural reaction?"

Aha! What would Wesley say to that?

"Of course, but according to Dr. Ducharme, there was more, much more," he said, determined to uphold his loyalty to his superior.

"Tell me."

Wesley cleared his throat. "Well, he claimed that she was so wild with grief that she often became physically abusive, and he had no recourse but to restrain her."

Pierce regarded the man over the tips of his steepled fingers. "Did she treat all the members of her family in this aggressive manner?"

Wesley appeared to think back. "Not that I'm aware of.

The family did say that she *was* sometimes belligerent toward the doctor. Sometimes accusing him of lying and trickery. Some days she was quite calm, sleepy, even bordering on comatose."

Cade wrote in his tablet. "What kind of trickery?"

Lilly was glad he'd asked the question.

"She would accuse him of taking things or moving them so that she couldn't find them and then putting them somewhere else just to confuse her."

Cade and Pierce shared a considering look, which increased the distress in Wesley's eyes.

"Did he say whether or not he'd administered any sort of calming drug to her before bringing her here?" Cade asked.

"Oh, he had to! For a while after her daughter was . . . murdered and before she was brought here, he was forced to give her laudanum from time to time, but he was fearful of her becoming dependent on the opiate, so he stopped it soon after the funeral. I believe he switched to chloral hydrate—but only as needed of course. As far as I know, Dr. Ballantine is continuing that treatment."

That would do it all right. "Chloral hydrate?" Lilly piped up, shooting an apologetic glance at Pierce for not keeping her mouth shut. "Is that really necessary?"

Dr. Wesley gave her a look that said plainly that, as a woman, she, like a child, should be seen and not heard.

"From time to time, I'm afraid it is, but it's perfectly safe," he assured them with a negligent wave of a plump hand. "As I'm sure you know, it releases the patients from worry and calms them down. They usually fall asleep, and the episode passes."

"Is there anything else you can tell me that might shed light on the situation?" Pierce asked.

"Not that I'm aware of." Wesley's expression said that he was eager to get the consulting doctor out of his office.

Pierce gestured toward Lilly, who stood. He and Cade followed suit. "Then I'd like to see the patient now."

"Well, I don't know. . . . She isn't allowed visitors."

"Dr. Wesley, I have traveled hundreds of miles at the urging of my friend. I will see the patient. Now, if you please."

"Oh. Yes, I'll take you to her . . . room." Clearly agitated, he preceded them to the door and started down the hall. "I'm afraid we must pass through the common area."

"It's nothing I haven't seen before," Pierce said, tugging on the cuffs of his coat.

Lilly had firsthand knowledge of it as well from her visit with Robbie.

Wesley led them down a hallway to a large room where approximately twenty women were busy idling away the lives they were only marginally aware of living. Today the situation was different. One sprawled naked on the floor. Another sat cradling a pillow as if it were a baby and sang "Hush, Little Baby" in a pure, clear soprano.

Wesley leaned nearer. "That's Chloe. When she kept losing babies, she just went round the bend."

A young woman, no more than twenty, sat alone, her arms crossed. Her eyes were clear and filled with loathing as she watched them cross the room.

"Kleptomaniac," Wesley said.

Yet another woman marched around the room, a Bible clasped against her ample bosom, her chin high. Every few seconds she cried out, "Repent, sinners! The day of the Lord grows near."

When the trio passed her, she grabbed Cade's arm and looked up at him, her eyes blazing with a fervor that seemed to emanate from her very soul. "Do you know the Lord, young man? Every knee shall bow . . ."

Wesley physically removed her hand from Cade's arm. "Yes, he does, Betty, now go convert those lost souls over there." She stared at him with a blank expression and turned and wandered away.

"Religious mania."

Wesley turned into another hall and led the way to a small enclosure with three walls and bars. It was more of a cell than a room, but it did have a few of the amenities of home. A settee sat against a wall, and an expensive rug covered the rough floor. The Fontenot fortune at work.

A woman sat in a blue wingback chair in the corner. As before, Lilly noted that she was not dressed in the loose-fitting dresses of rough white fabric provided by the asylum. Patricia Ducharme wore a simple shirtwaist of blue-striped dimity. Her sable-brown hair was coiled into a sleek chignon at the nape of her neck.

Wesley unlocked the door and they stepped inside. As they neared her, Lilly noted the dark lashes that lay against her cheeks. She didn't think she was reading at all. She thought the patient was asleep. A drug-induced sleep?

"Patricia."

Wesley's voice had no effect on her.

"Patricia," he said louder. He reached out and lifted her chin. As Lilly suspected, her eyes were closed, but as the supervisor kept speaking to her, they began to flutter and she managed to open them. They were green and quite lovely, filled with haziness and maybe a question.

"You have company, Patricia. Wake up and talk to them, won't you?"

Though an obvious effort, she did her best to focus.

"These two gentlemen are doctors from back East," he said, repeating the background information they'd come up with for the occasion. "The young lady is a student. They've come to help you." Wesley spoke loudly and slowly and enunciated each word with care, as if she had a hearing problem instead of a psychological impairment.

"I don't like doctors," she said, trying to focus on Pierce. "My husband is a doctor. He put me here."

What a wealth of information that was, Lilly thought, shooting a glance at Cade, who gave a lift of his dark eyebrows.

"Do you know where you are, Mrs. Ducharme?" Pierce asked.

"Oh, yes. Henri believes I have lost my mind, but I haven't. I just . . . lose things." Those incredible green eyes filled with tears. "I lost my baby and my daughter, and, well, it's always something. But I haven't lost my snuffbox. I hid it so that no one can take it and say I lost it."

"You don't have a snuffbox, Patricia, because you don't use snuff," Wesley told her.

"I don't?" She looked confused; then she sighed. "But I was so sure it was mine. The boy brought it to me. He told me he threw out the snuff because it made him sick."

Lilly's heart skipped a beat. So Robbie *had* taken the snuffbox from Mrs. Fontenot's room. She felt somewhat better about the theft knowing he hadn't taken it for himself. But when had he had time to visit Patricia again, and how had he arranged it?

"What boy was this?" Pierce asked, unaware of the things that had been going on at the house on Rampart Street.

Wesley offered them an apologetic smile. "There was no boy, Dr. Pierce. She insists a boy visits her when she's in the yard, and that he gave her a filigree snuffbox. She claims he's one of the workers. The problem is that we only hire adults. And even if we did hire a child, where would a youngster who worked here get a fancy snuffbox?"

Patricia's eyes had drifted closed once more.

"From her appearance and mannerisms, I assume Mrs. Ducharme has had her medicine this morning," Pierce commented.

"Of course. Unless there is a need to administer an extra dosage for some reason, we give medications immediately after breakfast."

"And is this how she spends her days? Sleeping in a chair, pretending to read?"

Wesley appeared baffled by the question. "Well, uh, yes. What else can she do?"

"She could do many things if she were not so sleepy," Pierce said in a stern voice. "Times are changing, Dr. Wesley. There are new advances in medicine and psychiatry. Good heavens, man! It's been almost a hundred years since Dr. Pinel urged institutions to treat their patients more humanely. One hundred years, sir, and we are still restraining patients and administering various drugs just to subdue them, mainly so they won't cause any trouble."

Wesley's face had turned beet red. Whether or not it was from embarrassment or anger at "Dr. Pierce" for giving him a dressing-down that rightly should have gone to his director was hard to say.

"Well, I—"

"The goal now is not just to lock up these unfortunate individuals because they're not a fit in polite society, but to try to rehabilitate them," Pierce said, interrupting whatever the poor man was about to say.

"We do categorize disorders," Wesley told him, grabbing on to anything to try to redeem himself and his superior.

"I'm aware of that," Pierce said, "and you and Dr. Ballantine are to be commended." His tone and manner softened. "Forgive my passion, Doctor. It's just that I have such commitment to changing things for the better."

A look of relief settled on Wesley's face. "I understand."

Pierce started across the room.

"Are you going?" The question held disappointment and sorrow.

The group turned back to the woman in the armchair. Tears glistened in her eyes.

"Yes, Mrs. Ducharme, we must," Pierce told her.

"I want to go with you." Two tears slid down her pale cheeks. "I want to go home."

"We're working hard toward that end," he said, offering another comment. "We want that, too."

Patricia's eyes drifted shut and her shoulders began to shake with her silent weeping.

Pierce gave Lilly and Cade a look she couldn't interpret and started once more to leave the room. "Of course I only spoke with her for a few moments," he said to Dr. Wesley, "but Mrs. Ducharme seems quite rational to me. She is sad and a bit confused, but that might be the effects of the drugs. I regret that I cannot do a proper evaluation with her under the influence of so much medication. Since she doesn't seem violent, I'd like her taken off all her medications at once."

Obviously appalled at Pierce's high-handedness, Wesley said, "You have, of course, spoken to Dr. Ducharme about changing her routine?"

"I'm off to see him at this very moment," Pierce assured the man. "And I'll be stopping by tomorrow sometime to check on her condition, after say . . . twenty-four hours of being medication free. We should have some indication by then if we're on the right track and I can give Henri my honest opinion for the future."

"Certainly."

"I suggest that someone trained in the science of psychotherapy spend time talking to her. Listen to what she has to say. Perhaps if she isn't under the influence of the drugs, she will make more sense, and there can be a rational conversation about why she feels the way she does. In fact, I would do this for all the patients. And I beg you to stop referring to them as crazy and lunatics, as some are so fond of doing."

"Excellent idea," Wesley said. "I'll suggest it to Dr. Ballantine. But you'll see him tomorrow when you come, won't you?" He looked relieved that he would not be the one to tell his supervisor to change his methods of running the hospital.

"Certainly," Pierce assured. "Most importantly, they need something to do besides sit. If they are not violent, and if they are able to take simple instruction, why not give them small tasks to keep them busy?" Pierce smiled amiably. "After all, Wesley, we all know that an idle mind is the devil's workshop."

Wesley's reply was only a sick sort of smile.

"Patricia is no more insane than I am," Cade said the moment they exited the building.

"Agreed." Pierce headed to the buggy tied at the street, his long stride eating up the sidewalk. "What do the two of you think?"

"I don't know if chloral hydrate calms violence or not," Cade said, "but I lived on the streets long enough to know that it's commonly slipped into the drink of a victim, rendering them comatose and making them easy targets for robbery or rape."

"True," Pierce verified. "And along with cannabis, morphine, and opium, chloral hydrate can be purchased in any drug store for a mere twenty-five cents a dose."

"I'd say Ducharme has kept her drugged to keep her out of the way," Lilly said. "The question is why?"

"So that he can carry on with Mrs. Abelard. And maybe the woman Robbie and I saw him with," he added.

"People have done far worse for less reason," Pierce agreed. "The question is how long will he be satisfied with keeping her out of the way? Will he decide to have Patricia succumb to some unexpected malaise one of these days?"

"That's the concern," Cade said.

"I saw a certain look in your eyes when Wesley mentioned

the snuffbox. Do you know something?" Pierce asked the younger man.

Cade explained how Mrs. Fontenot's pretty gold box had come up missing before she and Lilly had gone to River Run. "Lilly's pretty sure Robbie filched it when she was ill. She may be right."

"I'm certain of it," Lilly said.

"Fine. But if he did, did he have a chance to give it to Patricia, and more to the point, why would he?"

"We know he went to see her once before," Lilly told Pierce. "He feels sorry for her and thinks she's being neglected, but I don't know—"

Cade swore suddenly. "He must have taken it to her when I went to pick up Lilly at River Run. He didn't want to go with me because he had 'things to do.' That would have been after his round of sickness, too, so he'd have been able to pull it off, since he'd gone off on his own once before. No one would have thought a thing of him being missing for a while."

"It might be a good idea to have a talk with that young man."

"I intend to."

At last the case was beginning to shape up, though Cade knew they had miles to go before putting all the puzzle pieces together. The first thing he would do was ask Robbie why he'd dumped the snuff from the box.

"So we're going back to check on Patricia tomorrow?"

"Of course not. I'm taking a train back to Chicago first thing in the morning. You and Lilly will do your checking on the Roswell woman. And Ballantine will . . ." Pierce let his voice trail away and smiled, the naughty smile of a boy who'd just done something very mischievous. "And Ballantine will show up tomorrow and his wards will be pure bedlam. Literally."

Satisfied that things were looking up in their case, Pierce

took Lilly aside to say his good-bye. She thanked him for putting his life on hold to help them and told him to give Rose a hug for her and then she wished him Godspeed. Pierce placed a kiss on her forehead and said, "He'll do."

"I beg your pardon."

"McShane. You're in good hands."

Lilly couldn't have been more surprised. Something about Cade must have impressed Pierce. He was not known for suffering fools.

Without waiting for her to comment, he said, "He's professional, always alert, and very street-smart. I've a feeling you can learn a lot from him."

High praise, indeed.

"Listen and learn, Lilly."

She nodded, and Pierce hugged her once more before turning and starting down the street.

When she returned to Cade, he was staring at Pierce's back. "That is a brilliant man, and one of the best actors I've ever had the privilege to work with."

Lilly smiled up at him, a rather sad smile. "More importantly, he's a good man."

Instead of replying, he took her hand and said, "Let's go have a talk with our little brother."

They found the boy outside in the garden, sitting on a concrete bench and watching the lightning bugs flickering in the semidarkness. When he heard them coming, he stood, almost as if he were readying himself for battle.

"I didn't take it for myself."

They all three knew what he was talking about.

"I know. Sit down, Robbie." Cade indicated the bench.

"I always planned to put it back, though I've no doubt it's worth a small fortune," he told them. "Like you always say, McShane, I've turned over a new leaf and I can't do those things anymore."

"That's true. So why did you take it to begin with?"

He gave a lift of his narrow shoulders. "I just wanted to try the snuff and see what the hubbub was all about. I figured there must be something good about it, like chewing or smoking, since so many people take a dip now and again."

Typical boy, Lilly thought. Typical child. She recalled how she and the daughter of one of the other actors had snitched a paper and enough Bull Durham for a single cigarette, which they smoked in secret. It made them sicker than dogs. . . . She hid a smile. Robbie's sickness while she was away made perfect sense now.

"And?"

"And it took me a bit to get up the courage to do it, since I'd been so sick when I tried the other tobacco."

Cade nodded. "But you were determined."

"Aye. Started out by just trying to smell it, but I accidentally sucked some of it up my nose."

Cade laughed. "Serves you right. And how was it?"

"Terrible. You were here. Threw up my toenails, didn't I?" Remembering, he gave a little shudder.

"Why did you take the snuffbox to Patricia instead of giving it back to Mrs. Fontenot?" Lilly asked.

He sighed. "I had to think on that a while. I was afraid that if I put it back in Madam's room, everyone would know that someone in the house had taken it, and since we're new, I thought they'd suspect one of us."

Cade gave Lilly a look that as much as said, "I told you he was smart."

"Besides, I didn't want Mrs. Fontenot to take any more of the nasty stuff, not with her just gettin' over being so sick and all. Then I thought about Miz Patricia there in that terrible place all alone, and no one coming to visit her. I thought she might like some reminder of her home and her family."

"That was very nice of you, Robbie," Lilly told him.

He shrugged. "I dumped out the rest of the snuff before I gave it to her. She's awful nice, but she's a little barmy. I didn't want her to be sick *and* barmy."

Lilly gave a little sigh. Perhaps there was hope for the boy after all.

"Good job," Cade told him, giving him a pat on the shoulder.

"You're not mad at me?"

Cade smiled at him. "No, I think you learned a valuable lesson and did some good, too."

"You've taken a liking to Patricia, haven't you?" Lilly said, recalling how he'd been so adamant about someone visiting her since she'd been abandoned by her family.

"She's been through some tough times," he said. "I feel sorry for her."

This from a child left in a cemetery by his parents. A child who lived on the streets and survived by his wits. A child who knew all about tough times.

CHAPTER 20

Lilly and Cade rose before daylight and left on the early train to Baton Rouge. It took some time to find Corinne, who was no longer Corinne Markham, but Corinne Chambers. They finally located her in a small white house on the outskirts of town, complete with a picket fence and blue shutters . . . just the sort of home Lilly dreamed of owning one day.

"It's perfect," she said, as Cade tied the rented rig to the gatepost.

"What's perfect?" he asked, lifting her down from the carriage.

"The house. It's just what I want someday."

The statement seemed to surprise him, but he made no comment. Instead, he opened the gate and offered her his arm. For this leg of the investigation, they were in agreement that they should show their badges. There was really no reason to hide their true identity.

The woman who came to the door was younger than Patricia but older than either of her daughters, a plump, pretty woman with a toddler on her hip. "May I help you?" she asked with a pleasant smile.

Cade showed her his Pinkerton badge and introduced himself. "This is Miss Long, my associate. We understand that Henri Ducharme and your mother were married at one time. Is that right?"

The woman couldn't hide the surprise in her eyes. "Yes, they were. Is he in some sort of trouble?"

"Not at all," Cade said, which was the truth at this point. "May we come in?" He softened the request with one of the rare smiles that was guaranteed to make the woman's heart flutter.

"Oh, of course." She stepped aside for them to enter the small parlor.

When they were seated and the baby was bouncing on her knee, Cade spun the lie. "We represent a client who has left Dr. Ducharme a fairly substantial sum of money."

The ends justify the means. Reminding herself of Allan Pinkerton's favorite saying made the falsehood a little easier for Lilly.

Corinne Chambers looked relieved.

"You look as if you were expecting a problem of some sort," Cade said.

"Well, I was only twelve when he married Mama, but even to me, it seemed that wherever Henri went trouble followed."

"How so?"

"He was a divorced man when he got engaged with my mother, and my aunt was very much against their marriage. She was afraid Mama's reputation would be in ruins. Divorce was really frowned upon back then."

And still was, Lilly thought, recalling how difficult it had been to find an attorney who was willing to handle her divorce from Timothy.

"Divorced? Really?" Cade was saying, playing his role to the hilt. "Do you know who the woman was?"

"Everyone knew, because his wife's family was none other than the high-falutin' Roswells. Henri was married to the judge's youngest daughter, Sophia."

Cade and Lilly exchanged a look of feigned surprise. It seemed as if they were about to get a few details on that first marriage.

"What happened?"

"Oh, she'd already had a previous relationship and a child by some misfit the judge didn't think was good enough for his little girl. When he pitched a fit, she and her lover ran off. I've heard the judge spent two years looking for her. When he found her, he brought her back home and then sent her to the country."

"You remember a lot for a twelve-year-old," Lilly commented, wondering if they were being led down a rabbit trail.

"Oh, I picked up a lot of this through the years. It's one of those stories people loved to talk about. Still do."

"What happened between Sophia and the man? Did they divorce?"

Corinne bounced the baby on her knee. "I'm not sure they ever married."

"Does anyone know how she met Henri?" Cade asked.

"Well, the story is that Sophia was in the country when she went into labor, and Henri was the closest doctor. He delivered the child, a boy, and over the course of a few months the two fell in love. They married, but the judge didn't like Henri any more than he did the first guy." She glanced from Cade to Lilly and gave a disdainful sniff. "You know how rich people are. If someone isn't from their world, they always suspect they're after their money."

Which was too often true, Lilly thought, as their current investigation proved.

Cade nodded in understanding. "So they divorced and he later married your mother."

"Yes, rumor has it that the judge paid Henri a huge sum of money if he'd take Sophia's bastard baby and get out of her life for good."

"Are you saying that when he married your mother, he brought Sophia's illegitimate son to the marriage?" Lilly asked, appalled by the notion, and hoping she'd misunderstood. What kind of woman would allow her father to talk her into giving up her child? A cold dose of common sense told her that in all likelihood, Sophia had had little say in the matter, since the Roswell family name was at stake.

"That's my understanding, but my sister and I never saw him. Henri must have left him in the care of a relative or someone."

Interesting.

"And you haven't seen Ducharme since your mother's death?" Cade stated.

"No, my sister, Delia, and I went to live with our aunt."

"Do you think she would have any idea about Henri's whereabouts?" Lilly asked, casting a look at Cade.

"Oh, no. We lost track of him long ago."

Corinne seemed to be answering honestly, but it never hurt to press a little. "Do you have any idea who else might know something about where we might find him?"

"Well, they probably won't be happy about dragging up the past, but I'm sure the Roswells can tell you a lot more than I know."

"What do you think?" Cade asked Lilly as he helped her into the buggy.

"I didn't get the feeling she was hiding anything, did you?"

"No, in fact, she seemed pretty adamant that Delia knew nothing. Do you think she's keeping her relationship with Henri a secret from Corinne?"

"Nothing would surprise me at this point." Lilly gave a

shake of her head. "My brain is spinning just trying to keep all those relationships and marriages straight.

Cade laughed, one of the few genuine expressions of emotion she'd seen from him.

"Maybe we should write it down when we get home."

"Maybe we should," she agreed.

The Roswell mansion was located east of town. There were no similarities between it and the small, cozy home of Corinne Chambers. The huge three-story structure was a perfect example of Queen Anne architecture.

"What if the judge is in court?"

"I'm sure he's retired by now," Cade said. "All this happened a long time ago."

"You're right."

A black-frocked maid greeted them. Cade told her they were making inquiries about his former son-in-law, and after checking with the master of the house, she bade them come inside. She led the way to the library, where an unsmiling gray-haired man with a tidy beard and wire spectacles sat behind a desk, working over some sort of ledger. He stood when his guests entered the room.

"Come in," he said, coming around the desk to shake hands. "I'm Ethan Roswell."

"Andrew Cadence McShane, Pinkerton National Detective Agency." He gestured toward Lilly. "My colleague, Miss Long."

With the social niceties satisfied, the judge invited them to have a seat on the camelback sofa while he settled in a large paisley wingback chair. He ordered coffee brought, and after the maid left the room, he said, "I confess that I've been in the business of law for many years, but I don't think I've ever had a visit from the Pinkertons or worked with them in any way."

"We promise not to take up too much of your time," Cade said.

Their host drummed his fingertips on the arm of his chair, and his face wore an amused expression. "Why is it that I feel you're here about Dr. Henri Ducharme?"

Wanting to find out everything they could about Henri's past, Cade and Lilly chose a different tack with the judge than they had with Corinne Chambers. Truth all the way.

"We are. Would you like to explain things to the judge, Miss Long?"

She was a little taken aback by the unexpected move, but quickly donned a professional persona and launched into all the happenings leading to Patricia's confinement in the asylum, as well as what had transpired since they'd been at the Fontenot home.

After contemplating what he'd just heard, Roswell said, "It doesn't sound as if he's changed much."

"Do you mind elaborating, sir?" Lilly asked.

"Well, it's been my experience that his kind never vary too much from their basic strategy. Meet a woman with money, woo her, marry her, and then get all he can get."

Though Lilly was not, and never would be, wealthy, that is exactly what Timothy had done to her. Taken every last dime of her savings.

"So this sounds like something he'd do?"

"Oh, yes."

"Do you think he's capable of worse?"

Roswell's smile was without doubt jaded. "If you're asking in a roundabout way if I think he would have his wife declared mentally incompetent to get his hands on the Fontenot money, I'd say yes. He's just the type. Everyone thinks I'm paranoid, but I have a fair amount of experience with this sort of thing, and I can spot his kind a mile away."

"Are you referring to Sophia's first husband?" Cade stated.

"Gregory?" Frowning, Roswell nodded. "There was nothing smooth or polished about him, but he had a charismatic personality and was exceptionally good-looking. I think it was that rough-around-the-edges quality that intrigued Sophia. He was so different from the young men in our social circle. Of course I recognized him for what he was the first time I set eyes on him, so I made the fatal mistake that many parents make: I forbade her to see him, and she repaid me by running away with him."

Cade leaned forward. "You eventually found them."

"I did, but only two years later, after Sophia contacted me." He offered them a weary smile. "I didn't use the Pinkertons, you see."

The maid brought in a sterling silver coffee tray. Roswell excused her and asked if Lilly minded pouring. For the next few moments they busied themselves with pouring the steaming brew and selecting cookies from an enticing array.

"So *she* contacted you?" Cade said, in an attempt to get the conversation back on track.

"Yes, she sent me a telegram telling me where she was. I believe she was tired of living hand to mouth and wanted to come home. Of course, Gregory wanted that, too. I believe he thought I'd be so happy to have my daughter back that I would accept him as one of the family with open arms."

"I wonder why he hadn't already married her?" Lilly asked.

Roswell shrugged. "I assume he thought there was no reason to since she was cut off from her family and the money, but when she tried to make amends with us, he changed his tune."

"Did they ever marry?"

"No, I wouldn't stand for it, even though she was expecting his child by then."

"That's a very unusual position for a father to take," Cade said. "Most fathers would be happy for a proposal."

"Not this father. I learned a long time ago that two wrongs never make a right, Detective. And during the time they were gone, I'd found out he had a little sideline. Forgery."

Cade and Lilly exchanged surprised looks. This case got stranger and stranger.

"I told him I knew all about it and if he didn't go somewhere far, far away, I'd have him thrown into jail for rape and kidnapping. He tried to hold out for money, but I told him it was a train ticket to Boston or jail. He took the ticket."

"Have you ever heard from him?" Cade asked.

"I like to stay on top of things, Agent McShane, so I've made it a point to keep tabs on him. A few years ago, he was picked up for forging some bearer bonds and sent to the state penitentiary. He died there a month or so ago."

"And after he left, you sent Sophia to the country until the gossip died down."

"And she met Henri there, and they married," their host said, nodding.

Lilly's head was whirling. "Do you mind my asking how you managed to get rid of Henri?"

His smile was rueful. "There are several advantages to having money, Miss Long. It really wasn't that hard. I simply asked him how much it would take to get him out of my daughter's life. He was a little smarter than Gregory, and to my knowledge he hadn't committed any crime against Sophia, so I had to count on his greed.

"He turned down my first offer, so I sweetened the pot. I offered him a large sum of money to sign the divorce papers and told him that if he'd take Gregory Easterling's son when he went, I'd make a deposit into an account for him every month." Once again, Roswell's lips curved upward into a bitter smile. "He couldn't sign fast enough."

Lilly felt her world shift and several of the missing puzzle pieces slipped into place. As Pierce always said: There was no such thing as coincidence.

"Easterling?" Lilly and Cade repeated in almost perfect synchronization.

"Yes, Gregory Easterling. The child's name was Preston."

Though they could hardly wait to get away and talk over what they'd learned, Lilly and Cade finished their coffee, thanked Roswell for the information, and told him they needed to get back so they wouldn't miss the evening train to New Orleans.

They didn't speak until they were in the buggy and rolling down the road. Cade turned to her and said, "Are you thinking what I'm thinking?"

"I don't know. I'm thinking that Henri and Preston are in on it together."

"Exactly. I'll even go so far as to speculate that Preston inherited his father's skill with a pen and learned his trade."

"Oh! I hadn't made that connection," Lilly said. "But now that you have, I'll go out on a limb and say that Henri's medical degree from Ohio came from the Easterling School of Forgery."

Cade actually laughed. "My thoughts exactly."

They rode in silence for several minutes while they each tried to absorb the flood of information they'd received from Corinne and the judge.

Lilly was first to break the silence. "Do you think Henri means to get rid of Patricia somehow? Permanently?"

Cade glanced over at her. "I do, but he's smart enough to know that it can't be too soon. With everything that's happened to the family, he has to be very careful or the whole setup will look fishy to the authorities."

"Good heavens!" Lilly said as a new and terrifying thought leaped into her mind.

"What?"

She looked at him with horrified eyes. "Do you think Henri and Preston had anything to do with Suzannah's death?"

He didn't reply for long seconds. Finally, he said, "After what we've heard this afternoon, I wouldn't put anything past either of them."

Silence reigned once more.

"The Fontenot family has amassed a lot of money and property through the years," he said at last. "It's pretty much a given that Henri married Patricia to get his hands on her money, and I'll give you two-to-one odds that Preston married Cassandra for the same reason."

"No bet."

They were almost at the train station when Lilly's fertile imagination came up with yet another possibility. There was a bleak expression in her eyes when she said, "Cade, I've been thinking about how Mrs. Fontenot's illness comes and goes, and how distrustful Lamartine is of the doctor and his remedies. You don't think he's been giving her something harmful, do you?"

"Harmful? Like poison?"

"That's exactly what I mean."

"Holy mother of pearl!" he said, using Robbie's favorite phrase. His blue eyes were filled with a sudden revelation of horror. "I think they mean to get rid of all the Fontenot women. Every single one of them."

Dusk was creeping through the trees and melding with the shadows when the hired hack dropped off Lilly and Cade at the house on Rampart Street. Since Henri had no idea that they were on to him, they doubted that he would make any overt moves, but they wanted to confront him before he had a chance to do anything else to the women.

When Amos and Bernard saw them dressed in their fancier clothes, they looked surprised but didn't say anything.

"Is Henri here?" Cade asked, his intensity unmistakable.

Amos looked from one of them to the other. "Yes."

"Where's Robbie?" Lilly asked Bernard.

"He went to sit with Mrs. Fontenot a bit."

"What's the matter, Bran?" Amos asked, confused and troubled by this new and very different side of his friend.

"We think the doctor plans to harm Mrs. Fontenot," Cade said. He took Lilly's arm and started for the house, not waiting to see Amos's reaction.

They entered the kitchen door and found Lamartine in the wide foyer, listening at the door. Like Amos, she looked surprised to see how Cade and Lilly were dressed. Henri was talking to someone, and if the tone of his voice was any indication, he was not happy.

Putting a finger to his lips, Cade guided the cook back to the kitchen. "What's going on?"

Lamartine wrung her hands. "Dr. Ducharme came in and started in on Mrs. Fontenot." She gestured toward the stove, where the pots still sat, filled with food. "They haven't even had supper yet."

"What's he so angry about?" Lilly asked.

"I've just been hearing bits and pieces, so I'm not sure. All I know is that something happened at the asylum yesterday and he is not happy about it."

Cade and Lilly knew exactly what had happened. Henri had found out about the visiting alienist he was supposed to have sent.

"Stay here," Cade said, giving Lamartine a comforting pat on the shoulder. Taking Lilly's elbow, he started toward the swinging door to the dining room.

"You aren't going to go in there, are you?"

"We have to," Lilly said.

"This isn't any of our business, Brona. You'll be fired for sure."

Lilly just smiled. The pocket doors leading to the parlor were open, enabling them to see what was happening. Mrs. Fontenot was seated on one of the small settees, Lucifer curled in her lap. Robbie sat beside her, a belligerent expression on his face, and wonder of wonders, he was stroking the ferocious feline. Henri stood a few feet away, glaring at them as he threw curses and accusations their way.

Together, Lilly and Cade made their way around the large dining room table toward the confrontation. Henri noticed them before they got to the doorway. It was impossible for him to hide his surprise, not only at their mode of dress, but their audacity in daring to interrupt.

Mrs. Fontenot's shoulders seemed to relax, and Robbie welcomed them with a broad smile.

"Is everything all right, Madam?" Lilly asked.

"Everything was fine before you barged in here," Henri snapped. "What the devil are you doing here, Sullivan?"

"Lamartine said that there was a problem at the asylum. I thought perhaps I could explain if it had anything to do with Dr. Pierce's visit yesterday," Cade said as he and Lilly moved closer to the two adults.

Lilly was impressed by his ability to remain so cool and un-ruffled.

"Dr. Pierce?" Henri frowned. "How do you know what his name is, and how on earth would you know anything about what goes on there?" Henri asked, clearly at a loss to what was going on.

"Dr. Pierce came at my request," Lilly said, beginning to take a bit of pleasure from Henri's bewilderment.

"Your request?" Henri set aside his confusion long enough

to try to reestablish his control. "Who do you think you are, coming in here as hired help and presuming to interfere in things that don't concern you?"

"Oh, but it does concern them, Henri," Mrs. Fontenot said as she handed Lucifer to Robbie. "They have every right, since I asked for them to come."

Good grief! What was she up to?

"You asked them? Have you gone as mad as Patricia?" Henri spat. Lilly was so close to the doctor that she could see the twitching of his lips beneath his mustache.

"Hardly." Mrs. Fontenot smiled as she stood to face him, a self-satisfied smile if ever Lilly had seen one. "Henri, I doubt that Bran and Brona Sullivan are even their names. You see, I'm beginning to believe that they are with the Pinkerton Agency, and they'd like to ask you a few questions."

Lilly darted a surprised look at Cade. How had Mrs. Fontenot figured out who they were? And why choose this moment to break the news?

"Pinkertons? You *are* mad." Henri dismissed the notion with a wave of his hand.

"Actually, Mrs. Fontenot, I believe most of our questions were answered today by Corinne Markham and Judge Roswell," Cade said.

There was a certain satisfaction in seeing the color drain from Ducharme's face.

Cade flashed one of his smiles at their employer. "By the way, Mrs. Fontenot," he said, as if they were discussing the weather, "the judge said to tell you hello, and you'll have to come visit him and his wife soon."

"That would be lovely."

"I'm not sure if you know it or not," Cade began, "but Henri and Preston have known each other since Preston was a baby. In fact, Henri is Preston's stepfather."

As LaRee Fontenot's sharp mind began to piece things together, an expression of shock entered her dark eyes. "You and that dreadful man planned everything together?" she asked, her quavering voice little more than a whisper.

Henri must have realized that his scheme had just come to an abrupt halt. His nervousness was replaced with a boldness Lilly had seen before . . . on her husband's face. Even his words were reminiscent of Timothy's taunt. "Your precious daughter-in-law was an easy mark, and so was Cassandra. Needy women always are."

Needy? The word was like a slap in Lilly's face. Mrs. Fontenot's next words brought her thoughts back to the confrontation taking place right in front of her.

"You and Preston planned to marry into the family, get rid of the girls, and take everything we've worked so hard for. That's why you were so eager to have Preston take over the legal matters from Armand. Correct me if I'm wrong."

Lilly was about to tell her she had it exactly right when Henri piped up. "Why else?"

"I must say, you were patient . . . at least in the beginning, but you're getting a little greedy now, aren't you?" the matriarch accused.

"Only because I have a few gambling debts, *Grand-mère*."

"There's nothing wrong with Patricia, is there?"

"Nothing that won't cure itself if she's off her drugs a few days," he said in an offhand manner.

That admission seemed to be the last straw. Mrs. Fontenot straightened herself to her full height, which wasn't much. "Brona, will you please have Lamartine send Amos for the police. I'd like this thief out of my home as soon as possible."

"Yes, Mrs. Fontenot."

As Lilly turned to leave, Henri pulled a small derringer from his pocket.

"Stay right there, Brona," he said, pointing the weapon at her.

Lilly stood very still. Robbie, who was always so unflappable about everything, looked truly dismayed. Cade's gaze was thoughtful, considering, and she knew that various scenarios about how best to handle the situation were running through his mind.

Without warning, Robbie scooped the black cat from Mrs. Fontenot's lap and tossed him right at Henri's face. The surprised feline gave a menacing yowl and swiped at the doctor before sinking his claws into him and making a leap to safety.

Unwilling to go down without a fight, Henri gave a yelp and made a grab at Lilly. He wound up with a handful of her hair. With mayhem erupting around her, she dug her nails into his hand and gouged as hard as she could, trying to pull free. She heard the unmistakable sound of Henri taking a blow to the midsection, and he let her go. A loud crash followed as she staggered in an attempt to keep from falling. She stumbled into someone and small hands reached out to steady her.

"I gotcha."

The words came from Robbie, who was struggling to keep her upright. His eyes held relief. She gave him a breathless smile of thanks and turned to survey the damages.

Lucifer was perched on the back of the second settee, giving the whole assemblage the evil eye, as if he were considering his next victim. Mrs. Fontenot's expression was nothing short of victorious. Cade, who was not even breathing hard, stood over Henri, who was lying on the pretty carpet, flat on his back. It looked as if he'd landed on a delicate gold-leaf table on his way down. The remnants of a gorgeous blue and green vase lay in shards behind him.

Three parallel scratches ran down his face from his forehead, through his eyebrow and all the way to his mustache. Lucifer's mark. It was somehow reminiscent of the cat's own wounds, and even resembled Cade's scar. Somehow, Lilly didn't think the doctor would be so accepting of his new battle wound as those two were.

Of course, where he was going, it didn't matter.

Cade turned to Lilly, genuine concern in his eyes. "Are you all right?"

"I'm fine."

"No thanks to you, McShane," Robbie told his mentor in a scathing voice. "You were supposed to be teaching her to defend herself, and she had to be rescued by a ten-year-old and a cat."

CHAPTER 21

When the police came, Cade invited the Lagasse family to join them while he and Lilly recounted the long and convoluted tale of Henri and Preston to the authorities. Mrs. Fontenot listened with tears in her eyes.

"So he is not a medical person at all?" she said.

"No."

"And there is nothing really wrong with Patricia?"

"Probably nothing but normal grief," Lilly told her. "But you'd be wise to have someone with some real knowledge check her over."

Once Mrs. Fontenot's basic questions were answered, Cade and Lilly promised to explain more later, but told her they needed to go to the police station and get some more answers from Henri. They planned to travel to River Run early the following morning to let Cassandra know what they'd found out and get her away from Preston before something happened to her. It would be a perfect time, since the attorney would be in New Orleans working.

Lilly wondered how Cassandra would take the news that her husband was nothing but a scam artist and crook. Lilly had firsthand knowledge of how hard that was to accept. It would not be pleasant for the young mother-to-be, but if there was any silver lining in all this darkness, it was that Cassandra and her child would be free from the wretched man and his hurtful ways.

It was almost midnight when they reached the police station. One of the night officers took them back to the cell, where they found Henri sitting on the narrow cot, his head in his hands.

He looked up when Cade spoke his name. He was disheveled, and there was dried blood all along the scratches Lucifer had inflicted. He looked as if he'd been crying.

Lilly's heart was not moved one bit.

"Are they treating you okay?"

Henri glared at them. Instead of answering, he asked, "Who the devil are you two anyway?"

Both Lilly and Cade showed their badges. "Lilly Long, Pinkerton."

"Andrew Cadence McShane, Pinkerton."

Cade indicated that they wanted to be let inside the cell while they questioned Ducharme, and the guard brought them each a straight-backed chair.

The night watch slapped his nightstick against his palm a couple of times. "Do you want me to stay close in case you need me?"

"Thanks," Cade told him, "but I think I can handle it."

"I think you're right." With a jaunty salute, the man left them locked in the cell with the prisoner.

"It will go a lot better for all concerned if you answer the questions honestly, Ducharme," Cade told him.

"I'll be out of here in no time. I've already sent for my lawyer."

"Oh, who's that?"

"Preston, of course."

"It will be hard for him to defend you when he's sitting there beside you," Lilly told him.

Henri shook his head. "He's too smart. You might pick him up, but you'll never hold him."

"We'll see."

Too much nervous energy was racing through Lilly for her to sit, but Cade stood, spun his chair around on one leg, and straddled it, resting his arms across the top. "You've already admitted that you teamed up and decided to steal the Fontenot ladies' money, but there are a couple of other things bothering me . . . like Suzannah."

"What about her?"

"Why did you kill her?"

Henri leaped to his feet. *That* rattled him. "I never killed anyone."

"Sit down, Mr. Ducharme," Lilly said in a dulcet tone that held a note of steel. As she stood looking at him, everything that Timothy had done to her came rushing back. She clenched her fists at her sides, fighting the urge to pummel him for all the terrible things he'd done. Instead, she grabbed a handful of his hair and jerked his head back until he was forced to look at her.

Ducharme yelped in pain.

"Of course you did. You killed her so there would be one less person to split the money with."

"I'm telling you I didn't kill her. I would never kill anyone."

"Then who did?" Lilly asked. "Preston?"

Seeing the handwriting on the wall, Ducharme caved in like a one-egg pudding.

"He wanted me to. I'd have been happy with my marriage to Patricia and all the money and benefits that came with being part of the famous Fontenot family. Preston wanted more, and he threatened to expose me for a fraud if I didn't help him with his plan. If there was any killing done, I didn't do it."

"You're saying Preston blackmailed you?" Cade asked.

"That's exactly what I'm saying."

Lilly felt the fight drain out of her. Maybe she was just tired, and maybe it was foolish of her, but she believed him. Ducharme wasn't a leader; he was a follower. Always looking for the easy way. Easily led. Weak. Suddenly realizing that she had a death grip on his hair, she released her hold on him and stepped back, appalled by her actions.

Cade pulled his watch from his pocket, flipped up the outside cover, and smiled. "So much for honor among thieves, Lilly. It took him all of three minutes to give up his partner."

Lilly couldn't answer for the guilt pressing down on her. She began to pace the small cell.

"So Preston wanted you to kill Suzannah. What about Mrs. Fontenot and Patricia?" she asked, determined to have all her questions answered.

"Yes, them too. I was supposed to give *Grand-mère* small doses of arsenic to sicken her gradually."

"Arsenic!"

Henri shrugged. "It would have been easy. She's old and frail, and when she finally . . . succumbed, there wouldn't be a single suspicion about what had happened. I tried, but I couldn't do it."

"How did you give it to her?" Cade asked. "I know it's caustic and has a bitter taste."

"I mixed it in her snuff so that she wouldn't taste it. The problem is that she doesn't dip that often."

Lilly's heart seemed to stumble. Mrs. Fontenot's unexplained bouts of sickness suddenly made sense. "Dear God!"

"What?" Cade said, hearing the panic in her voice.

"Robbie. Robbie took the snuffbox so he could try the snuff, and *he* got sick."

She thought she saw Cade's face go a little whiter. She waited to see what he'd do, but he only dropped his forehead on his hands that rested on the top of the chairback.

"What about Patricia?" Lilly asked, taking up where Cade left off. "How did you plan to kill her?"

"I'm telling you I never planned to kill anyone. I gave her the chloral hydrate and had her committed, the way I promised Preston."

"Did you plan to leave her there forever?"

Perhaps she'd finally touched some last lingering bit of decency in him. Henri buried his face in his hands. Lilly had to lean nearer to hear what he was saying.

"I'd planned to put her in a new private hospital somewhere out in the country. Or build her a little place and hire someone to stay with her."

"Dear sweet heaven, Henri!" Lilly cried, shocked anew by his callousness. She began to pace the cell again. "She's your wife! Didn't you care at all for her? How could you see her suffering over the death of the baby . . . *your* baby and not feel any compassion for what she was going through?"

Henri lifted his head and looked at her. There were tears in his eyes. "He isn't dead."

She stopped pacing. "What did you say?"

"The baby—Carlton—isn't dead. He's with my stepdaughter Delia." He jerked his head toward Cade. "Ask Agent McShane. He and the boy drove me out to see him."

She looked at Cade, who looked as surprised as she felt.

Lilly stared at the doctor for long seconds and called him a very unladylike name. Then she curled her small hand into a fist and swung at his face with every ounce of strength she had.

The sound of his head striking the wall was very satisfying.

CHAPTER 22

Everyone was asleep when they got back to the house, and Lilly and Cade were so exhausted they both fell across the bed with their clothes on. She didn't even notice he was beside her. He woke her early, they dressed in their everyday clothing once more, and they were on the road to the plantation by first light. They left a note for Mrs. Fontenot telling her that they hoped to be back with Cassandra by late evening and that they would explain everything when they returned.

It was midmorning when they arrived at River Run, and Rollo greeted them with a worried expression on his face.

"What are you doing here?" he asked, grabbing the horses' leads.

Cade leaped to the ground and helped Lilly down. Then he pulled out his Pinkerton badge. "We're not really Bran and Brona Sullivan," he explained. "I'm Cade McShane and this is Lilly Long. We're with the Pinkertons."

"Pinkertons!" Rollo looked as if the news had knocked him sideways to Sunday. "Why are Pinkertons pretending to be hired help?"

Lilly smiled. "Pretending to be someone we aren't is an excellent way to get the goods on someone who's under suspicion. We were hired to try to find out if Henri Ducharme was the caring husband he seemed to be, or if he was after Patricia's money."

"We found out last night that he's the latter," Cade told him. "In fact, the doctor and Preston created the whole scheme together."

Emotions chased one another across Rollo's face. Relief. Joy. Thanksgiving. His dark eyes filled with tears.

"It's over?"

There was no need for him to explain what he meant. Cade placed a comforting hand on the other man's shoulder.

"It's over. The police were going to Preston's office this morning to arrest him. Lilly and I have come to take Cassandra back home. You and your family, too, if you want."

Rollo looked troubled. He shook his head. "Mr. Easterling's not in the city. He's here."

"What!"

This would change everything. Both Lilly and Cade had expected it to be an easy matter to pack up a few things for Cassandra and take her back to her grandmother's. They hadn't counted on having to deal with Preston. Lilly knew that any animal was dangerous when he was cornered, and she worried about what might happen when she and Cade confronted Preston with his crimes.

"What's he doing here in the middle of the week?" she asked. "We expected him to be in the city."

"I don't know. He come home in the middle of the night, drunk, yelling about everything around him going to Hades, and how stupid the doctor was." Rollo shrugged. "He finally passed out. What's he talkin' about, Bran?"

"We've discovered that Preston was behind Suzannah's

death, and that he and the doctor planned to get rid of all the Fontenot women and take control of their money."

"Dear Lord," Rollo said. It was hard to say if the words were shock over what he'd heard, or a prayer.

"Is he in the house?" Cade asked.

"No, sir. He came stumblin' out 'bout thirty minutes ago, carryin' a bottle of bourbon. Told me he was goin' into the woods to drink and think."

"Are the women all right?" Lilly asked, more concerned about Cassandra and Neecie.

"As far as I know," Rollo said, nodding slowly. "After he passed out, Neecie went to check on Miz Cassie. She was awful upset. Cried herself to sleep with Neecie holdin' her. She kept sayin' she couldn't take much more. This mornin' when I went in for my breakfast, Neecie said Miz Cassie been walkin' around like a zombie, mumblin' to herself and cryin'."

Mutual suffering made strange friends, Lilly thought. "If Preston is away from the house, now would be a good time to get Cassandra and leave."

"I agree. Rollo, why don't you hitch up a buggy and follow us back to town? Our main concern is the women, and I don't think this will be a good place to be when Preston comes back and finds that his wife is gone."

"You're right about that."

"If we can slip away before he knows we're gone, we'll send the law here to arrest him."

Rollo nodded. "Will you tell Vena and Neecie to get some things together?"

"Of course."

They found Vena in the kitchen pacing and wringing her hands. She was as surprised to see Cade and Lilly as Rollo had been. They gave her the briefest of explanations, promised to fill her in on the details when everyone was safe, and told her to pack a few belongings.

"Where are Cassandra and Neecie?" Lilly asked.

"I don't know where Neecie is. I went up to make the beds and when I come down, she was just . . . gone. She does that sometimes. Says she needs time by herself to think about things."

Poor thing. She was so afraid of saying or doing anything that might make her daughter look bad.

Cade placed a hand on her shoulder. "Vena, we know about Preston and Neecie, and we know it's not her doing. Do you think she's with him?"

Vena wrung her hands. "Lord, Lord, Mr. Bran, I don't know. If he told her to meet him, she would. She's so afraid of him. Not for herself, but the baby . . . and Rollo."

"He's threatened to harm Rollo?"

"Yes, sir."

"We think Cassandra knows what's going on," Lilly offered.

"Course she does. Women know these things. That's what worries me. I saw her slippin' through the woods after Mr. Preston, and if Neecie is there . . ."

Her dark eyes filled with tears and her voice trailed away, as if the thought of what might happen if the three of them had a confrontation was too terrible to put into words.

Lilly took both of Vena's hands in hers. "We'll find them," she promised. "It's going to be fine."

Vena nodded, but the expression in her eyes told Lilly she wasn't convinced.

Without any more talk, Lilly and Cade left the house and made their way to the woods, following the well-worn trail.

"Do you have your derringer?" he asked.

Lilly stopped in her tracks. She'd left the little gun hidden in her things in their room. Not having the pistol when she needed it was beginning to be an annoying habit. There'd been more than once during her last investigation when she'd needed protection, only to realize she'd left it behind somewhere.

Expecting an upbraiding, she was surprised to see Cade smile.

"Robbie's right. I need to work with you."

She followed him down the path toward the clearing where the voodoo ritual had taken place. As they got closer, they heard the unmistakable sounds of raised voices. Reaching a place where they were near enough to see and hear what was being said, Cade held out his arm to stop her from going any closer.

As Lilly took in the scene before her, something akin to panic rose inside her. Preston and Cassandra faced each other. Preston, who looked to have a tight grip on Neecie's arm, stood swaying unsteadily. His free hand was coiled into a fist at his side. Cassandra's pretty face was contorted with fury. With tears streaming down her face, a trembling Neecie was doing her best to maintain her modesty by holding the torn pieces of her bodice together. Her mouth, which was swollen and bleeding, was moving as she mumbled something low and incoherent. It did not take a veteran agent to figure out what Cassandra had interrupted.

Cade held a finger to his lips and they inched closer.

"Suzannah was right," Cassandra cried. "You're nothing but a filthy swine. She tried to warn me about marrying you. She told me how you were always undressing her with your eyes."

Preston gave Neecie a little shove, as if he were bored and found this new exchange more to his liking. She staggered backward, then turned and ran for the safety of the woods.

He raised the half-empty bottle to his lips and took a deep sip. Then he wiped his mouth with the back of his hand and shook a finger at his wife.

"Your sister was the most irritatingly virtuous young woman I've ever seen," he noted almost thoughtfully. Then, as if he were remembering, he smiled a smug smile. "But I fixed that. And I undressed her with more than my eyes before it was over."

Cassandra's hands covered a cry of agony. Even from where she stood, Lilly saw the tears in her eyes glittering in the sunlight.

"And then . . ." He paused, almost as if to maximize the effect of his statement, almost as if he were savoring the moment, he said, "I gave her to one of my associates to do with as he wished for the rest of the evening."

A shiver of sickness and loathing slithered down Lilly's back. She had never in her life heard anything so wicked, cold, and insensitive. Cassandra made a noise that almost sounded like a feral growl.

Preston didn't seem to notice. From the rapt expression on his face, he was reveling in his twisted, obscene memories. "Of course, when she fought and screamed, he had no choice but to quiet her."

With a scream of sorrow and fury that seemed rooted in her very soul, Cassandra launched herself at her husband, her fingers curled into claws, intent on inflicting some kind of damage.

It was almost like reliving that moment she'd attacked Timothy in much the same way when he'd flaunted his theft of her savings. Just as Tim had, Preston swung a hard, backhanded blow at Cassandra, knocking her to the ground. With a maniacal roar of his own, he dropped to his knees, straddling her prone body, and placed his hands around her throat.

Lilly was marginally aware that Cade had left her side and was running toward the pair. He'd almost reached them when Neecie burst into the clearing, screaming like a demented banshee. There was murder in her eyes and the hatchet used to slaughter the chickens raised above her head.

Cade stopped dead still. "Neecie! Don't."

Hearing the warning, Preston turned just in time to see the blade slice downward. Neecie swung with hate and purpose. She buried the hatchet squarely in his forehead.

He didn't even cry out, but there was a question in his eyes as he looked at her, almost as if he couldn't believe she'd done such a thing. Then he toppled to his side and Cassandra pushed him off her and scrambled to her feet.

She was crying, but she was much calmer than Lilly expected. Neecie, who looked as if she were coming out of a trance, as full awareness of her actions began to sink in, stepped away from the body, muttering something about her loa protecting her.

Cade took a tentative step toward the trio, and Lilly emerged from her hiding place and stepped nearer to Preston's prone body. The man who had wreaked such havoc on the Fontenot family was quite dead. Lilly, who had never seen a dead body besides her mother's, had to turn away for a moment.

"Are you okay?"

She drew in a deep, steadying breath. "I'll be fine." She glanced at Cade over her shoulder. "We need to get the authorities."

"No!"

The harsh denial sent them both whirling around. The man who'd come crashing through the undergrowth to see what was going on burst into the clearing. Rollo took in the scene with a single piercing glance and shook his head, as if processing it all was just too much.

"No." This time the word was softer, but no less emphatic. Cassandra stood regarding them all with an almost regal bearing. "No authorities."

"There's been a murder, Mrs. Easterling," Lilly said. "I know you have all been living a nightmare, but we can't just . . . let this go. We can't go on with our lives and act as if this never happened."

"Why not?" she challenged, looking from one to the other. "Preston intended to kill me. He all but killed my sister, and God knows what else is on his black soul. Why should Neecie have her baby in jail and Rollo be left with no wife, just because she was trying to keep my husband from killing me?"

"I'm sure her punishment won't be too harsh, considering the circumstances," Lilly told her.

Cassandra laughed, a world-weary sound devoid of joy. "You're more innocent than I am, Brona. What kind of justice do you think a black woman who killed a prominent attorney will get? None. The good Lord knows that she and Rollo have suffered enough. I hold no ill will toward her, especially since she gave me back my life."

The subtle choice of words was not lost on Lilly. Cassandra felt as much that Neecie had given her back what she lost when she married Preston as that she had physically saved her. Cade made no comment but stood silent, watching the drama unfold with his usual intensity.

"What are you suggesting?"

"I'm suggesting that Rollo get some rope to tie rocks to Preston's body. Then we take him deeper into the swamp and bury him there. The gators will finish him off in no time."

Cassandra's voice held no hint of victory or elation. She sounded weary. Drained. Beaten down. As if her plan were the only solution that made any sense, yet Lilly was stunned by the ruthlessness of the proposal. The tiny, well-bred, sheltered daughter of one of the most prestigious families in the state did not seem capable of such subterfuge.

Everything inside Lilly rebelled at the notion. "Cade, tell

her," she begged, looking to him for help. "Tell her we can't do that."

"Sure we can, colleen," he said with a gentle smile. "The ends justify the means, remember?"

Allan Pinkerton's favorite saying.

Before, it had always sounded so right, made so much sense, but today, Lilly was having a hard time defending the adage. "Trying to hide this is a mad scheme if ever there was one."

"Then how about that line from *Hamlet*?" he said.

She frowned, trying to think. "Which line?"

" 'Though this be madness, yet there is method in't.' "

EPILOGUE

Chicago
Pinkerton Offices

When Lilly and Cade entered William Pinkerton's office ten days later, she was surprised to see him engrossed in a week-old edition of the New Orleans *Picayune*. The headline proclaimed there were no new clues in the disappearance of New Orleans attorney Preston Easterling.

"I assume the two of you have read this," William said.

"Several times, sir," Cade told him. "As well as many other accounts."

William laughed. "It might very easily be taken straight from one of my father's dime novels."

He was right. The reporters by no means had the details, and as far as Lilly was concerned, if they wanted them, they could dig for them just as she and Cade had done.

The gist of the article was that law enforcement had followed up on every lead, hoping to locate the missing husband of Cassandra Fontenot, young heiress to the Fontenot fortune, all with no success. The prominent young lawyer seemed to have disappeared from the face of the earth after he and his equally notorious stepfather, Mr. Henri Ducharme, had

charmed their way into the Fontenot family for the sole purpose of gaining control of the Fontenot holdings.

Tragedy after tragedy followed. First, Mrs. Patricia Ducharme's newborn baby had died, and only months later, her
younger daughter had been kidnapped and murdered during a
suffragist rally. Mrs. Ducharme had suffered a mental break-
down and was placed in the New Orleans City Insane Asylum
for evaluation.

Feeling there were far too many calamities besieging the
family, Mrs. LaRee Fontenot had decided it was time to take
action.

When Mrs. Etienne Fontenot hired the prestigious
Pinkerton National Detective Agency, agents from the
Chicago office uncovered the truth about the two men.
Henri Ducharme was in fact the stepfather of Preston
Easterling, whose biological father was notorious forger
Gregory Easterling. There is no record of the identity of
Preston's mother.

Besides obtaining a law degree, the younger man had
taken up his father's trade and used his forgery skills
whenever it became necessary to further his agenda,
including the falsification of Ducharme's medical degree.

When the Pinkertons confronted Ducharme about
drugging his wife so that she would appear to have lost
her mind, and his collusion with his stepson, Ducharme
confessed everything, including the fact that Preston was
the one responsible for the murder of Suzannah
Fontenot. Easterling disappeared the night of Ducharme's
incarceration, and the theory is that he has gone to
Europe to escape prosecution for his crimes.

The Fontenot luck has changed. Mrs. Patricia Ducharme was released from the asylum where her husband

had put her, and has learned that her son did not die at birth as she was led to believe. They have been reunited.

Henri Ducharme is currently awaiting trial.

"I've read your reports," William said, finally laying aside the paper, "and I must say that it appears the two of you worked well together." When neither operative corroborated the statement one way or the other, he continued. "I have a few questions."

"Of course, sir," Lilly and Cade said in unison.

"Who put the blasted voodoo doll in Preston's shirt drawer? Neecie or Cassandra?"

"Cassandra," Lilly told him. "She knew there was no way she could change things, but she knew how superstitious he was, and that he would be petrified at the thought of someone using voodoo against him."

"Clever girl."

"Are Patricia and the baby doing well?"

"Yes, sir. As far as we know," Cade said.

"And Mrs. Fontenot?"

Lilly gave a slight shrug. "She's had no more gastric bouts since she no longer comes into contact with arsenic."

"We can thank Robbie for that piece of the puzzle," Cade told their boss. "If he hadn't sneaked the snuffbox to try the snuff for himself, it might have been weeks before we figured out the source of the poison."

"Ah, yes," William said, regarding them over the tips of his steepled fingers. "What do you plan to do about him, McShane?"

"I can't very well leave him on the streets, and if I leave him with the nuns, he'll just run away, so I plan to try one more time to get him to stay with Meagan and Seamus."

"He has a taste for law enforcement now, so we believe

that if Seamus will include him in little things, it will satisfy that wild spirit of his, at least to some degree," Lilly said.

"Lilly and I both think he should be in school this fall, and surprisingly, he's eager to learn. In the meantime, he's staying with the Fontenot ladies for a few months. Mrs. Fontenot has taken quite a liking to him, and I think the Lagasses will be a good influence."

"Well, it certainly seems as if he's getting on the right track, thanks to you, and from reading both reports it sounds as if he was invaluable."

"There's no doubt he uncovered some things neither Lilly nor I ever could have."

"Did you ever hear how Mrs. Fontenot figured out who you are?" William asked.

"She said it was my reading habits that alerted her."

"Your reading habits?"

Lilly nodded ruefully. "Yes, sir. I didn't read the kinds of materials she felt a young Irish housemaid would be attracted by. My taste was much too 'sophisticated,' she said."

"Your choice of reading material gave you away?"

"Yes, it seems that I still have a lot to learn, sir," Lilly said with a grimace.

"And you're learning." William rose. "Well, I believe that's everything. Do either of you have any questions?"

Cade cleared his throat. "Yes, sir. About the fight in the tavern."

"Justified, McShane. Your job is not in jeopardy for defending yourself."

Lilly could almost feel his relief. "Thank you, Mr. Pinkerton."

"You two take a few days and rest. I'll give you a call when something comes across my desk."

They said their good-byes and Lilly and Cade went down the stairs and out onto the street.

"Do you have any plans for the next few days?" Lilly asked.

"I plan to sleep in a real bed until I wake up. And I hope not to muck any more stalls for a while."

"I'm hoping my . . . our . . . next assignment is something different from housekeeping."

Cade bestowed one of his rare smiles on her, and for the briefest instant, they shared a moment of true camaraderie.

"Oh, thank goodness I caught you, Miss Long!"

Lilly turned to see Harris was running toward her, waving an envelope in his hand.

"What is it, Harris?"

"This was delivered to us a couple of weeks ago," he said, holding out the cream-hued envelope. "I guess the sender had no other way to reach you. I hope it's good news."

"Yes, that would be nice. Thank you, Harris." She watched the secretary walk back inside the building, and turned over the envelope to check the return address.

Simon Linedecker, Attorney-at-Law.

Her heart skipped a beat and she tried to slide her fingernail beneath the flap.

"Important?"

"It's from my attorney. Something to do with the divorce, I suspect."

"Here." Cade handed her his open penknife.

She slit the envelope and handed back the knife. Cade closed it while she pulled the pages free and opened them.

Dear Miss Long, she read. *Enclosed you will find a check for the amount of the retainer you paid me, less a small amount for cab fare when I went to the courthouse.*

What on earth was going on? Eager to know why Simon was returning the money she'd paid him, she skimmed the typewritten pages impatiently. There was a lot of information. Three other women . . . faked certificate . . . imposter . . .

"What?"

It was more than her already weary mind could take in, but the last line summed things up nicely.

"What is it?" Cade asked, seeing the shock on her face.

"It seems I won't be needing a divorce after all."

"Really? Why?" He held out his hand for the letter.

"Just read the last paragraph."

He did. Out loud.

" *'So you see, Miss Long, you were never married to the man at all. He has a history of setting up fake marriage ceremonies, using his friends as preachers, priests, or whatever. When you next come in, I'll be happy to show you everything I found and point out the discrepancies in the certificate itself. I'm so sorry to be the bearer of such bad news, and wish you all the best in the future. Respectfully, Simon Linedecker.'* "

Cade folded the letter and handed it back to her. Then he whistled for a cab.

"That's it?" she said. "You have nothing to say?"

"What can I say, Lilly?"

"Well, say *something!*"

He shrugged. "Fine. I think you should be celebrating with a nice glass of wine. He's a sorry excuse for a human being and you're better off without him."

Lilly looked into his blue eyes for long seconds. Then she nodded. "For once, McShane, I think you're right." She looped her hand through his arm. "I'll buy."

Don't miss the next Lilly Long Mystery

by Penny Richards

coming to you in the Spring of 2018

from your favorites booksellers and e-tailers.

Connect with Us

Visit us online at
KensingtonBooks.com
to read more from your favorite authors, see books
by series, view reading group guides, and more.

Join us on social media

for sneak peeks, chances to win books and prize packs,
and to share your thoughts with other readers.

facebook.com/kensingtonpublishing
twitter.com/kensingtonbooks

Tell us what you think!

To share your thoughts, submit a review,
or sign up for our eNewsletters, please visit:
KensingtonBooks.com/TellUs.